DOUBLE BOGEY MURDER

BOOK THREE

THE BOB ROOSEVELT MYSTERY SERIES

by

Robert K. Swisher Jr.

Text copyright © 2013 Robert K. Swisher Jr.

OPEN TALON PRESS

OTHER PUBLISHED NOVELS BY ROBERT K. SWISHER JR.

Historical Fiction: Trade and E-book
Published by Sunstone Press
The Land
Fatal Destiny

Contemporary Western Fiction: Trade and E-book
PUBLISHED BY SUNSTONE PRESS
How Far the Mountain
The Last Narrow Gauge Train Robbery
The Last Day in Paradise
Love Lies Bleeding
The Man From the Mountain

Literary: Out of Print
Published by Samisdat Press - Canada
American Love Story

Young Adult: Trade Only
Published by Echo Press California
The Weaver
Published by Sunstone Press
Only Magic

Humor: E-book only
Conversations With the Golf God

Mystery Series: E-book and Trade
Bob Roosevelt Mystery Series – 4 novels

Contemporary Fiction: E-book only
Hope
A Circle Around Forever

Trade and E-book
Published by Open Talon Press
Vent
Grammar Nazis Are Not Always Rite, Right, Write
Vent Revisited
The Lonely Cowboy
How Bridge McCoy Learned to Say I Love you

Short stories and poetry in literary journals, articles in outdoor magazines. Reviews by Publishers Weekly, Best Sellers, Library Journal, and many others.

PUBLISHED BY
OPEN TALON PRESS

EDITORS: Sheila Awalt

COVER DESIGNER: Samantha Fury...Mike Nguyen
PRINT FORMAT: Samantha Fury

Part of this book is a work of fiction. For the fiction segments names, characters, places and incidents are either products of the author's imagination or are used fictitiously. Any resemblance to actual events, locales, or persons either living or dead, is entirely coincidental. Part of this work might be construed as non-fiction. If any of this book reminds you of yourself and you get offended by certain comments or remarks (corporations included since you are by law considered people) no harm, malice, libel, racism, discrimination, in any of the previous terms multitudes of forms and definitions, and any term that would come to mind by any other person, was intentionally intended either by me, my wife, my dog, my cat, my goldfish, my hanging plants, or any relative - this includes all and any life forms in the known and unknown universe that might share some of my DNA, and unknowingly, by either cosmic intervention, or a form of communication as yet unknown to mankind had anything to do with the writing of this book.

If you wish to use portions of this book for anything but reviews you must contact OPEN TALON PRESS or the author. Sorry, what can I say? We all know lawyers run the world. And to be honest we all know our politicians are controlled by big business interests who are also controlled by lawyers.

Library of Congress - In Publication Date

Swisher, Robert K, 1947 -
DOUBLE BOGEY MURDER: A novel / by Robert K. Swisher Jr.
Summary: mystery, humor, satire
ISBN is 978-0-9979096-7-8
LCN is 20200923331

DEDICATION

FOR RENO

TO HELL WITH THOSE CATTLE OLD PARD
IT'S TIME TO LET THE FENCE FALL DOWN

RIP

DOUBLE BOGEY MURDER

BOOK THREE

TABLE OF CONTENTS

CHAPTER ONE
I SHOULD HAVE GONE TO IDAHO

I was sitting in the living room of the upscale, second story, furnished apartment that I'd rented in Scottsdale, Arizona. The walls are covered with western prints that go with the Southwest style furniture and there is a patio that overlooks an Olympic sized heated pool and a Jacuzzi. No slumming for Roosevelt this time. The old hippie in me was enjoying a good dose of modern materialism. I felt as snug as John Wayne surrounded by fake Indians.

My Guardian Angel gave me a troubled look like he had just had a serious revelation. "You know, Roosevelt, at first I thought it was a good idea for you to come to Arizona, but now I think we had better get out of town."

"Why? Life is good. I still have a little money. The weather is nice. I am living in a gorgeous place and I have no doubt I will meet the woman of my life. Plus, I am about to take up golf again. What can go wrong, it's the American dream."

"No Roosevelt, we had better go, if not you are going to golf yourself right into the middle of a murder, a gang of wanted bank robbers, some thieves, police who don't give a hoot about their public image, and to top it off more than one person is going to try and put the big hurt on you. By big hurt I mean the really, really big hurt. The big hurt that is so bad it doesn't hurt anymore."

"You are not right all the time," I said.

"That's true," he said.

"Exactly," I replied, ignoring his warning.

"You'll be sorry," he said, sounding like my sister when I was a kid and had done something wrong and I knew she was going to snitch me out.

I went out onto the patio.

"Oh Roosevelt," my Guardian Angel sighed looking toward the pool.

By the pool was a golden-skinned, longhaired brunette, who had a body most women would consider illegal and was wearing a white bikini that was little more than a string and two band-aids. "She is beautiful," I murmured.

"You should go down and introduce yourself," my Guardian Angel said trying to keep his tongue in his mouth.

"You only want a closer look," I said.

My Guardian Angel has been with me since Vietnam but he is not a normal guardian angel. He is snide, sarcastic and lecherous. He thinks that by going against the grain of what a guardian angel should be like makes him an individual. How he got into heaven is beyond me. But, like all long-term relationships, at times I wonder if it's been worth it. I can as easily be a 'famous for 15 minutes' private detective without carrying a guardian angel around as excess baggage. But, he has saved my life numerous times and it's not his fault he is assigned to me - God can be mysterious in His ways even to guardian angels.

"Listen," I said to my Guardian Angel. "In the past six months I've been shot in the head, been beaten up more times than I want to remember, locked in a bomb shelter, hand-cuffed to a bed, and fallen in love with a woman who only wanted to kill me. I came to Arizona to play golf, try to find out who I am, and hopefully meet the love of my life. But, that girl in the pool is too young for me."

"I didn't say go ask her to marry you, just go talk to her."

"You just told me a minute ago to get out of town."

"We can get out of town this evening."

I am the only person who can hear my Guardian Angel and when I talk to him it is through my mind, which is a good thing, if not, people would think I talk to myself all the time. And, thankfully, I am the only person who can see him. He is not a pleasing sight. My Guardian Angel is a 14th century monk with a shaved head. He is 5'2" tall and in his early 60's. His eyes are tiny brown slits that show he is not to be trusted. His eyebrows are so bushy birds could nest in them. He has a splotchy uneven black beard and his complexion is close to watery flour paste. He wears sandals with no socks, a knee-length, stained, brown wool robe, which exposes mats of black curly hair on his bowed legs. To top it off he does not bathe. For many years he would not tell me his name saying it was none of my mortal business, but then in a weak moment, which we all seem to go through, he informed me his name was Wright, which is completely out of character, so I nicknamed him Pea Brain. A name he does not really like, but what the hell, I am his boss, and how many people in life like their boss? But, in an effort to be nice, I only call him Pea Brain when he peeves me off. I have also discovered he used to take money to forgive sins and slept with as many women as he could informing them he was a blessing from God. In a lame excuse he told me the Bishop made him do it.

The girl in the pool rolled over on her back and started doing backstrokes. She was a lovely creature, at the most in her mid-twenties. She was tall, close to 5'8", thin, but not so thin her ribs showed. She had to exercise a lot as her arms and legs were well defined and perfectly proportioned. She stopped swimming, shook the water from her hair and noticed me. To my surprise, she waved. I waved back, trying to look nonchalant. She waved again and called to me. "Come on down, it's no fun swimming alone."

I was off the patio, through the living room, into the bedroom, changed into my bathing suit, down the stairs, and into the pool quicker than Lois Lane can say, "Watch out Superman, it's Kryptonite."

I swam over to the girl trying in a manly fashion to look like I could swim lap after lap, when truthfully I swim like a rock. Two feet from the girl I stopped. The band-aids that were the top of her swimming suit were as useless as trying to cover my face with a postage stamp. I looked her straight in the eyes.

"You're new," she said, with a smile that would make a cheerleader envious.

"No," I said, "I'm 62 years old."

She giggled like a little girl but her lavender eyes moved around nervously. I've always been good at noticing people's subtle body language - the girl was in trouble and needed help.

"Help her into bed," my Guardian Angel said with a twinkle in his eye.

Like I said, my Guardian Angel is one of a kind.

"Where did you come from?" she asked me.

For a reason beyond me I decided to tell her the truth. "I just came down from Colorado where I busted up a porn ring," I said, leaving out the fact the only thing I had wanted to do in Colorado was go trout fishing.

My statement startled her.

"I'm a part-time private detective," I added quickly, figuring she was afraid of cops, which seems to be an American trait - especially now that our police dress like Gestapo agents.

"Oh," she said, in what I took as relief. "That must be exciting."

"As exciting as making popcorn," my Guardian Angel said.

I had a feeling the most exciting thing she does is paint her toenails.

"Ask her if you can paint her toenails?" my Guardian Angel said.

On a scale of one to ten for class and morals my Guardian Angel is a minus two.

"Why are you in Scottsdale?" she asked, looking at me imploringly, almost lost, her eyes begging for help.

"I'm taking a break" I said. "I'm going to play some golf and I hope to fall in love and find out my true calling in life."

"That sounds noble," she said.

"God help me," my Guardian Angel said rolling his eyes toward the sky.

I smiled.

"My boyfriend and I play golf," she said. "We have a tee time tomorrow at the, OUR GREEN FEES ARE SO HIGH ONLY FOOLS PLAY HERE, course," she laughed at her own joke, but her eyes once again darted from side to side nervously.

I should follow my gut feeling and ask her if she is in trouble or needs help, but I didn't.

"Smart move," my Guardian Angel said. "Heed my warning, Roosevelt, but don't get out of the pool yet. I really like her band-aids."

The girl gave me a questioning look, seemed to ponder a question in her mind, than ran her hands through her hair nervously. I noticed how long her nails are and was surprised they were unpolished and she was wearing no rings. She started to speak, dismissed the idea and then smiled tentatively. "It's been nice meeting you, whatever your name is."

"Bob Roosevelt," I said.

"I'm Gloria Simpson," she replied, looking around like at any second little green men would jump out of the bushes and carry her away.

I started to ask her if she needed help, but she turned quickly and swam toward the side of the pool. After she was out of the pool she picked up her towel and walked to the gate. By the gate she stopped and waved, hesitated, started to walk back toward me, but then turned quickly and was gone. The clang of the metal gate rang over the pool like the recess bell at an elementary school.

"You could have asked her out to eat," my Guardian Angel said.

"I think she is in trouble," I said.

"You, trying to think is trouble," he said.

I went back to the apartment and got dressed, still troubled with my feelings about Gloria. My plan for the day was to buy a set of golf clubs.

"You should listen to me and let's get out of here," my Guardian Angel said.

Driving toward the, ONLY HACKERS BUY GOLF CLUBS HERE, discount golf shop, I could not stop thinking about Gloria Simpson. Not about her lack of tan lines or perfectly proportioned body, but the fact I felt she needed help. I erased my guilt by telling myself I would see her again and this time I would ask her if I could help her. Maybe she just needed someone to talk to - life to many is lonely.

"Since you are not going to leave Phoenix, I hope you see her again in her bed," my Guardian Angel said.

"You know I will only sleep with a woman I love," I said.

"You don't have to remind me," my Guardian Angel frowned.

The golf shop was confusing. Standing in the middle of the store I was bewildered by all the clubs - cavity backed, counter weighted, off set, square, closed, mid-sized, senior sized, beryllium, titanium, steel, low kick point shafts, high kick point, mid-kick point, bubble shaft, enlarged shaft, graphite shaft, cord grips, rubber grips, reminder grips, sticky grips, half cord grips, long distance golf balls, high flight, low flight, soft, extra spin, mid spin. Years ago when I used to play there were only blade irons, two kinds of grips, and about four types of golf balls. A sales person walked over to me who reminded me of a cross between a stockbroker and a heart surgeon. The smile on his face hinted that if I bought a set of clubs he would tell me the latest stock market tip and toss in one free open-heart surgery. Two hours later I walked out with an old set of Ping irons, 3 iron through wedge, a Bristol sand wedge, a carry bag that had PING embossed on it, three used metal headed woods with matching head covers that cost more than my 1966 black Volkswagen, Matilda, a putter that the salesman told me a blind man with no hands could sink a putt with, a dozen golf balls guaranteed to fly longer than any ball on the market and stop on a slab of concrete within twelve feet of where they landed, two pairs of short pants with what I guessed were matching shirts, a pair of white golf shoes with spikeless cleats on the bottom - the only place they won't slip was in my bedroom - and, last but not least, a straw hat that if I gave up golf I could wear trekking through Africa in search of ivory poachers.

"You spent $1,000 on that garbage?" my Guardian Angel snickered.

My Guardian Angel has a way of getting to the point.

"If I can break 75 it's worth every dime," I defended myself.

"You are a lost soul, Roosevelt," he said and went to wherever Guardian Angels go when they don't want to be bothered with trivial, human being, useless endeavors.

Before going back to the apartment I stopped at a convenience store and bought a twelve pack of beer and stopped at a hamburger joint and got two hamburgers and fries to go, telling them to throw on some extra grease - my cholesterol count is falling. After being

a hippie for many years and only eating organic food I need a shot of grease every so often to threaten my heart to toe the line or else.

Back in the apartment I scarfed down the hamburgers and fries, gulped down a beer, and then changed into one of my golf outfits. Standing in front of the full length mirror that was on the closet door I am a golfer with shoulder length white hair, a close cropped white beard, 5'11' tall, and 185 pounds, with green eyes,"

I was ecstatic.

"You are a middle-aged man who looks like an idiot in plaid short pants, a green shirt, and a straw hat," my Guardian Angel said.

Even with my Guardian Angel's sarcastic remark I couldn't wait to go out in the morning with all the other people dodging reality, tee up that little white ball and whack the pepper out of it. Every tee shot would hit the fairway, every iron shot would hit the green. I would either two putt or one putt every green. I got another beer, sat down in my chair surrounded by golf magazines and day-dreamed how in a few weeks I would be on tour waving at all my admiring fans.

"Listen, dreamer," my Guardian Angel said. "Try murder, bank robbery, and your death on for size, if you don't take your golf game to another state."

I went to bed. What does my Guardian Angel know?

The morning dawned - no clouds, no breeze, the air was a pale brown, filled with pollutants, dust, car exhaust, factory waste, and radioactivity left over from the last atomic test that the government tells us we need so we can kill 7 million people at a time and sterilize the earth for at least a million years. It was a perfect day to play golf and drink too much beer.

The rush hour traffic sped past Matilda, my 1966 black Volkswagen bug that years ago in the old hippie days I'd painted two white daisies and a yellow one on the headliner. As in all big cities, traffic was bad, terrible, or worse. "You poor idiots," I thought. "Speeding your life away," ignoring the fact I was also on the freeway and driving as fast as I could, which in a 66 Volkswagen isn't much past a fast walk.

The golf course was a jewel in the brown sand of the desert. The greens were perfect. The fairways were gently rolling green ribbons meandering through the desert landscape. People were scurrying around in non-matching outfits smiling like they had just kicked the President. The waitress in the restaurant was so happy she didn't care that she was only making $5.75 an hour plus tips. The pro took my money, looked at my short pants, chalk white legs, and tried to make me feel like I am a mere priest and he is a bishop - golf pro's anymore think they can stop global warming and raise the dead. "We will put you in with a threesome, Mr. Roosevelt," he said. "Do you need a cart?"

"I'll walk," I said.

"While you're waiting, would you like a bucket of balls?"

I strutted away letting him know that practice is for sissies.

"Murder, bank robbery, your death, all for some stupid game," my Guardian Angel warned.

"Pea Brain, I don't want to listen to any of your dribble, I am here to play golf, understand?"

"You don't have to be rude," he said with a huff. "You know I hate being called Pea Brain."

"And don't talk when I swing," I ordered.

I was enjoying the unreality of my surroundings when my name echoed throughout the golf course. "Mr. Roosevelt, you can join the Parker threesome on the first tee," a voice boomed over an intercom.

At one time I was a fairly good golfer. When I was a young man, before going in the army, I played golf consistently in the 70's, using, of all things, forged irons, wooden woods, and a blade putter. None of which a self-respecting golfer would use now. But that was before pro golfers cried when they won a tournament.

The three men waiting for me at the first tee had to be locals. Their skin looked like lizard hide and their eyebrows were bleached blond. I know that if I asked they would all say, "Skin block is only for people from the Midwest, we don't care about any stinking skin cancer."

They hadn't rented carts. There were at least four of us on the course who still have legs.

All three of the men were about my age and from looking at their graphite-shafted woods, taped putter grips, and high spin golf balls, I know they play more than casual golf.

Since I have never been good with money, I agreed to play in their skin game - $5.00 a hole, one tie all tie, carryovers and we would play from the longest tee boxes.

"Besides losing a lot of money you are making one big mistake, your golfing and falling in love fantasy is about to sink," my Guardian Angel said.

"People don't like to be talked to when they play golf," I told him.

"Don't listen to me oh dumb one," he said and shrugged his shoulders nonchalantly. "I have tried to do my job."

The first hole was a dogleg left, par four, 428 yards long, with nothing but sand dunes covered by small bushes and large cactus on either side of the fairway. Beyond the sand dunes to the right were brand new stucco homes big enough a man's parents, all his grown kids, his first wife, his new wife and her three kids, and her ex-husband, could all live in and never see each other. They probably started at around a million and were owned by rich people from Belize who left South America to get away from Americans.

The first of the lizard skins hit his drive down the middle of the fairway. The second lizard skin hit it down the middle. The third lizard skin hit it down the middle. I took out my metal wood, took two practice swings, lined up, and hit it hard, but pushed the ball to the right deep into sand dunes. "It's a tough shot from there," one lizard skin said.

"You'll find it," another lizard skin said.

"Get out your money," the last lizard skin said, smiling like a cat playing with a mouse.

"Please, don't go look for your ball," my Guardian Angel begged.

"What did I tell you about talking," I warned him.

"Is Roosevelt annoyed he hit his little white ball into the rough," he taunted.

My Guardian Angel doesn't really care what I tell him.

I'd kept a good eye on the flight of my ball and marched determinedly after it. Once I was in the sand dunes I could no longer see the fairway. After a few minutes of futilely looking for my golf ball, but seeing nothing but lizards, cactus, and Inca doves, I was about to drop another ball when I saw a small hill of sand no more than two feet tall and six feet long that had a Mesquite bush growing out of it that I hadn't looked behind. I prayed my ball was there. Taking a two shot penalty on the first hole isn't exactly the way to start off a leisurely afternoon.

"Forget the sand hill, take the penalty," my Guardian Angel said.

Walking around the sand hill my Guardian Angel gasped. "I told you," he said sadly, shaking his head.

There was my ball. I had a clear shot to the green. Five yards in either direction I wouldn't have had a shot because of other sand dunes. But, from where my ball was, there was an alleyway between the dunes. There was only one problem. I had a bad lie - my long distance golf ball that was designed to stop within twelve feet if it landed on concrete rested between the breasts of a naked lady - a naked lady with a short piece of rope around her neck and her dry tongue hanging out of the left side of her mouth. Ants were crawling on her eyelids. It was Gloria Simpson and she had looked much better in the swimming pool. I felt both sad and guilty. I knew she had needed help and I had not acted on my feelings.

"Roosevelt," my Guardian Angel implored. "Why didn't you hit the ball straight?"

"I should have listened to you. You have never steered me wrong. I should have gone to Idaho. They don't play golf up there in the winter. All they do is sit around and drink, talk about over throwing the government and eat elk meat."

"You have always been good at wrong decisions," he said.

CHAPTER TWO
BAD LIE

One of the lizard skins walked into the sand dunes to find me, making sure I wasn't cheating and teeing my ball up in the rough. Seeing the body, he faded two shades of brown and stammered, "It's Gloria."

"You'd better go in and call the police," I said.

"I wonder how he knew Gloria?" my Guardian Angel asked.

The man scurried off like a rabbit with a coyote on his tail.

A deep sense of loss came over me knowing Gloria had wanted me to help her. I had sensed it. It was not fear she had emitted when I had told her I was a private detective, it was need - she had wanted to tell me something. She needed help and like most people in this wham bam, thank you ma'am world, I had ignored her unspoken cries. I looked at her naked body, the lifeless skin, the large black ants crawling on her eyelids, the dried tongue protruding from her mouth, my golf ball between her breasts. "I will find your killer," I swore, "you needed me and I ignored you."

"No, Roosevelt, please, don't do anything. Pick up your ball and let's get out of Arizona. You can play golf anywhere," my Guardian Angel beseeched me.

His plea fell on deaf ears. I looked around the body - there were no footprints in the area except mine. There were no drag marks in the sand. The sand was as smooth as a freshly vacuumed carpet. So smooth it couldn't have been swept with a broom to remove footprints. The rope around her neck was hemp, not the modern plastic rope, but woven hemp, about three feet long. It was drawn up around her neck in a slipknot and the end had been cut with a knife. She had either been hung or strangled. I could see no marks on her body except the bruises caused by the rope around her neck - no bruises on her arms like she had been held down, no sign of a gag on her lips, no cuts. Her feet were unscratched. Her long fingernails were unbroken - she had not fought with her killer. She lay on her back with her hands resting on her stomach. Whoever had put her here took care to position the body, carefully, lovingly, even closing her eyelids. I pondered the situation.

Arizona has enough open spaces to bury every murder victim in the country. Why would somebody dispose of a body on a golf course? My mind has always been filled with questions that can't be answered. Once, during my hippie days, I wondered for three days why people always say ‘fall down'. If you fall, you fall, you don't fall down - down is understood. But, if we can fall down then can we fall up? Strangely, the answer is yes, you can fall up in outer space. See what I mean about questions?

One of the black ants crawled off of Gloria's face. I looked around and could see no line of ants coming and going from an anthill anywhere in the area.

I walked away from the body toward the houses that circled the golf course, on my way going around half a dozen tall sand dunes and noticing once again how smooth the sand was. On the edge of the sand dunes was a concrete cart path. If our foursome hadn't been walking we would not have been allowed to take our golf carts off the path. On the other side of the path was a wrought iron fence separating the houses from the course. I figured there were entrances through the fence so residents could walk around the course during the day, or ride their bicycles, or bring a golf cart from their home to the golf course. Looking down, next to the paved path in the sandy ground were six distinct holes - each about a quarter of an inch wide and two inches deep. The holes were about a foot apart and went for close to three feet into the sand dunes and toward where Gloria was. I examined them carefully and what I thought caused them didn't make any sense.

I walked back to the body following my own footprints. The black ants were gone, replaced by smaller red ants. I glanced at my cheap water-resistant watch with its authentic plastic band. It was only 8:45. I examined Gloria closely. I touched her right hand, it

was cold. I pulled gently on her hand. Rigor mortis was setting in. I looked closely at everything about her but disturbed nothing. I noticed her ears were pierced, each with three holes in them, but she wasn't wearing earrings. A few minutes later I heard the siren. Johnny law was on the way.

An unmarked car followed by two police cruisers sped down the middle of the first fairway. I know the greenskeeper was cringing as clumps of expensive turf flew through the air. The three cars skidded to a stop not three feet from where I was standing on the edge of the fairway. Two men dressed in dark suits got out of an unmarked car, looked around like communists were hiding in the rough, looked at me, looked at each other, and then back at me. "Where's the body?" one of the suits asked me - much to my surprise in a civil tone.

The uniformed patrolmen from the cruisers were telling people to stay back. Crime scenes draw onlookers like free beer draws fraternity brothers.

I led the suits to the body. "Strange place to hit a golf ball," one of the suits said.

"Yes, and it's a bad lie," I said, feeling no need to tell the detectives I knew the dead lady.

We stood and said nothing for a few moments then we walked back to the car. One of the suits got on the radio and then went and talked to the uniformed police. For all I know they were wondering if they could get in a quick nine while the forensic people messed up the crime scene.

"My name is Detective Richards," the suit who stayed behind told me, holding out his hand.

"Bob Roosevelt," I said, shaking his hand - an old hippie and a cop shaking hands - don't tell me life doesn't go in circles.

Detective Richards was taller than me, blond headed, around 35 I would guess and in as good of shape as me although slightly heavier. He had a short, reddish moustache, thinning brown hair, and pale blue eyes that look bored and tired. He had a clean-cut air about him and probably cared about his job and what crime is doing to his community.

"How many kids do you have?" I asked Richards, noticing the ring on his finger.

"Two, 12 and 10 years old, never divorced," he smiled.

I was impressed. Most cops, what with the stress and odd hours of their job, end up having ten or eleven wives.

"Do you need me to make a statement?" I asked.

"After the lab boys get here you can give a statement. I know that lady didn't die from being conked by your golf ball. Around here we find bodies all the time," he added, almost as an afterthought. "Chances of solving this case are slim and none unless it was her boyfriend or husband."

"I think it is strange whoever murdered her dumped the body on a golf course," I said.

"Strange somebody killed her," Detective Richards said, adding, "Maybe whoever killed her couldn't stand to get beat."

The other detective came back. "The lab boys are on the way, as soon as they get here we can leave," he said to Richards and then looked at me. "You look kind of familiar but I can't put my finger on it."

"You haven't seen me in a line up," I joked.

"No, it has to do with TV or a movie."

"This is Detective Brad Williams," Detective Richards said to me. Detective Williams was in his late thirties, extremely short black hair, with a potbelly and looked like he enjoyed beer and cigarettes. His hands were pudgy but not soft and his eyes, though happy looking, had a tinge to them like he enjoyed beating the crap out of punks he knew were guilty but he didn't have enough evidence on them for a case. I noticed he didn’t have a wedding ring.

"Bob Roosevelt," I said, shaking hands with Williams.

"I know you now, you were on that crime show on TV. I saw you on the original and twice on reruns. You're that private detective from Florida that solved that kidnapping case."

"That's me," I confessed, one never gets away from 15 minutes of fame - 45 minutes counting reruns. "It's been over two years," I said. "You have a good memory."

"Strange, you being a famous private dick and all hitting a golf ball that lands on a dead body," Detective Richards said.

It's a good thing I'm the only person who can hear my Guardian Angel as he said, “You think strange, you follow this idiot around the country. Everything he does is strange. This boy is two pieces of bread short of a sandwich. A fish hook short of being a fisherman."

Luckily I was saved from more descriptions of my inadequacies when two unmarked patrol cars came tearing down the fairway followed by two white vans.

Soon yellow tape was fluttering in the desert breeze and men wearing latex gloves, who obviously had not heard about latex poisoning, ran around looking at the ground and discussing where they were going to eat lunch. Fifteen minutes later the ambulance came and Gloria Simpson was on her way to the city morgue. "Listen," Detective Richards told me. "I have another body I have to go check out. Why don't you come down to the office around 8 tomorrow morning and give me your statement." He took out his billfold and handed me his card.

"What's your address?" Detective Williams asked. "In case something comes up and we need to contact you."

"The Breckenridge Apartments, number 212," I told him.

While I could still hear the ambulance siren the yellow tape came down, the police piled back into their vehicles, and a foursome waiting on the tee prepared to hit. The three lizard skins appeared from nowhere. "Hey," one of them said. "We'll give you a break and start the match on number two."

I looked back at the tee. I looked at the sand dunes. I looked up at the green. The death of Gloria would not change the course of the world. There was no need to go home. Life goes on. Life is tough. "Ok," I said, as we walked to the number two tee box, "but number one is a carry over."

"Of course," the three lizard skins agreed in unison, already counting my money, "you can even hit first."

My Guardian Angel tapped me on the shoulder. "Play the ball a little more forward in your stance and clear your left hip quicker and you won't push it. I'd like to see you beat these guys."

My Guardian Angel and I might fight a lot, but he is always in my corner. I hit the ball with a slight draw about 285 yards right down the center of the fairway. The three lizard skins didn't say a word.

It's fun to sit at a golf course bar and buy the drinks after you have thoroughly thrashed your golfing opponents. I don't know for sure, but I think my Guardian Angel is buddies with the golf god because I won every skin. I'd chipped in for par, hit a sand wedge in for par, and won a carry over with a bogey, besides having two birdies. I'd never missed the fairway. 18 skins from each player at five bucks a pop is a whipping and yes, I am smart enough I would never play them again. I'm not the United Nations. Being fair went out when Girl Scout Cookies started costing more than a buck.

The lizard skins were not enjoying their beers as much as I was, and after two they all stood up. "You sure played good after you found that body," one lizard skin said.

"Pure luck," I said.

They didn't invite me to join them for another round in the morning. After they left without even a handshake I got back to business. I went to Matilda, changed shoes, and locked my golf clubs in the car. I found where the cart path started by the number 1 tee and followed it. As I suspected there were accesses from the housing area to the cart path. Several of these I followed and they all led to cul-de-sacs. All the houses around the golf course were separated from the course by the wrought iron fence. None of the houses had a private gate that opened directly onto the course. I walked around the entire course, following the cart path, and then went to the pro shop.

The golf pro was still on duty practicing how to ring up a cash register. "You're the guy who found the body," he said to me like I had just won a free trip to Tucson on a mule train.

"Did the police give you a description?" I asked, making a mental note that he was around 26, over six feet tall, well built, tanned, and his brown hair was combed back and perfectly in place. He had to be the world's ultimate frat rat except he had one bad habit - he bites his fingernails.

"Mr. Bradshaw, the man who came in to call the police, told me it was Gloria Simpson," the pro said. "She used to work here driving a refreshment cart. She moved to Phoenix from L.A. but never told anybody why."

"Did she play golf?" I asked.

"Not to my knowledge," the pro replied.

A customer came in so I went back outside. People were

hitting balls on the driving range. People were putting on the putting green. A pro was giving a chipping lesson to an eighty-year-old lady. I was about to go to Matilda when the refreshment cart drove in. A petite woman, in her late 20's, no more than 5'1" tall, got out of the cart. She was pretty and had short blond hair and a cute little button nose. She was wearing a blue shirt with the club logo on it, brown short pants and tennis shoes.

"Excuse me, miss," I said as she headed toward the bar, I presumed to restock the beer and soda for the cart.

She stopped and smiled a smile the size of Texas. Smiles on golf courses along with nice legs and short pants bring big wampum in tips, especially from older men who know they don't have a chance but really don't care anymore, they merely want to look.

"I like watching," my Guardian Angel said.

"I hate to bother you," I said to the young lady, "but I was wondering if by chance you knew Gloria Simpson?"

Her smile vanished as quickly as Tide takes out dirt spots, at least on TV. "It's so tragic," she said. "She had one tough go."

"How?" I asked.

"Listen, I really can't talk here," she said, lowering her voice. "I need this job, the tips are great and this is a tough place to work. We only have so much time to reload our carts."

She turned and got a pencil and scorecard out of the refreshment cart, scribbled a few lines and handed me the card. "This is my phone number and address. My name is Linda. Why don't you come by this evening, around seven?"

"You don't even know me," I said.

"I know you're that private detective that was on TV," she smiled.

I didn't bother to ask her how she had found out so fast, but I did notice when she said TV her blue eyes sparkled.

"If you were a true celebrity you would take advantage of her," my Guardian Angel said.

"I'm not that way," I said.

"Bummer," my Guardian Angel said.

I put the card in my pocket and as I turned to walk to the parking lot I noticed the pro looking at me from the window of the pro shop. He didn't look happy.

Matilda, as usual, started with one turn of the key.

On the way back to the apartment I stopped at a Mexican food restaurant and had the El Grande Special and a Corona. Food and drink tastes better when lizard skins have bought it for you, plus, I needed time to think about how I was going to proceed to find Gloria Simpson's murderer. My Guardian Angel won't bother me while I'm eating. He loved to eat and drink when he was alive and now that he no longer eats, it bums him out when I really enjoy food and he shuts up and sulks.

CHAPTER THREE
CRAB LEGS OR LOBSTER

I took a long hot shower, trimmed my beard and put on my usual Levi's, western shirt, and well-worn brown cowboy boots. After all my years of travel I've never been able to get the cowboy out of me - working on a ranch after my stint as a hippie saved me from going completely insane. I put on my $10.95, waterproof, glow in the dark watch with an authentic brown plastic band. I only recently started wearing a watch again, something about middle age has made me time conscious. I want to know how fast I'm dying. I took my 9 m.m. out of my suitcase, checked it, put on a pair of leather gloves to load the clip - no fingerprints on spent brass - and stuck the pistol under my pillow.

I know it is legal to carry a pistol in Arizona as long as it is visible. I also know it is easy to get a concealed weapons permit - the state gives classes at all the local libraries. But, being able to carry a gun does have its drawbacks. The police in Arizona have a 30 foot kill zone, which means if you are within 30 feet of them and they tell you to raise your hands, you do it or bang you're dead. And, dear dead one don't think your relatives will sue the state for 97 million dollars and win. You won't even make the paper. All the locals will only shake their heads and say, "Stupid idiot, should have stuck up his hands." Freedom has its price.

I got my spiral notebook and a pencil and sat down to write down the few things I know concerning the case of Gloria Simpson. I do not own a laptop. I have this thing about batteries that for some weird reason bothers me. I also do not own a cell phone. By law conversation on cell phones are considered open airways and can be listened to without a warrant. I don't want Big Brother, your sister, nobody, listening in on my conversations so I make my phone calls from pay phones and never use the same one twice. My Guardian Angel thinks I am being paranoid. I call it being cautious. With all the laws on the books now who knows when anybody is breaking one.

"I'm warning you, Roosevelt," my Guardian Angel said. "You don't want to get involved with this."

"If I would have listened to my inner self Gloria might not be dead," I replied.

"You can't blame yourself."

"But I do."

"Morals one day are going to get you killed," he said.

It took me thirty minutes to write down my clues. I have eleven major clues and eight minor clues - all of which lead nowhere - but everything starts from nowhere. I am an optimist with a pessimistic outlook.

Reading over my clues I had a sudden idea. "Spare me any ideas," my Guardian Angel said.

I ignored him, put my gloves in my back pocket and walked to the main office of the apartment. The office had a red tile floor and a western print on the wall of three pink coyotes howling at a yellow moon. I figured it was painted by some white guy who wished he was a gay Indian. A plate of cookies was on the counter. I took a cookie and just as I took a bite, the apartment manager, a young oriental man named Wang, came out of a back office. "Mr. Roosevelt," he smiled. "I hope there is nothing wrong with your apartment."

"Good cookies," I said, "oatmeal is my favorite, and no there is nothing wrong with the apartment. I was just wondering if you could help me with a slight problem."

He looked at me with his wise oriental eyes and said nothing, waiting to hear what the problem was before he committed to an answer.

"I was swimming with a very beautiful young lady yesterday afternoon and she told me what apartment she lived in, but, being that I have the brain of a telephone pole, I forgot." I shrugged my shoulders and gave Wang my best - I am a stupid idiot round eye look.

"I observed you two," Wang said, and winked. "Gloria lives in apartment 273. She is single."

"How can I ever thank you?"

Wang held out his hand. "Five dollars will do nicely."

I took a five-dollar bill out of my billfold and handed it to Wang while reconfirming my belief that one-day the Chinese will control the world. They are patient, smart enough to know when not to talk, and know the American government likes to give money to its enemies.

I located apartment 273. It was on the bottom floor. I went to the door and knocked.

"Dead people don't answer the door," my Guardian Angel said.

I tried the doorknob, it was locked, but the window next to the door was raised slightly.

"Roosevelt, Roosevelt, you are dumber than a flounder," my Guardian Angel warned.

Bottom floor apartments are the easiest ones to break into. That is why, when I do rent apartments, I always make sure I get the second story. If a thief is stupid enough to crawl up your balcony to try and rob you, you can shoot him in the head as his head pops over the edge of the railing. It took five seconds to take off the screen, one second to raise the window, two seconds to get inside the apartment, and another few seconds to put the screen back on. Contrary to popular belief most apartment burglaries happen during daytime. The majority of honest people work during the day and nobody is at the apartment complex except fugitives and guys cooking small batches of crank, who, I guarantee, won't call the cops.

The apartment had the same floor plan as mine - a good-sized living room connecting to a small dining room. The kitchen sat off to the side of the dining room separated by a counter. A bedroom was to the right, off of which was a small bathroom. There was a large closet.

Gloria's apartment was neat and sparse. She had not rented a furnished apartment. There was a sofa in the living room, a small TV on top of a wooden fruit crate and another fruit crate with a lamp on it. There was no table in the dining room and no pictures on the walls. There were no pictures, recipes, or cute magnets stuck to the refrigerator and the refrigerator only had three apples, two oranges, and a head of lettuce in it. The cupboards would make a bachelor proud, empty except for paper plates, paper cups, and plastic utensils. There was a set of knives on the counter in a wooden holder. I have always liked good kitchen knives and I looked at each of them - they all needed sharpening. In the bedroom, next to the bed on the floor, was a phone with a phone book next to it, and on top of the phone book a small black personal phone book. I put the personal phone book in my pocket - I felt no guilt - Detective Richards had told me he had little hope of solving Gloria's murder unless it was a boyfriend or a husband who had killed her. The bed was made but it looked like somebody had slept on top of the covers. Like the living room there were no pictures on the walls, but on top of a small dresser was a five by seven framed photograph of Gloria's face - it looked like a glamour shot. I took the photograph. I went through the top drawer of the chest of drawers. There was nothing exciting unless you are into women's underclothes. The second drawer had pantyhose. The fourth drawer contained a coil of hemp rope -it glared at me like a rattlesnake about to strike. The ends were flared out from being cut and it looked to be the same size that had been around Gloria's neck.

"Every modern woman keeps hemp rope in her drawer," my Guardian Angel said.

There was a straight-backed wooden chair by the wall with a blouse draped over the back. There were ten dresses in the closest, all with designer labels, short pants, the various little tops to mix and match outfits with and a half dozen pairs of shoes, all flats, and an empty spot where a pair of shoes had been. There were two matching leather suitcases. Gloria traveled light. Lighter than any young modern woman I have ever met. Most of the women I have known need a moving van to move their clothes and six suitcases to pack their jewelry.

Gloria's bikini hung over the shower curtain in the bathroom.

I walked slowly through each of the rooms. She could have been a nun that took a vow of poverty, but nuns don't go swimming wearing a string and two band-aids. I opened up all the drawers and cabinets one more time in the kitchen. I went back to the closet and went through the pockets of her clothes. I shook out the phone book. I looked underneath the mattress and underneath the bed. I looked in the folds of the towels in the bathroom. There was nothing. I did find it strange there wasn't a jewelry box. I wondered if Gloria was running from the law and if Gloria Simpson was really her name? Back in the living room I noticed a pillow and a light blanket on the sofa, either she slept on the sofa or somebody had spent the night. I looked under the sofa. There was one man's black silk sock, calf length, the kind of socks that cost more than most men spend for shoes. I noticed a spill mark on the rug. Touching it, it was dry but it smelled like whiskey.

"You didn't look in the medicine cabinet," my Guardian Angel said.

I went to the bathroom and looked in the medicine cabinet - there was Midol, ibuprofen, tartar fighting toothpaste, an empty prescription bottle of Elavil, another empty prescription bottle for Imipramine, and a toothbrush. Under the sink were enough cosmetics to open up a beauty shop. I walked out the front door calmly and was back in my apartment before it dawned on me. There had been no purse in Gloria's apartment. I put her photograph and phone book with my notebook. "Something else should dawn on you," my Guardian Angel said.

"What?"

"You have gloves in your back pocket but you didn't put them on when you broke into the apartment," he said.

"Thanks for reminding me," I said.

"I'm a lot of things but I'm no thief," he said.

I went back to the office. Wang was all smiles. "No five bucks this time," I told him, "but, does Gloria have a car?"

"No, Mr. Roosevelt," she does not, Wang informed me.

As I was about to leave, Wang told me in a tone like he wanted to sell me a fake jade bracelet that his great grandmother had brought over from China, "If she does not want to go out with you ask her if she is in to exotics?"

"Wang, you are a dreamer," I said.

He smiled at me like he was a prophet whose prophecies had

been going down hill ever since he ran out of opium.

Back in my apartment I added three more clues to my notebook and read over them several times. When I was done it was close to seven and I called Linda, the cute refreshment cart driver from the golf course.

"Hello, this is Linda," her voice was happy and carefree.

"Hey Linda, this is Bob Roosevelt, you told me to call you."

There was a hesitation before she answered. If we had been going together I would have guessed I was about to get axed for a younger man with a new car and a real job. "Can you be here within twenty minutes," she said, sounding urgent and surprising me.

"I'm at Bell and Tatum," I told her. "What's the quickest way to your place?"

"Go down Tatum and take a right on Greenway, after you go through the third stop light you'll see an apartment complex, go to the back and park. I'm in apartment 170."

"I'll be there quicker than a Baptist preacher about to convert a Born Again Christian," I said.

She didn't laugh.

"Religion isn't very funny," my Guardian Angel said.

I was about to close the door behind me when I went back and got my pistol, stuck it in the back of my pants, and put on a Levi jacket to cover it.

The sun was about to go down and the sky was a deep purple tinged with dark red, the deep red of drying blood, and the purple from four million cars pumping pollutants into the air. It took ten minutes to drive to Linda's apartment. When I pulled into the parking lot the security lamps came on. I found a parking spot next to a trash bin that had a tree growing by it, which I thought was strange, unless Arizona is into making sure their garbage has shade.

"They don't let homeless people sit under bridges during the day so what's the deal about garbage?" my Guardian Angel asked.

I wandered around for five minutes before I found apartment 170. Knocking on the door it opened immediately. Linda was wearing a light green, above the knee summer dress, with spaghetti straps and a low cut bodice, the type of dress young ladies in soap commercials wear when they dance barefoot through a field of

blooming white daisies. She had on a pair of sandals and her toenails were painted blue. She smiled at me like I was her older brother who had been at war and was finally home. "I'd like to see Linda naked," my Guardian Angel said to me.

"Now, now," I told him.

The apartment was small, very neat, and the walls were covered with Sierra Club prints - Save the Whales, Save the Owls, Save the Forest. I think the only thing we will save from our planet is a Master Card. There were potted plants hanging in front of the window, sitting on the end tables by a small sofa, on a glass coffee table, on the dining room table, on the counter that divides the dining room from the kitchen, on the kitchen counter, and on top of the refrigerator. It was a mini jungle without the land mines, leaches, mosquitoes, and humidity. There was a wall unit along the wall opposite the sofa but no TV. The shelves of the wall unit were covered with unicorns ranging in size from an inch to six inches tall and in every color known to man. "I don't watch TV," Linda told me, noticing my gaze. "All it does is steal mankind's brain cells and turn them into non-thinking, non-producing zombies that the government can walk all over because they are too stupid to know anything but government controlled news, pie in the sky family shows, and movies produced for people who can't count to 25 either forward or backward."

"I bet you majored in political science in college," I said.

She smiled and nodded her head.

"I wonder if she would sleep with you if you read environmental books?" my Guardian Angel asked.

I wished it was 1968. I was a hippie and she was my age and we had met at a commune in New Mexico. She and I could sit around and laugh about the absurdity of the world.

"Would you like a beer?" Linda asked me, turning and walking toward the kitchen before I had a chance to answer. I guess I look like a beer drinker.

I admired the back of her legs and her young enthusiastic steps.

I sat down on the sofa that had a blanket over it stitched with various animals. Linda came back and sat down so close to me the sides of our legs touched and handed me a Fosters.

We each took a big swallow. "So you're a private detective," she said. "You look like an old hippie to me."

"I was a hippie when you were a little girl," I said.

My Guardian Angel whispered in my ear, "You poor, poor little guy, he is getting so old."

He loves being snide.

"I wish I was older. You all had a cause, a purpose in life, a direction, peace and love," Linda said in a dreamy voice.

I wanted to tell her it all sounded good on paper, but history is filled with lies and being a hippie had not exactly been like being the Jolly Green Giant in a field of tall ever-producing green beans. But, dreams are dreams, and I really don't like to be the one in a person's life that comes along to say welcome to reality.

Linda sipped her beer and took a deep breath. "Let me tell you what I know about Gloria," she said, looking at me with sad eyes.

I nodded.

"Gloria started working at the golf course about the same time I did. She would work one cart and I would work the other. It's not a bad job. I put on my shirt and short, smile at all the men as I give them beer or a mixed drink and get great tips. The golf course only pays us minimum wage but on a good day I still bring home over a hundred dollars. Gloria and I would meet at the bar when we had to come back in and restock and at first we never said much. We both were hammered on by all the young golf pro's who think they are God's gift to the world, but we both said no. Neither one of us liked golf jocks. If you do go out with one of them all they talk about is putting and doglegs. In time Gloria and I would talk every so often and then one evening when we both had to work late, we decided to go to a bar after work. She didn't have a car, and normally her boyfriend would pick her up, but that night he must not have been coming."

"Did you ever see him?" I asked.

Linda shook her head. "All I know is he drives a new silver Jaguar and Gloria would meet him out front. He never got out of the car but I always sensed she was afraid of him."

"How do you know it was her boyfriend?"

"She said he was."

"How do you know she was afraid of him?"

"She would always get nervous when he was about to pick her up. We women have a way of knowing these things."

I took another sip of beer. "Go ahead," I said. "I shouldn't butt in."

"Just like a man," Linda smiled and then continued. "As I was saying, we decided to go to a bar. We went to a sports bar on Bell and as things go we had a few beers, started talking, had a few more beers, and before you know it she was telling me more than I really wanted to know about her life. It seems her ex-husband was looking for her and she was afraid. She told me if he ever found her he would kill her."

"Did she say why?" I asked.

"No, and I didn't ask. I really didn't want to get involved. Life is scary. Lord, Bob, I'm scared to go out of my apartment alone at night. I'm scared to drive to work alone, go to the grocery store, stop at a bank machine. I didn't want to get in between some crazy ex-husband who might kill me because I was a friend of his ex-wife."

"I understand that," I said. "We live in a country of paranoids. We live in cities where people are afraid to look at each other, afraid to talk, afraid to communicate, afraid to reach out. Truthfully, I'm glad I'm older. I wouldn't want to be young now."

Linda smiled a, 'I'm looking for a protector smile.'

"I wonder if she wears lace panties," my Guardian Angel asked.

I gave Linda my, 'I will be your protector smile.'

My Guardian Angel gagged.

Linda continued, "Gloria and I would talk at work, but only about light things, you know, men who had asked us out, tips, things like that, but we never went out again,"

I finished my beer. "Do you have another one?" I asked.

Linda went to the kitchen and brought back two more beers.

"Three days ago," Linda said after taking a drink. "Gloria and I happened to meet on the cart path by the fifth tee box. There were four men about to tee off and they walked over. As one got close to us I looked at Gloria and it was like she had seen a ghost. One of the men looked at her and the air seemed to get cold. As I was serving the other three men beer I heard the man say to her. "You weren't that hard to find. I'll pick you up after work, in a tone that she had better do as he said."

"Can you describe the man?" I asked.

"Tall, dark black hair, a thin black moustache, he was wearing sunglasses and had on expensive silk pants with a matching shirt and was in his early thirties. He wore a Rolex and a gold bracelet and had a large diamond pinky ring. After work I watched the parking lot, and instead of a Jaguar picking her up, she was picked up by the man who had talked to her on the golf course in a new glossy black B.M.W. He got out of the car and opened the door for Gloria and then two men walked out of the bar and got into the car."

"You didn't get the plate number did you?"

"No, but it was a Florida plate."

"Did Gloria come back to work after that?"

"She never came back," Linda said and then sobbed. "I should have been able to help her. I was so thoughtless. I could have called the cops."

I reached over and touched her on the shoulder. She fell into my arms and started crying. Big tears splashed on my neck.

"You're a regular male Joan of Ark," my Guardian Angel said.

After a few minutes Linda regained control of herself and pushed away from me.

"Did you by chance ever see the license plate on the Jaguar her boyfriend drove when he picked her up?" I asked.

"Not the numbers but it had Arizona plates."

"The young man that works in the pro shop, did he have a crush on Gloria?" I asked as I handed her my handkerchief.

"Kevin, he asked her out several times but she would never go out with him. After that he treated her like she was nothing but a hairball. He's a big jerk."

"Has he asked you out?"

"Once," she replied. "I told him I was married and had two kids," Linda smiled.

"That wouldn't stop me," my Guardian Angel said.

"Who told you I was a private detective that had been on TV?" I asked Linda, trying to ignore my snide Guardian Angel.

"A Detective Williams. He thinks you're the best private

detective in the country."

"I guess he's never heard of J.J. Arms out of El Paso," my Guardian Angel said.

Linda took another sip on her beer. "Would you like to take me to dinner?" she almost pleaded.

My Guardian Angel perked up, "Now you're getting somewhere," he commented, but not thinking about dinner.

"Sure," I said to Linda. "How about seafood?"

Linda went to her bedroom. When she came back she smelled like lilacs.

I opened the door to Matilda for Linda to get in. "I knew you were an old hippie," she smiled, seeing the daisies painted on the headliner.

I was about to open my door when my Guardian Angel hollered, "Incoming, Incoming."

I turned just in time to see a large white man swinging a ball bat in the direction of my head. He was doing a bad impression of Babe Ruth. Instead of jumping away from the swing, I lunged into the body of the man, kneed him quickly in the groin, and when he started down, crashed my fist into his Adams apple. He lay on the ground making noises like a leaking water faucet with air in the line. I was about to thank my Guardian Angel when a Mexican man ran from behind the Dumpster with a large knife in his hand. Spinning, I fell to one knee, at the same time pulling out my 9 m.m. and shot him twice, once in each leg. The look on his face reminded me of a pig who didn't think he would ever be turned into bacon. I know one thing he would never try out for a football team. As he thrashed around I made a decision to leave and not call the cops. I don't want the cops to know I had been involved. I jumped into Matilda, turned on the ignition, and as always my beloved Matilda started. As we drove away, nobody had come from the apartments to the parking lot. Gun shots in big cities have a way of keeping people indoors, glued to their TV's and hoping some street punks don't knock on their door warning them that if they talk to the police they will kill their pet bird.

In the dim light from the dashboard Linda looked strangely calm. "That was a lousy ambush," I told her.

"Only because of me," my Guardian Angel said proudly.

Linda didn't say anything but I felt she agreed.

"Maybe Linda isn't what she seems," my Guardian Angel said. "She is the only one who knew you were going to her apartment?"

"Maybe the two men were out to rob anybody?" I said. But then I thought. If they were, why didn't they grab Linda and hold her and make me give them either my car keys or billfold?

As we sped away from the apartment complex I asked Linda, "Crab legs or lobster?"

She didn't answer.

I thanked my Guardian Angel. "Good work, I owe you once again."

"Take Linda home with you and get her naked and let me watch and we'll call it even," he said.

"She is too young for me. It wouldn't be right," I said. "And besides, she might be instrumental in me finding out who killed Gloria. I don't want emotions getting in the way of decision-making."

"Emotions, who cares about emotions? I'm talking about sex, lust, passion, a good time, a one-night stand."

I shook my head. My Guardian Angel is bewildering.

CHAPTER FOUR
FASTER THAN AUNT JEMIMA FLIPS A PANCAKE

Linda and I were sitting by the window at the Seafood Grotto. The view wasn't much, unless a steady stream of headlights turns you on, but a dozen oysters on the half shell for $8.00 I ordered for an appetizer was so cheap I figured they were clones.

Linda ordered a scotch and water. I ordered a beer. She drained the drink like she had been walking in the desert for six hours and was dying of thirst. "You knocked that one guy down and shot that other man and I don't think your blood pressure went up," she said, looking at her empty glass like it should refill itself.

I couldn't tell if she was freaked out or impressed. I ate an oyster. "People who go around and try to knife somebody or beat somebody over the head with a ball bat should be shot," I said.

After serving in Vietnam with an infantry unit, getting two purple hearts, and being a private investigator for years, I can be as cold as a Brit eating a cucumber sandwich.

"The regular mister tough guy," my Guardian Angel said.

Linda ordered two more scotch and waters. After the drinks came and she drained one she seemed to gain control of herself, if she had ever lost control. She was hard to read. I couldn't tell if she was happy I was still around or trying to figure out why her two goons hadn't taken care of me.

"Well, I must say," Linda said, as chipper as a drunk squirrel with a bag of shelled peanuts, her third drink half gone, "you can handle yourself."

"She thinks you are her knight in shining armor, her Robin

Hood, her Romeo with a sword. She doesn't know you as well as I do," my Guardian Angel said.

"Shut up. I think she might be the Wicked Witch From the North."

"Don't think too much," he answered smugly. "Thinking has never been one of your strong points."

Linda's scotch and water eyes were now dreamy pools of seduction. She picked up an oyster and sucked it out of the shell as quickly as a robin pulling a worm out of the ground. She shivered, shut her eyes, and ran her tongue over her lips and ate another oyster. "Why don't we skip the main course and order more oysters," she said with a crooked little smile.

"Hon, you want oysters, I'll fly you to the ocean," my Guardian Angel said.

"Three more scotches later, three more dozen oysters, Linda was ready to slide out of the restaurant. I half carried her to the door. Older men sitting with their wives smiled a - 'you lucky pig you got a young one' - smile.

I smiled back my 'she is only a friend' smile. The older ladies sitting with their husbands glared at me - if they had a knife they would make sure I would never again go out with another younger woman.

I got Linda into Matilda. She put her feet up on the dash as I started to drive away. "You know, Roosevelt," she slurred. "I want you to take me home and both of us get naked."

"Will that save the whales?" I asked.

"I don't care about whales," she slurred. "I don't care about the owls or fish."

"O boy, Roosevelt," my Guardian Angel said. "You have one here."

Driving through her apartment parking lot there were no police cars. I parked in the same parking spot, saw bloodstains, and looked around for the brass from my spent rounds but I didn't find any.

I followed Linda to her apartment. We were no sooner in the door than she turned and slid the straps to her dress off her shoulders and let it slide to the floor. My Guardian Angel was right, she did wear lace panties.

Linda started to reach out for me. I stepped back. "You are lovely," I told her, "but I can't mix business with pleasure."

"No, reconsider," my Guardian Angel pleaded.

To my surprise Linda smiled and slowly slipped her dress back on. "It's nice to meet a real man," she said and sat down on the sofa, grinned at me, and passed out. I covered her with the blanket and tucked it under her chin.

"When are you going to learn you can mix business and pleasure?" my Guardian Angel asked me as I walked to the car.

It was slightly past midnight when I got back to the apartment. I cleaned my pistol, put on my gloves to reload the clip and got my notebook and pencil. About forty minutes later I finished writing. I now have 19 major clues and 11 minor clues, but I also have some burning questions in my mind. Number 1: How does somebody kill a person and dump them in a desert area without leaving footprints? Number 2: Who was the supposed boyfriend who drives a Jaguar? Number 3: Who was the mystery man who picked up Gloria in the B.M.W.? Number 4: If Gloria was so afraid and didn't go back to work after being picked up by the mystery man why was she swimming the day I met her? Number 5: Why would anybody dump a body on a golf course when there is a wide-open desert everywhere? Number 6: Did Linda try and ambush me? Number 7: Why is my Guardian Angel so twisted?

I got a beer out of the refrigerator, sat back down and opened Gloria's private phone book I had taken from her apartment. There were six phone numbers in the book with no area codes or names by any of the numbers. I figure the missing area codes have to be either Florida, California, or Arizona - Florida, because the mystery man's car had Florida plates. California, because Gloria had told Linda she was from California and Arizona because Gloria's boyfriend's car had Arizona plates.

I finished my beer and headed for bed. I have to go see Detective Richards at 8 in the morning and then I am going to make another visit to the golf course. There might be something the cops had missed.

I woke up at 6 a.m., cleaned up, checked the address on Detective Richards' card, and was headed out the door with time to spare. I decided to leave my pistol at the apartment. The traffic was already bumper-to-bumper. The locals blame the traffic on the snowbirds, but you can go to Phoenix in the middle of the summer when it is 174 degrees in the shade and the traffic is still bumper-to-bumper, then the locals blame it on Arabs who are trying to get away from the heat.

"It's funny, during the summer all the locals blow out of Phoenix as fast as a dust twister, wherever they go nobody calls them desert birds or heat stroke cowards," my Guardian Angel said.

"Another thing funny about Arizona," I said. "During the winter all the green fees in Arizona go sky high. Even at the muni-courses if you are not from Arizona you have to pay more - in fact they ask you for identification. I would make it a standing rule that anybody from Arizona who plays golf in any other state has to pay three times what everybody else does and must wear a Road Runner on their head."

My Guardian Angel laughed.

The Scottsdale police building was like everything else in Scottsdale - new and expensive. The one story brick building was on the edge of a park and landscaped like it should have been a day care center. The front of the building had tinted glass. In the main lobby behind a marble counter sat a receptionist who could have been Miss May except she doesn't sell videos of herself taking a bubble bath and say things like, "I think exposing one's body is art."

"I'm here to see Detective Richards," I said.

"Sixth door on the left," she smiled.

"I wish she did sell videos," my Guardian Angel said as I walked down the industrial strength blue carpeted hall.

All the offices I passed had glass fronts. I guessed bulletproof glass by its thickness. A secretary sat in each one tip-tapping away on her little computer, ruining her eyes and chipping her nails. The sixth door down was no exception. When I walked in, the secretary looked up from her tip-tapping - she could have been Miss April. She was tall and had long straight blond hair, dancing blue eyes, graceful hands, and a chest big enough for Alaska. "You must be Bob Roosevelt," she said, "go on in."

The lady took my breath away. I felt my heart flutter and I

smiled at her.

"I'll wait here," my Guardian Angel said, staring at the secretary.

I opened the door and went into a large office. The walls were covered with photographs of baseball teams - I figured Richards was in each one. Scattered on various shelves and tables were baseball trophies. Detective Richards didn't bother to stand from behind his desk nor did he look as friendly as he had the day before.

"Take a seat, Roosevelt," Richards ordered more than asked.

"What, no coffee," I said as I obeyed orders.

"You can get coffee at McDonalds. At your age you can even get a senior discount," Richards said, then smiled and pressed his intercom button. "Miss Stone, would you please bring two cups of coffee, black."

"I figured by your boots and Levi's you don't put milk in your coffee," he said, leaning back in his chair.

The secretary brought two cups of coffee, in real cups, and handed us each one. "Don't send any calls through," Detective Richards told her as she left. Miss Stone was wearing stiletto high heels.

"Nice office, nice building, nice secretary, fighting crime pays in Scottsdale," I said.

Richards ignored my remark. "I put out some feelers on you Roosevelt, that little deal you got involved with in Colorado was quite the feather in your cap."

"I only wanted to go fishing," I replied, sipping the coffee, which, if I guessed right was Kona. "I didn't want to catch a body."

"And before that you busted up that big gun and heroin ring in Iowa. You're a busy boy."

"I was just blowing through town," I said.

"And I suppose you decided to come to Phoenix just to play golf for the winter?"

"That's why you're a detective," I grinned.

Richards shook his head but he was smiling, "Seems to me you have a knack for finding trouble."

"My karma has always been bad. It started when I volunteered for Vietnam."

"It started when he was born," my Guardian Angel said.

I don't think Richards knows what karma is and after a few moments he said, "Ok, let me tell you what I know. I know you and Gloria lived in the same apartment complex. I know you were seen swimming with her in the pool. I know you went to play golf without making a tee time, got put in with a threesome, hit your first drive dead right and your ball came to rest between the breasts of Gloria which would have been great if she hadn't been dead. Would you care to fill me in on any other details?"

"This boy is smart," my Guardian Angel said.

"Boy Scout honor Detective Richards there are no other details."

Richards gave me a look like he knew the truth and I are not bedfellows. "And now," he said, "protector of the poor and underprivileged like you are, you are going to try and find out who killed Gloria, if for no other reason, she ruined a good round of golf."

I started to say, "No she didn't," but didn't have the chance.

"She didn't exactly ruin a good round," Richards continued, "you won 18 skins for five bucks a skin, 3 ways."

"You've done a lot of work in one afternoon," I said, "and yes I am going to try and find the murderer or murderers, which ever the case may be."

"I'll help you in anyway I can," Richards said, much to my surprise. Most detectives think that private detectives are lower than I.R.S. agents. "Let me tell you what I've found out about Gloria but you have to tell me what you took out of Gloria's apartment."

I tried to play dumb, innocent, framed. I started to open my mouth. "Don't bother, Roosevelt, your fingerprints are everywhere and Wang told me you asked where she lived. I'd think you would be smart enough to wear gloves."

"Breaking and entering isn't my specialty," I said meekly.

"Obviously," he replied.

"Having gloves and wearing them are two different things," my Guardian Angel said looking at me like I am dumber than a crab.

"I didn't find anything in the apartment," I lied to Richards, adding, "did you and Detective Williams find the man's silk sock

under the sofa?"

"I sure did, but Williams didn't go with me, he had a bunch of paper work to catch up on. But it's strange there was only yours and Gloria's fingerprints in the apartment," Richards said, giving me a look to let me know that if he wanted to he could put me in one of his expensive Scottsdale jail cells.

"What do you think about the rope in the chest of drawer?" I asked.

"It's the same type rope that killed her," Richards said. "Whoever killed her must have been in the apartment."

"But why would she have hemp rope in her apartment?" I asked thoroughly puzzled.

"That is the million-dollar question," Richards said.

He took a sip from his coffee and then picked up a folder and removed a computer printout sheet. "Gloria Simpson was 26 years old. She was born in Portland, Oregon. Her parents were killed in a car wreck when she was seven and she moved to L.A. to live with her wealthy aunt. She was a good student, a cheerleader in high school and on the Dean's List. She went to U.C.L.A. on a full scholarship and got a degree in Education, graduating when she was 22. When she was 22, her Aunt died, leaving her a nice endowment, and she moved to Florida for several months but returned to L.A. where, within a year, she married a Cecil Hoffman. The marriage lasted three years during which time Cecil spent all her money. Also during those three years Gloria called the police five times after being beaten by her husband, but she never pressed charges. She was never in trouble, not even a speeding ticket."

"Anything on this tough guy Cecil Hoffman?" I asked.

"If you sit there and listen I'll get there," Richards said.

"He's a testy homicide detective," my Guardian Angel said.

"After her divorce, Gloria moved to Phoenix. She'd been here 14 months. She worked various odd jobs, secretary, waitress, bank teller, and then took a job at Tatum Ranch Golf Course where we found her dead, or I should say you found her dead." Richards sipped his coffee. "Now, concerning this Cecil Hoffman. He is a different story. Hoffman is 31 years old. He was born in L.A. to a wealthy family and went to various private schools around the country. He got excellent grades, played football and baseball, and got a full ride to U.C.L.A. where he majored in computer programming. Up to this time he had never been in trouble except for school pranks, drinking, girls in the room, stuff like that. After graduation something happened and according to the F.B.I. Hoffman is suspected of being the mastermind behind six unsolved bank robberies in California that grossed over 2 million dollars. He is smart and has enough money from his family he can live a lavish lifestyle and not worry about cleaning any of the robbery money. He likes fast cars, good clothes, jewelry, and good-looking women."

"Remember my warning, Roosevelt, murder, bank robbery, big hurt," my Guardian Angel said.

"Do you have a photograph of Hoffman?" I asked Richards, disturbed that my Guardian Angel has been right twice.

Richards handed me a 5" by 8" computer printout.

"Can I keep this?"

"Frame it and put it on your wall for all I care," Richards said.

"Was the money from the bank jobs marked?" I asked.

"All unmarked bills," Richards answered.

"Does anybody know what Gloria did in Florida?" I asked.

"She didn't work. The only reason we have all the information we do on her is because of her marriage to Hoffman."

"Did Hoffman mastermind these bank jobs before, during, or after Gloria?" I asked.

"After."

"I wonder why he spent all her money if he has money." I mused more than asked.

"Some guys get their jollies by using people, especially young innocent ones," Richards replied coldly.

"Good girls like bad men," I commented.

Richards didn't say anything.

"I went out with a lady from the golf course last night," I said. "She told me Gloria had met a man on the course who she was afraid of, and that the man and two of his goons had picked her up after work. The next time Gloria was seen she was dead."

"I wondered if you were going to tell me about Linda," Richards said.

"You had me followed."

"Did Linda tell you anything else?" Richards asked, ignoring my question.

"She said she couldn't I.D. the guy but he drove a black B.M.W. with Florida plates and wore flashy clothes and jewelry."

"Did she teach you anything?"

"Roosevelt is too dumb to try and learn," my Guardian Angel said.

I gave Richards my, 'I don't kiss and tell look'.

"I have the autopsy report on Gloria," Richards went on. "She had enough Elavile and Imipramine in her system to not know she was dead. She was strangled to death, no signs of struggling, no flesh underneath the fingernails. She was not molested."

I stood, I know when a party is over. "If I find anything out I'll let you know," I said and started for the door.

"By the way," Richards said as I started to open the door. "You wouldn't happen to know anything about some guy getting shot in the legs, and another guy getting his Adams apple turned into apple butter last night at the apartment complex where Linda lives?"

I rubbed my chin, pretending I was deep in thought, something that has always been a problem to me - the deep thought bit - not rubbing my chin. "No, not that I can remember."

"I didn't think so," Richards said.

I was halfway through the door. "Oh yes, Roosevelt, I have something for you."

He opened his top drawer and set two 9 m.m. bullet casings on his desk.

I looked at him carefully before walking back and picking them up. "Vietnamese make ashtrays out of these," I told him.

"There's a litter law in Phoenix," he told me, "you'd better be careful."

I put the casings in my pocket. "You can carry your pistol for all I care, Roosevelt. If you get stopped have them call me."

Miss Stone smiled a beaming smile at me. My heart fluttered like a banjo. "Could this be the one?" I asked my Guardian Angel.

"I hope so," he said.

I wanted to talk to her but instead I walked by her feeling like a 14 year old boy who has fallen head over heels for a college coed.

I made my exit from the building as fast as Aunt Jemima flips a pancake and tossed the shell casings in the nearest bush.

I sat in Matilda for a few minutes. Why didn't Richards grill me for shooting my attacker? It was self-defense but still one would think it was worth a few questions. Richards knew more than he was letting on about Gloria. And why would he tell me I could carry my pistol if he didn't think I would need it again? I should have asked him if they had anything on Linda. I looked at the photograph of Cecil Hoffman and then put it in the glove box. I have a feeling he and I will meet and it wouldn't be to have a few beers and talk about fishing.

"Roosevelt," my Guardian Angel said, "maybe this time you will get your idiot self killed and I can get assigned to someone who does not have any morals."

"We all have to have dream," I said.

"Why didn't you ask for Miss Stone's phone number? I heard your heart flutter," my Guardian Angel said.

"It didn't seem like the right time," I said.

"Roosevelt, love is never at the right time," he said.

CHAPTER FIVE
LOVE NOTE

I decided to kill two birds with one stone and go to the golf course to both eat lunch and see Linda.

The golf course was doing a brisk business. Golf carts were zipping everywhere, people were putting, hitting golf balls on the driving range, and standing in groups discussing whatever people discuss while waiting to tee off - normally some excuse as to why they were going to play poorly.

Only two people were eating in the restaurant. I sat by a large picture window overlooking the putting green and watched what obviously was a putting contest between six men. They were not smiling and by their determined looks were not putting for quarters. The waitress came over to my table. She was young and bubbly and had a hickey on her neck. I ordered eggs and bacon, coffee, and wheat toast and tried to ignore the hickey. There is nothing uglier on a woman than a hickey unless it is a tattoo of a spider on her forehead that clashes with her blue lips and orange eyeliner.

"Who are you to pass judgment?" my Guardian Angel said. "Hippies weren't exactly the most beautiful people, except to other hippies, and then you had to be stoned."

Truth is not always a nice thing.

While eating my breakfast I watched the putting gamblers. They were so intent on their game they didn't see Linda drive by in her cart. For some reason I noticed she was wearing golf shoes.

I finished my breakfast, left the money on the table and went outside. Linda had gone the reverse way on the cart path so I walked the opposite way along the path past the number 1 tee. I followed the path until I came to the spot where I had noticed the six small holes in the sand - they were gone - the area had been raked. I took note that the sand dunes averaged about ten yards apart. They were probably designed this way so golf balls would hit the dunes and roll down so a person could at least hit the ball. I walked back into the dunes, amazed that the complete rough had been raked and found the spot where I'd found Gloria. There were no footprints anywhere, just neat little rake marks. There had been no rake marks in the area close to Gloria the morning I found her - in fact I remembered how smooth the sand had been. I looked at the spot for several minutes and then started walking around. About ten yards away I found a red anthill - the red ants were smaller than the black ants that had been on Gloria. I went back to where Gloria had been and looked in the direction I could have hit my golf ball if it had not been for my precarious lie. It was only about 30 yards to the fairway and the dunes formed an alleyway to the fairway. Whoever had disposed of Gloria could have come in from the cart path or could have come in from the golf course itself. I spent another few minutes looking around until a golf ball thudded about five feet from me and I went back to the cart path and continued on around the course. Soon two carts drove up behind me and I stepped to the side and said, "Hello."

None of the four men returned my greeting. I hope they all miss a one-foot putt and lose every golf ball in their bags.

I walked for about five minutes when Linda drove up behind me, obviously somewhere on the course she had turned around. She smiled a smile at me so large I could have tossed a softball in her mouth. "Snuck out on me," she grinned.

"You are pretty when you pass out," I said.

"I had too much to drink."

"I like you topless," my Guardian Angel said.

"Linda, not to be rude, but what is your last name?" I asked.

"Adams. I was born in Scottsdale and raised here and went to college at Arizona State. Anything else the private detective wants to know?"

"Yes there is, did you tell anybody I was coming over to your apartment last night?"

The smile vanished from Linda's face. "As a matter of fact I did. Kevin wanted to know why I was talking to you. And I told him you were coming over."

"Is Kevin the golf pro who was working behind the counter yesterday?"

"You don't think he sent those guys to attack you, do you? He's a creep, but not that kind of creep."

"I don't believe in accidents," I said, not saying it could have been you my little drunk sleeping beauty.

"Would you like to go out again tonight?" Linda asked me in a tone that promised more than a TV dinner and a video.

"Yes, yes," my Guardian Angel said.

"I don't know," I said, "I might be busy, but I'll give you a call this evening."

"You don't know what you might be missing cowboy," Linda said as she got into her cart. If the cart would have had more power I would have been left standing in a cloud of smoking rubber.

"Roosevelt, Roosevelt," my Guardian Angel said. "You really disappoint me."

I headed back toward the area where Gloria had been found, looking closely at the desert rough as I walked.

The ground was now covered with footprints of all different sizes with the tell tale cleat marks from golf shoes. Obviously a lot of people had hit balls into the dunes since I had last been here. I went to the small hill that Gloria had been placed behind and tucked into the mesquite tree was an envelope with, ROOSEVELT, typed on it. "Oh man, here we go again," my Guardian Angel said.

The envelope had not been there earlier or in my normal spaced out fashion I had missed it. I took the envelope, looked at it like it was a 'Dear John' letter and opened it carefully. Typed on cheap, lightweight typing paper like one buys at Walmart was: ROOSEVELT: BE A SMART GUY AND TAKE YOUR LOUSY GOLF GAME TO TEXAS. THERE IS MORE ROPE LEFT.

Folding the letter I put it in my shirt pocket and went back to the cart path. I stood on the path and looked both directions, and then at the house on the other side of the wrought iron fence. I headed toward the pro shop and as I was about to go in I saw Linda talking on a pay phone.

Kevin, the pro, was working behind the counter. Two people were looking at golf hats. "I bet you don't get a lot of practice in," I said to Kevin.

He started to talk but I cut in. "I understand that you asked Gloria out once but she wouldn't go out with you and you treated her like scum."

He started to talk but I cut in again. "I also understand you wanted to know why Linda was talking to me."

He was getting angry and started to talk but I cut him off. "You listen to me you no putting jerk," I told him in a tone like I was talking to a guy who had just run into Matilda with his Buick. "If you ever want to mess with me, I'll put such a hurt on you, you won't ever pick up a golf club again."

Looking into my eyes he saw something that scared him, death, uncaring, lost, too many acid trips, stale beer, something, but his eyes softened and the anger left him. "I haven't done anything," he said meekly.

"I'm not so sure of that," I told him and started to walk away, but stopped. "When do they rake the rough?" I asked.

"Every evening, why?"

I didn't answer him but had a sudden hunch and walked behind the counter where Kevin was. I looked at his feet. He had on golf shoes. "You supposed to where those in here?" I asked.

"I just finished a golf lesson," he replied, "and besides, they're spikeless."

"Temper, temper, Roosevelt," my Guardian Angel said.

I don't know what it is about Kevin but I don't like him. I think he knows something about Gloria and the only way I am going to find out what he knows is through fear. Human nature being the way it is, sugar and spice a lot of times gets you nothing but bloody lips - fear gets results especially when you are working with the dredges of society.

Heading toward Matilda I took the envelope out of my pocket and read the note again. At least they had spelled my name right. I hate it when somebody sends me love notes and can't spell my name.

A new Cadillac pulled into an empty parking spot next to

Matilda as I was unlocking the door and four men started to get out. I saw a four door black Mercedes, with a driver and another man, start down the row where I was parked and then it suddenly speed up. "Duck, idiot," my Guardian Angel hollered as the Mercedes was almost even with me.

As soon as 'idiot' reverberated through my brain I hit the pavement and a shotgun blast ripped over my head and blew out Matilda's rear window. I reached for my pistol, which was where all pistols are when they don't do any good, home. The Mercedes squealed out of the parking lot.

The four men by the Cadillac gingerly looked around. "Sore losers," I told the driver as one of the men ran toward the clubhouse to, I presume, call the cops.

Fifteen minutes later Detective Richards and Williams drove in. Richards got out of the car, looked at Matilda, looked at me, scratched his ear, rubbed his left eye, and said, "Roosevelt, you'd better pick another course to play."

"It was a four door black Mercedes. There were two men, one driving and one shooting. He fired a shotgun."

"That's good," Williams said. "There are over 22,000 four door black Mercedes in this town and at least 800,000 shotguns. Do you happen to know what year the car was?"

"They all look the same to me."

"Did anybody witness the shooting?" Richards asked.

"Four guys, but they didn't see a plate or get a good look of either of the men so I told them to go ahead and tee off."

Richards and Williams got back in their car. Richards rolled down his window. "That's one ugly car you got there," he said as they started to drive away.

"Hold up," I called. "I found out Linda's last name, it's Adams. You might want to check her out."

"Already did," Richards said seemingly bored that I had been shot at but not hit. "She's a local girl, born and raised, no trouble, went to Arizona State and majored in nursing. She worked at Memorial Hospital for a year and quit. The hospital said she was a good nurse but couldn't take the pain and suffering."

I waved as they drove off. I hoped Matilda had not heard Richards call her ugly - ugly is only in the eye of the beholder and to me Matilda is finer than a Volvo, finer than Cadillac, finer than a Mercedes, finer than a Bentley...well, maybe not a Bentley. I got in Matilda, even wounded, she started right up. As I drove away I couldn't help but think, "Whoever left me the love note is also a lousy shot."

"Not even thanks for saving your life," my Guardian Angel said after I had driven for a few minutes, as if his feelings were hurt.

He can't fool me. I know he doesn't have any feelings.

"Thanks," I said, "I owe you one." At times it's best to butter up my Guardian Angel.

"You owe me one is right, so you call Linda tonight. And try to seduce her."

My Guardian Angel had to have bribed his way into heaven.

I drove to Bell Road and within five minutes came to a car window repair shop. For some reason Phoenix has more car window shops than any town I have ever seen. Within thirty minutes Matilda was as good as new, not one pellet had hit her paint. The repairman hadn't said a word about my window being shot out - I guess in Arizona it's common.

I drove back toward the golf course and took a leisurely drive through the houses that surround the course. They were all two stories, tile roofs, with double connecting garages and southwest styled yards. Every house around the course was occupied and had a little sign in the yard stating what alarm company they were connected to - it's great to live in a place where crime is rampant.

I drove back to the apartment. I got my notebook and a beer. Sitting, I took a deep breath. "I really am glad you saved my life," I told my Guardian Angel.

He didn't answer. "I really am glad," I repeated.

He still didn't answer.

"I'll call Linda in a few hours," I said. "But I am not going to try and seduce her."

I read over my notes again and remembered the photograph in the glove box and went and got it. I looked at Cecil Hoffman's photo - Gloria's ex-husband. He has dark hair, a thin neat moustache, and has the air about him like he is on top of the world. He matched the description of the man Linda said was on the golf course that told Gloria she had not been hard to find. But if it was Gloria's ex-husband, and he was smart, why would he expose himself by going to the golf course? If he knew where she was why wouldn't he go to her apartment? Maybe he is too confident. People who get away with a few crimes start thinking they will never get caught. I laid the photograph down on the table and read over my notes again.

It was 3 p.m. when I finished and I had a rash idea to drive over to Linda's apartment and break in. "No, no," my Guardian Angel said. "When you go over tonight you can snoop around without her knowing it."

"What if she doesn't want me to come over?"

My Guardian Angel was silent for a few moments before he sheepishly replied. "I never thought of that."

None-the-less, breaking and entering after being caught by Detective Richards would be pushing. There are a few times in my life I know when to not push it.

Now was a good time to try to call the six numbers in Gloria's phone book. I decided to first try all the numbers using no area code. The first number was not in Arizona. The second number was Linda's - "Hi, this is Linda, leave a message. The third number was Tatum Ranch Golf Course. The fourth number was a Tony's Pizza. The fifth number was a man's voice on an answering machine - "Hello, you know what to do." The sixth number was out of state like the first number. I got out the phone book and Florida has eight area codes so I started from the top. I dialed six area codes with no connection but on the seventh call a recorded message said. "This is Cecil Hoffman's. Leave your name and number and I will get back with you." Cecil Hoffman, Gloria's ex-husband lives in Miami. I then dialed the other number that had not gone through. All Florida area codes drew blanks. I then dialed the remaining number with the L.A. area code. "This is Cecil Hoffman. Please leave your name and number." Cecil Hoffman, the ex-husband got around. But why, if she was so afraid of him would Gloria have his phone numbers? I have no doubt Hoffman had caller I.D. - all crooks are paranoid and they never answer the phone unless they have to, especially when most people who call they owe money to. Out of curiosity, I dialed the fifth number again that had been in Arizona. "Hello, you know what to do." I dialed it again. "Hello, you know what to do." I dialed the number in L.A. "This is Cecil Hoffman, please leave your name and number." I dialed the number again that was in Florida. "Hello, this is Cecil Hoffman. Leave your name and number and I'll get back with you." By the voice I knew all three were Cecil Hoffman. I then dialed the forth number and ordered a pizza with everything on it. If Cecil Hoffman delivered it, I would shoot him.

The pizza was delivered by a young man with gold earrings in his eyebrows, lips, nose, and through the tip of his tongue. His pants were six sizes to big and his shirt would have fit a baby whale. I tipped him a quarter. If I gave him more he would have bought another earring. The pizza was excellent. Even though Gloria's choice in men had been lousy, she had known where to get good pizza.

While I ate the pizza I read over my clues one more time. I now have 29 major clues and 14 minor clues and have barely escaped being clubbed with a ball bat, knifed, and shot. I looked at the note I had pulled out of the tree - all it told me was somebody knew my name and knew how to type.

"You know, Roosevelt," my Guardian Angel said. "You're not getting paid for this. You could just boogie on out of here."

"I could," I replied.

"But not till you see Linda tonight," he added quickly.

After eating the pizza I called Linda. "Hi, this is Linda, leave a...." the answering machine stated. My Guardian Angel was bummed out...."Hang on, hang on, stupid machine, I missed it...sorry...this is Linda."

"This is Roosevelt."

"Lord, Roosevelt, somebody tried to kill you again," she gasped.

"I take it you don't want me to come over?"

"Yes... no... oh.... I don't know what I want. Maybe we should meet at a neutral site," she said, then changed her mind. "No, you come on over in about an hour."

"You're not going to be Mr. Moral again, are you?" my Guardian Angel asked me.

I didn't answer him.

CHAPTER SIX
IT'S TOO EARLY FOR HALLOWEEN

My Guardian Angel was singing a bawdy medieval song while I was taking a shower. I wished he would stop because his voice was somewhere between a croaking frog and a braying donkey.

After my shower I put on a deodorant guaranteed to keep me dry and smelling good even during a war. I splashed on cologne that hinted in all its magazine ads that when I wore it even fish could not resist me. I trimmed my beard with my battery powered beard buster and dressed in clean Levi's, a blue western shirt, a brown corduroy jacket, my stepping out pair of ostrich cowboy boots, and tucked my pistol in the back of my pants. I have become a disgrace to my old hippie roots but at least I don't look like Mick Jagger.

The apartment complex I live in is landscaped in the Southwestern style - colored rocks and cactus with a few palm trees to waste water. As I walked to Matilda, a young Mexican man with a gas powered leaf blower was blowing dirt and pieces of trash off the brown rock and into the parking lot, where another man with a gas powered leaf blower was blowing the dirt and trash into a pile so his buddy could sweep it into a large plastic garbage can. Only in America would people in the desert try to control the dirt and sand. We are definitely a people who love futility.

Driving toward Linda's my Guardian Angel wouldn't shut up. "You know Roosevelt, you could buy her a bottle of wine and some flowers," he said.

"She might not like wine," I replied pragmatically.

"All girls like flowers."

"She is into saving wildlife. She might be offended because the flowers were cut."

"How about a potted plant?"

"She has enough plants in her house to replant Colombia if it ever has a freeze."

"How about a bottle of perfume?"

"I don't know what kind she likes."

"You don't know what romance is," he said scornfully.

"Listen, the main reason I'm going over to Linda's is to snoop around her apartment not to satisfy your lecherous heart."

"Roosevelt, if I could only inhabit your body for a few months I could show you what a woman wants."

"Let me handle my own love life."

My Guardian Angel thought my last words over for a few minutes then replied solemnly, "Do as you wish oh master, I, your humble Guardian Angel will be as quiet as a nun confessing her sins."

My Guardian Angel is as full of poop as a dog that has eaten five cans of Alpo. But I did stop and buy a twelve pack of Fosters. In the parking lot I put my pistol beneath the car seat.

Linda answered the door, still in her work clothes. "Roosevelt, you dear," she said taking the beer from me. She set the beer on the table, took out two, quickly handed me one, popped the top on hers and guzzled half of it. "This has been one hell of a day. I've never seen the course so busy and then right at the busiest time two detectives came out to see me."

"Richards and Williams?" I asked.

"No, their names were Lugo and Suzzi."

"What did they want?" I asked as I sat. Linda remained standing.

"They wanted to know if Gloria and I had ever gone anyplace together. And if so, where did we go? They wondered if she confided in me and wanted to know if I knew anybody else that she knew. They even wanted to know where you live."

"Where they nice?" I asked, taking a sip of beer and hiding my concern.

"They were both nice but they didn't seem like cops. They didn't even ask me if I had any ideas who would have killed her." Gloria chugged the rest of her beer and opened another one.

"Oh boy, Roosevelt," my Guardian Angel said. "This is perfect, keep her talking and drinking."

I knew he couldn't keep his mouth shut.

"Did you ask the detectives for identification?" I asked.

"They showed me their badges."

I drained my beer and got another one.

Gloria finished her beer. "Why don't you make yourself at home while I take a shower," she said.

"Ask if you can take a shower with her," my Guardian Angel begged.

Linda headed to the bedroom, shutting the door that separated the bedroom and bathroom from the living room. In about five minutes I heard the water running in the shower. I waited a few minutes in case she was not in the shower and only letting the water warm up. Standing by the door, I listened, and then opened the door slowly. The door to the bathroom was closed and I can hear the water hitting the shower curtain. Linda's dirty clothes were in a pile by the bathroom door. I quickly checked her closet. There were several rows of dresses, a ski outfit, ski poles, ski boots, assorted shoes including six pair of high heels and a pair of golf shoes. I picked up each pair of high heels and examined them carefully. I then went into the bedroom. The bed was a twin with a bedspread decorated with dolphins. There were two chests of drawers, with plants and a jewelry box on each one. There were two bookcases with shelves covered with stuffed animals and more unicorns. I was about to go through the chest of drawers when I heard the water shut off and I dashed to the living room - barely getting the door shut as Linda came out of the bathroom. I walked to the counter that separated the dining room from the kitchen, where the phone is, and thumbed through an address book. Under S was Gloria Simpson, address and phone number. There was nothing under H. But under T there was Tony's Pizza and Tatum Ranch. Using a pen and paper by her phone I wrote down the Tony's Pizza number and stuck the paper in my pocket. I picked up my beer and looked at all the unicorns on her shelves. It's strange what people collect: Some people collect guns, others unicorns, ceramic elephants, match book covers, stamps, arrow heads, tiny spoons, dolls, salt and pepper shakers, old keys, butterflies, bugs, books, shot glasses, ashtrays, money - some people, like myself, collect trouble.

Linda strutted in all clean and squeaky. Her hair was towel dried but still wet. She had on gray cotton short pants, a gray sports bra and she was barefoot. She hadn't put on any makeup. My Guardian Angel sighed. I admired her simplicity and smiled warmly to myself. As she walked by me to get another beer she smelled like vanilla bath soap.

We sat on the sofa. "Boy, I feel better now," Linda said and took two deep breaths.

"Did the two detectives leave their cards with you in case you thought of anything that might help them?" I asked.

"No, they said they might be in touch, but they did tell me they didn't have any leads."

"Enough of this murder case Roosevelt, ask her if she wants to get naked?" my Guardian Angel said.

"Good thing you were a monk," I said to him. "With your way for words women wouldn't give you the time of day." I said.

"I never wanted to know the time of day," he said and winked.

"Who do you think killed Gloria?" Linda asked me.

"You are really pretty without makeup," I said.

Linda smiled and then said. "Tell me what you have found out about Gloria."

"I wish you were older," I told her, feeling a slight stir in my old gray heart.

Linda punched me playfully on the arm and smiled.

"Don't fall in love Roosevelt, keep it simple, only sex," my Guardian Angel said.

"I have a good idea what happened, but right now I haven't figured out how to put it all together and catch the people I think are responsible," I lied to Linda, in truth I don't know squat.

Linda looked disappointed.

"Hey," I said. "It's only been a few days."

"I've read that if there are no big breaks on a murder case within a few days the murder normally doesn't get solved."

"You must be reading some cheap murder mystery filled with violence and sports sex," I replied giving her a, 'I'm a smart private detective even though it doesn't seem like I know what I'm doing most of the time', smile. In truth, I don't know what I'm doing most of the time and when it comes to intelligence I'm about one step higher than a chimp, a dumb chimp at that - one that doesn't know how to peel his bananas.

"Are you having a low self-esteem week?" my Guardian Angel asked.

"Who do you think killed her?" I asked Linda.

"Her husband killed her," Linda replied, like even Favio knew who killed Gloria. "She told me she was afraid of him and if he ever found her, he would kill her. It's as simple as that."

"Is that too easy for you, Roosevelt?" my Guardian Angel said. "Or as usual, do you want to make a complicated mess out of it?"

"If he did then how do I pin the case on him?" I asked Linda.

"That's your job. I'm the dumb little blond who works at a golf course. But for starters I think I would try to find him," Linda said.

"That's a good idea. Maybe I should run an ad in the paper. Would the ex-husband of Gloria Simpson please contact Bob Roosevelt I think you killed your wife."

"Not funny," my Guardian Angel said.

"It must be tough. Especially doing a case you aren't getting paid for," Linda said, not at all offended by my sarcasm.

"Who told you I wasn't getting paid?" I asked.

Linda laughed. "Nobody, silly, Gloria is dead, who is there to pay you."

"You should be the private eye," I said, standing up to get two more beers.

"No," Linda said as I returned with the beers. "I don't want to be a private detective I only want to sleep with one."

Linda stood up, removed her sports bra and slid her shorts off quicker than I can wink and gave me a coy sexy smile.

"Ride 'em cowboy," my Guardian Angel hollered.

I looked Linda in the eyes and shook my head. "I can't Linda. It's not that I don't want to, or that I don't have feelings for you, but I don't mix business with pleasure and I made a vow I will only sleep with a woman I love."

"In your line of work that is probably a good idea," Linda smiled at me and put her clothes back on, seemingly not bothered by my rebuke.

"You are lovely," I told Linda.

"I won't stop trying to seduce you. A woman loves a challenge."

"Roosevelt's biggest challenge is putting one foot in front of the other one," my Guardian Angel said.

"Did Gloria ever mention anything to you about playing golf with her boyfriend?" I asked Linda, with the image of her pink freshly scrubbed body still swimming in my head.

"Not to me. In fact when she did make comments about golfers they were always negative. She thought anybody who would spend four hours hitting and chasing a little white ball around was as close to being crazy as a person could be without being committed. Why, is it important?"

"I was just wondering," I said.

Linda stood. "I have to get ready since you won't sleep with me this is the night I go to the spa."

My Guardian Angel shook his head sadly.

Linda left the room and came back dressed in one of those tri-colored spa outfits you see ladies wearing on TV who do fitness programs at four in the morning. The only people who are up at four in the morning are speed freaks and perverts and they could give a hoot about push-ups or toning up their abdominals, but they do like the ladies outfits.

We walked together to the parking lot and I escorted Linda to her car which to my surprise was a brand new gold Mazda. "Nice car," I commented, wondering how she could afford a new car when she is driving a refreshment cart on a golf course.

She stood on her tiptoes and kissed me on the cheek before she got in the car and zipped away.

"If I was alive I'd slap you silly," my Guardian Angel said as I headed to Matilda.

I stopped at a Taco Bell and bought tacos that were thrown together by a girl from Pakistan. Sitting in the neon ambiance I tried to sort my thoughts which was as hard as convincing myself

that what I was eating is a taco. There is no way the two men who had approached Linda were detectives. For one thing, they wouldn't have had to ask where I live. Gloria had to have had something they wanted and therefore they were not responsible for her death.

Back at my apartment I got my notebook and Gloria's phone book. I compared the phone number for Tony's Pizza from Gloria's book with the one I had written down at Linda's - they were the same. I picked up the phone and dialed the number for Cecil Hoffman that was in Arizona. The answering machine came on, "Hello, you know what to do."

I waited for the ring. "Hello, I am about to become your worst nightmare," I said, and hung up.

I dialed his number in Florida, waited for the machine, and said the same thing.

I dialed California and did the same thing.

Since I have an unlisted number his caller I.D. couldn't identify me.

I then called Tony's Pizza. "Tony's", a young lady with a voice that could have made her millions on a 900 number line answered. "What is your address?" I asked.

"I don't give out my address to strangers," she said slightly peeved.

"No, no, your business address."

"2245 Tatum Blvd," she laughed. "Would you like to place an order and we can have it ready when you get here?"

"No thanks," I replied. "It might take me a while, but what time do you close?"

"During the week we close at midnight," she purred. "On the weekends we close at 2 a.m."

I had a brief picture in my mind of the girl standing naked behind the counter with spaghetti sauce dripping down her body.

"I like that image," my Guardian Angel said.

"I hope you are not rubbing off on me," I said.

It was only 10 p.m. so I read over my notebook several times and added two more clues. Everything was a confusing mess. I know nothing but fragments, but I did have a gut hunch as to what had happened.

At 11:30 I drove to Tony's Pizza. It was in a strip mall between a cleaners and an ice cream shop. I parked about 50 yards away and got out of the car. At five to midnight a silver Jaguar with Arizona plates parked in front of Tony's. The driver, who had to be Cecil Hoffman, unless Cecil Hoffman has a clone and the photograph Detective Richards had given me was not Cecil Hoffman. He and two other men got out of the car who looked like they specialize in broken knees and improper English.

"I'll be dipped in pizza sauce," my Guardian Angel said.

At 12:15 Cecil Hoffman walked out of Tony's between his two knee breakers. He was carrying a night deposit bag. There is something about Tony's Pizza that smells more like fish than pizza dough.

I know it was no use to try and follow the Jaguar with Matilda. It would be like a chicken thinking it could out fly a hawk.

Back at my apartment I added one more clue to my list. I now have 34 major clues and 14 minor clues. I suddenly felt tired, not merely tired, but bone weary tired. I went to bed but couldn’t sleep. I thought about Miss Stone. I still haven't called her. I thought about Linda and it was strange, but I have warm feelings for her, not love, but good feelings. But she is far too young for me.

"Old age is a bummer," my Guardian Angel said.

I couldn't take it anymore and got out of bed, put my Levi’s on and went to watch TV. I seldom turn on the TV. In the old days drugs were better than TV and now TV is like snorting coke that is all Mannitol - all TV does is make your mind have diarrhea. On one channel a preacher was saving us from ourselves while his phone number flashed across the bottom of the screen so I could send him money so he could buy another diamond ring in God's name. On another channel a lady was trying to sell a machine that pulls the air out of freezer bags so I could stuff more food in the freezer that wouldn't get eaten anyway. On another channel a cop had just killed six men, three cows, two Indians, four women and seven kids with a pistol that only held six bullets. I turned off the TV and told myself I would go see Wang in the morning and tell him I wanted the golf channel. If I couldn't play golf then at least I would watch it. Watching golf is guaranteed to put a person to sleep.

I went back to bed knowing I wouldn't fall asleep. My Guardian Angel didn't care - he doesn't have to sleep. I've always wondered what he does while I'm sleeping. I wonder if Guardian Angels have all night parties where they sit around and laugh about the people they have to watch.

As my luck goes I was about to doze off when the doorbell rang. I put on my Levi's, walked to the door, stood as far to the side of the peep hole as I could, craned my neck and looked through the peep hole. I have always hated looking through peepholes. If somebody wants to dust you all they have to do is shoot you through the door when they hear you walk up to the door - that's why I stand as far to the side as I can. If I ever build a house I will have bulletproof doors.

"It's an old hippie paranoid thing," my Guardian Angel said.

To my surprise Detective Richards and Williams were outside.

I opened the door. "It's too early for Halloween," I said.

"Then the trick is on you," Williams replied with no humor in his voice.

CHAPTER SEVEN
TWO LITTLE WHITE LIES

Detective Richards and Detective Williams didn't wait for me to ask them in. They walked by me so fast somebody must have told them I never give to the policeman's fund.

I shut the door. "You boys are out a little late," I said.

Richards and Williams both sat, Richards in my chair, which I didn't like, and Williams on the sofa.

"Want a beer, a cup of coffee or a glass of water?" I asked.

It is good manners when people come to the house to be hospitable even if they are rude.

"Where were you this evening?" Richards demanded.

"He must be a man who needs eight hours of sleep," my Guardian Angel said.

"I take it you guys didn't come over to tell me I'm going to be a Publishers Clearing House winner?" I said.

"Answer the question, smart guy," Williams ordered.

I looked at Williams. "Listen up," I said in a cool and calm tone, which was difficult, being ordered to do things, has always settled in my stomach like two day old pizza. "Let's start from the top. Am I under arrest?"

Neither detective said anything.

"If I am, before I answer any questions, you take me downtown and book me and I'll call an attorney. If I'm not, get off your high horse and be civil. The good guy bad guy routine doesn't do a thing for me."

"You tell them, Roosevelt," my Guardian Angel said.

Williams looked at Richards like, 'let me beat the whites out of this egg'.

The day he can make me into meringue is the day the Jews give the Golan Heights back to Syria.

Richards seemed to weigh his options before saying. "I'll take a beer."

"Me too," Williams said begrudgingly.

I got three beers. "Roosevelt," Williams said, this is the cheapest beer you can buy."

"Hold your nose," my Guardian Angel told him.

"Ok, now why are you two fine specimens of the American legal system here?" I asked, cheap beer doesn't bother me.

"Around 12:30 this morning Cecil Hoffman was driving down Shea Blvd," Richards said.

"With two guys that would make a moose look intelligent," I butted in.

Williams gave me an inquisitive look.

"With two other men," Richards continued. "A black Volkswagen bug pulled up on their left side with two men in it. The guy-riding shotgun decided Cecil and his two friends were ugly and he cut loose with a pistol."

"That's a good way to get rid of suspects," I said.

"Nobody got killed," Williams said, taking a drink of cheap beer. He must have decided any beer is better than no beer.

"Cecil was shot in the left shoulder. His friend-riding shotgun took one in the ribs and the guy riding behind Cecil got shot in the left leg," Richards said.

"Sounds to me like the shooter only wanted to scare them. From a few feet he could have put one in Cecil's head," I commented.

"Or a lousy shot," Williams said.

"What kind of pistol was it?" I asked.

"We don't know yet but we'll know in the morning," Richards answered finishing his beer and holding out the can like he wanted another one.

I brought him another beer not bothering to ask Williams if he wanted one.

"So you guys came over to visit me merely because I drive a black Volkswagen and you think I might be the shooter. What type of plates did the shooter's bug have?"

"Arizona," Williams said, setting his empty beer can down. Feeling like a bad host I got him another beer.

"I have Florida plates," I said handing Williams a beer. "You guys didn't bother to look before you knocked on my door?"

Richards and Williams didn't know how to answer me without sounding dumb so they didn't say anything. Myself, when I sound dumb, I keep on talking and put my foot deeper into my mouth.

I went to the bedroom and brought out my 9 m.m. and handed it to Richards. "Be careful, it's loaded," I told him.

He released the clip, slid the breach back to flip out the chambered round - a pistol is no good unless it is ready to fire - and then smelled the barrel. He'd probably seen it done on a on a TV show.

"If I had shot at them they'd all be dead," I stated flatly.

"If you would have shot at them you might have hit yourself in the foot," my Guardian Angel said.

I sat on the sofa. "Since you guys are here I've had an interesting thing come up." I told them about the two men who had gone to see Linda. Richards confirmed my belief that the two had not been detectives. There are no detectives named Lugo and Suzzi in Phoenix.

"The bank robberies that Cecil Hoffman supposedly masterminded, does anybody know how many men were involved?" I asked.

"There were five men that went into the banks and one man driving the get away car," Richards said.

"And there have been no arrests?"

"None."

"How did the police get the idea Cecil Hoffman was the ringleader?" I asked.

"A man named Joseph Springer got picked up on an assault and battery charge," Richards said. "He was on parole for an armed robbery and didn't want to go back to prison and get his masters. He told the L.A. cops he had been in on six bank jobs and could get everybody involved for them if they would let him skate. After he gave the cops everybody's name they had him try to call Cecil Hoffman on a bugged line, but he never got through. He did

get through to a Randy Blackwell and Springer set up a meet at a bar. They put a wire on Springer and followed him. When he went into the bar he did the old run out the back door bit. He wasn't seen for three days then a lady living in an apartment complex went to dump her garbage and found him in a dumpster. His throat had been slit."

"It's hard to be a snitch with a slit throat," my Guardian Angel said.

"Nobody likes a snitch," Williams commented, which I thought was a strange statement from a cop, even though it is true.

"Springer did tell the L.A. cops the money hadn't been divided and he didn't know where it was hidden," Richards said.

"Is it possible I can get the other men's names that Springer fingered and maybe a description?" I asked.

"I can get you that by tomorrow afternoon," Richards replied.

"I'll stop by. If you can't be there leave everything with your secretary." As soon as the word secretary was out of my mouth my heart fluttered.

"Good Miss Stone," my Guardian Angel smiled.

"Who do you think killed Gloria?" Williams asked me.

"So far, of all the people who might be involved in this case, I don't see why any of them would want to kill her."

"Right now Williams and I are working on 14 homicides. You do know that you are mostly on your own?" Richards told me.

"That's how I like it."

Richards stood and Williams followed his lead. I opened the door. "Listen," Richards said, I could tell he was about to apologize for busting in, in such a huff. "Forget it," I said. "I promise you I won't break the law and I know crime doesn't pay."

They left and I shut the door. I had only told them two little white lies. I would break the law to catch a scumbag and contrary to what the police want the American people to believe, crime does pay.

I tossed the empty beer cans in the garbage, Arizona for some reason doesn't give back a deposit on aluminum cans. I reloaded my pistol and went to bed, falling asleep faster than a convict can say, "I didn't do it."

I woke up just before dawn. I hate to sleep late. Life passes by us so quickly I don't want to sleep my life away. After cleaning up, I got out the photograph of Gloria I'd pilfered from her apartment. "I wish you would have told me what you wanted to that day in the pool," I said to her image.

Certain sects of Mennonites and Amish won't let people take photographs of them. They believe a photograph steals part of a person's soul. Looking at Gloria's photograph, and feeling sad for her, I wondered if she had had a soul.

Within a block of the apartment complex was a large home improvement store that sells anything a person needs to work on their home. I figured it was easier to start close and if necessary, fan out to other stores. Most people in big cities shop as close as possible to where they live that way they get in more TV and bar time.

It was easier to walk to the store than drive so I walked, taking the photograph of Gloria with me.

The store could have held a 747 jumbo jet. A sign at the front of each isle told what merchandise could be found on that aisle. It took me 25 minutes to find where I could buy rope. They should have handed out road maps at the door. In the far corner were spools of every type of rope imaginable and every size, excluding rope big enough to moor up a destroyer. I found the spool of hemp rope that was the same size that I had seen in Gloria's apartment and around her pretty little neck. After about ten minutes a salesman walked up to me and asked, "Need any help?" Which I've always thought is a stupid question, but I didn't press the issue.

"You work this department everyday?" I asked.

He looked at me like I might be a person that management planted to check up on their employees. "I work Monday through Friday from 5 in the morning until 3 in the afternoon."

"How long have you worked here?"

"Going on two years, one more year and I should make manager."

"Good for you," I said. People with a job have always amazed me. Jobs seem futile to me. But I've always respected people who work for a living and like to let them know they are appreciated whenever I can.

The salesman smiled at me, a small bit of praise in our modern world is not a common thing. I held out the photograph of Gloria. "I was wondering if you helped this lady buy any rope."

"I sure did," he beamed as bright as a new halogen headlight. "She bought 8 feet of that 1/2 inch hemp rope you are standing by."

"You're sure?"

"Mister, I wouldn't forget a lady as pretty as she is," he said.

Back at the apartment I made a cup of instant coffee and stood on the patio drinking it. It was a beautiful day, temperature in the low 70's, sparrows were chirping, in other parts of the country people were shoveling snow and drinking flu medicine by the gallon. I finished my coffee and headed to the office.

"Mr. Roosevelt. I trust everything is fine with your apartment," Wang greeted me.

"I want you to have the Golf Channel added to my cable," I told him.

"There will be a slight charge," he stated, like I must be stupid and thought something in America was free.

"Has anybody rented Gloria's apartment?" I asked.

"No, business has been slow but two men came by yesterday and looked at it."

"Would you let me look at it? I have a friend moving to Arizona and he might be interested."

I followed Wang to Gloria's apartment. He told me they had put all of Gloria's possessions in a storeroom and if nobody claimed them within six months, they would sell them. He unlocked the door, opened it, and stood to the side to let me go in first. The apartment was empty, except somebody had been there. All the light sockets and switch plates had been removed and left on the carpet. The built in iridescent lamps in the kitchen ceiling had been taken apart. We walked from room to room, every wall socket had been removed. The air conditioner vents and heater vents had been unscrewed. The lid to the back of the toilet was sitting in the bathroom sink. Anything that could be opened had been opened. Parts of the carpet were ripped back. Wang stood in the middle of the living room looking bewildered. I walked slowly back through the apartment, looking carefully at everything. Standing in the closet, there were two large metal hooks in the ceiling that were used to hang a bicycle from - not necessarily by

Gloria. I hadn't seen them when I broke into her apartment. I reached up and was able to grab onto one with my right hand. Gripping my right wrist with my left hand I was able to lift my feet off the ground and hang from the hook. The hook had to be anchored in a ceiling stud.

Wang was still bewildered when I went back to the living room. "Somebody must have a socket fetish," I told him.

"In China we did not have this much crime," Wang said.

"The Tong has already stolen everything," I said, adding, "Can you remember what the men looked like?"

"They were both close to 200 pounds, one of the men had dark hair and was balding, and the other had wavy brownish hair and an earring."

"That could be any of nineteen million people," I commented.

I went back to my apartment and got my golf shoes and golf clubs and pistol. I put my golf clubs and shoes in the trunk and the pistol under the seat. Going to a driving range and hitting a bucket of balls seemed like a useful thing to do.

"Better than trying to kid yourself you are a detective," my Guardian Angel said.

I drove to Cave Creek Golf Course. The driving range was packed with teenagers who had either skipped school or been expelled, businessmen who were on their lunch break, and a few bookies and dope dealers.

There is something beautiful when I hit a golf ball the way I want. The sound of the hit, the flight of the ball, the way it hits the ground and rolls. I hit a large bucket of balls and then went to the putting green and was immediately asked by an 80-year-old man if I wanted to putt for a few dollars. "Why don't I just give you twenty bucks now and we don't have to putt," I told him.

He started to say something but I shook my head and he walked off mumbling something to the effect of, "How hard it was to make a living anymore and young people had no gamble in them."

After an hour I had reconfirmed the fact I can't make a three-foot putt and I went into the snack bar and ate two chilidogs and drank a coke.

With a good case of heartburn I drove to Detective Richards' office. Miss May was still behind the reception desk. I waved to her as I walked by. Miss Stone, Richards' secretary, was tip tapping away on her computer, seemingly as happy as a beaver who had found out beaver coats weren't in this year. "Detective Richards said you might be by Mr. Roosevelt," she said, "If you will take a seat."

Her smile sent goose bumps running up and down my spine.

"I don't think she is good for you," my Guardian Angel said. "But I don't care."

"I might be falling for her. The old love at first sight," I said.

"Second sight," he corrected me.

There were two chairs in the office separated by a coffee table that had a few magazines on it. I picked up a copy of LAW ENFORCEMENT, definitely not a magazine I was going to run right out and order a subscription for.

Miss Stone called Richards. "Mr. Roosevelt to see you, sir," she said. "Yes sir, I'll send him right in."

Her voice made me shudder.

Richards was practicing swinging a baseball bat when I walked in. "10th annual police tournament next week," he informed me. "My team has won it ten years in a row. It's a tough tournament, double elimination."

"I wonder how many murders get solved during tournament week?" my Guardian Angel asked.

Richards stood his bat up in the corner and sat behind his desk. "I have all the information you requested including mug shots of everybody except Hoffman, he's never been arrested, but you have a picture of him anyway." He handed me a manila envelope. "You can take it with you."

"Thanks," I said and started to tell him about Gloria's apartment being broken into but changed my mind. Right now his mind was on curve balls and change ups, not breaking and entering.

"Did you find out what type of pistol was used on Hoffman?" I asked.

"It was a 22."

"I was right. Whoever the shooter was didn't want to kill them. They only wanted to scare them."

With nothing else to say I left his office.

Miss Stone looked up from her computer. "You certainly are lovely," I told her.

"Well, thank you kind sir," she said.

I wanted to ask for her phone number. I wanted to tell her I thought I was falling in love with her. I wanted to take her to dinner and spend all my money on her. I walked out of the office with my tongue in a knot.

"That's my boy," my Guardian Angel said.

Miss May was talking on the phone when I went through the lobby, probably turning down an offer from Penthouse.

As I pulled out of the parking lot a white Chevy Nova pulled in behind me. I noticed it because both men in the car were wearing cowboy hats. I didn't think anything about it until six blocks later when they were still behind me, keeping their car about two-car lengths back. Turning left I sped into the parking lot of the Paradise Valley Mall. The Nova was still behind me. I drove slowly through the large parking lot, following the road as it circled the mall. I turned right between rows of parked cars. The Nova turned. I turned left. The Nova turned. There now was no doubt I was being followed.

"Great deductive skills," my Guardian Angel said.

I drove toward the outer edge of the parking lot where there were not as many parked cars - this is America - who wants to walk? The Nova followed, closing the distance between us. I suddenly slammed on the breaks, grabbed the pistol from underneath the seat, jumped out of Matilda and started running at the Nova, pointing the pistol at the windshield.

The driver, obviously not expecting my move, slammed the Nova into reverse and spun the tires, throwing a cloud of gray smoke into the air. The car sped backwards, swerving left and right and crashed into a parked red Ford pickup, headlight and taillight glass and plastic flew through the air. I still ran after the car, my pistol ready. The driver shifted the car quickly into forward and left me standing in a gray cloud of smoking rubber. I lowered the pistol. I know three things: The car was an Avis Rent a Car (there was a sticker on the bumper), it had Arizona plates, I couldn't tell if the men were white or Mexican because of the cowboy hats, and

there was no need to go to Avis and see who rented the car as the renters I.D.'s would be fake.

"You handled that well," my Guardian Angel said.

"Why didn't you tell me I was followed to Richards?" I demanded, a not too happy camper.

"You need practice, Roosevelt. I think you're slipping. Besides, if you needed me, I would have warned you."

I drove, deep in thought, back to my apartment. Gloria's murder was beginning to take shape in my non-fertile cerebellum.

I sat in my chair, drank a beer, and read Richards' report. It was like reading a minor Who's Who in crime. I read all about Cecil Hoffman, which was a rehash of what Richards had told me. I read about Joseph Springer, which was like closing the gate after the horse had gotten out as his throat had been cut. The other four were interesting.

BRANDON AWALT: 33 years old. Born in Kansas City, Kansas. Dropped out of high school. First arrest was for armed robbery - probation. Second arrest - armed robbery - victim would not testify. Third arrest - robbed a convenience store - five years. Discharged sentence. 6'2" tall, dark brown hair, normally keeps hair short, brown eyes, slim but muscular build, 170 lbs. no visible body markings on body or tattoos. Divorced.

CHUCK REID: 43 years old. Born in Chicago, Illinois. Graduated from Woodward High School. Four years in the Marines, explosives expert. First arrest - possession of a controlled substance, Methedrine - probation. Second arrest - possession of a controlled substance with intent to distribute - case dismissed. Third arrest - armed robbery - robbed a savings and loan - 15 years - served 8 years. 5'8" tall, blond wavy hair, blue eyes, stocky build, 250 pounds, tattoo of eagle on right forearm with words BORN TO DIE underneath. Divorced.

KIRT MCVEDE: 47 years old. Born in Phoenix, AZ. Graduated from Paradise Valley High School. First arrest - auto theft - probation. Second arrest - auto theft - probation. Third arrest - parole violation (possession of a controlled substance i.e. marijuana) - probation. Fourth arrest - possession of a controlled substance with intent to distribute - 10 years - discharged sentence. 5'9" tall, sandy brown hair, green eyes, stocky build, 195 pounds.

No visible body markings. Divorced.

RANDY BLACKWELL: 39 years old. Born in Salt Lake City, Utah. Did not finish high school. First arrest - assault - probation. Second arrest - assault - probation. Third arrest - assault - charge dropped. Fourth arrest - assault - charge dropped. Fifth arrest - armed robbery - probation. Sixth arrest - armed robbery - 8 years - discharged sentence. 5'6" tall. Black hair but balding. Hazel eyes, stocky build, 210 lbs. Normally wears gold loop in left ear. Divorced.

I looked at the blown up mug shots of all the men. None of them were men I would want my oldest daughter to bring home - that is if I had a daughter. I wondered which two had broken into Gloria's apartment. I also wondered why there was no mention of any of the men's ex-wives or if they had children.

"Wonder on wonder boy," my Guardian Angel said.

I added nine more clues to my notebook. I now have 43 major clues and 14 minor clues. Looking out my back window it was almost dark. The day had flown by. I thought about going to get something to eat but decided I would first read over my notes. I read for about five minutes when the doorbell rang. "Watch out Roosevelt," my Guardian Angel said. "I don't think it's a Jehovah's Witness."

By the tone in his voice I decided to heed his advice. Picking up my pistol I crawled to the front door. Moving to the side of the door I stood up slowly and keeping my hand on the wall side of the door jam tapped on the door with the barrel of the pistol. Two shotgun blasts ripped through the door so fast they sounded like one shot. Pieces of wood splintered through the air. I fired seven shots through the door - waited for a few seconds and fired two more. I then yanked open the door and leaped outside, landing in a shooting crouch. There was nobody. But there was a large blood spot on the patio floor and blood spots leading to the stairs. I followed the blood spots all the way to the parking lot where they ended. I know for sure Wang wasn't going to be happy. "You owe me again," my Guardian Angel boasted.

"Put it on my tab," I said. Getting shot at has a tendency to make me hard to get along with for a while, but I also realized by Guardian Angel has been right on all his warnings.

As I was about to go upstairs to my apartment Wang ran up to me. "You'd better call the cops," I told him. "My front door was murdered."

CHAPTER EIGHT
SURPRISE, SURPRISE

Wang and I were standing on my front porch when four patrolmen arrived. It had taken them thirty minutes. Not one neighbor had come over. If I had been shot, I could have bled to death six times over. Of course, I could have been a mad man and shot three or four of my neighbors for sticking their noses into my business. It's harder than it used to be to be a good neighbor. "It's ok," Wang called down to the police.

Two patrolmen came up the stairs without taking their pistols out of their holsters. I guess Wang has an honest face. The other two stayed below. The policemen looked at me. They looked at the door. "Guess they missed," one of them said.

Arizona police don't get overly excited about shootings.

"Arizona has a strange welcome wagon," I told the policemen.

The cops were efficient. I gave them my statement, which wasn't much. I told them the shotgun was probably a double barrel as I hadn't found any spent shotgun shells. I told them I knew I'd shot the shooter and showed them the blood. A policeman took a sample and placed it in a test tube. They would put out an alert to all the hospitals for a gunshot wound, but if the guy had any sense he'd go to Mexico to get worked on. They ran a N.C.I.C. check on me to make sure I wasn't a felon or wanted. They looked at my pistol, said it was a good make and I had better keep it loaded, and left in a hurry.

"It must be time for their coffee break," my Guardian Angel said.

I told Wang I wanted a new door put on immediately, a metal

door, not a wood door like had been on and exploded everywhere. And, as soon as possible, I wanted the shotgun pellet marks in the wall filled in and painted.

Wang didn't want to put a new door on until morning, but I told him. "Ok, then, I'll stay at your place and if the shooter comes back he can shoot up your door."

Wang gave me a dirty look, which made me feel proud. It was the first time in history an American has put something over on the Chinese. He started down the stairs as Detective Williams started up. They met halfway. "It's nice to see you again," Wang said to Williams.

Williams looked surprised at Wang but didn't say anything. I noticed Williams had a slight limp and his slacks didn't match his sport coat. "You missed the party," I told him. "Everybody's gone."

"I heard the report over the radio and thought I'd stop by. It seems somebody doesn't like you."

I hate it when people state the obvious and think they're saying something cute. "I wasn't voted the most popular boy in high school either," I said, adding, "What happened to your leg?"

"I fell down and twisted my knee playing handball. Hurts like the dickens."

"Are dickens related to chickens?" my Guardian Angel asked.

The maintenance man started up the stairs with a scrub brush and a bucket of water. "Before you clean up the blood I want a sample," I told him and went inside.

I took six Q-tips and rubbed one end of each into a blood spot, put the Q-tips in a plastic baggie and put the baggie in the refrigerator. When I went back to the porch Williams seemed worried. "You want a beer?" I asked.

"No, not really, no reason for me to stay," Williams said. "Glad you're ok," and he left.

"He is not too big into conversation," my Guardian Angel said.

The maintenance man was polite as he cleaned up the blood and put on the new door. It was all ‘no sir this', and ‘yes sir that'. When people know you have a pistol they are usually polite. I had a feeling he thought I was in the mob. If he had seen Matilda he would have known better - wise guys only drive Lincolns or Cadillac’s.

After the maintenance man left, I was famished and taking my notebook and pistol, drove to a Denny's. Drinking coffee and waiting for my chicken fried steak smothered in cream gravy I read over my notes. I have to get organized. Things are getting so complicated my pea sized brain can't handle the confusion. "Walking up stairs confuses you," my Guardian Angel said.

I finished the steak, drank another cup of coffee, and felt like I could challenge Stallone to a boxing match - one that wasn't held in Russia.

I decided to drive over and see Linda.

"It's not nice to drop in on people without calling," my Guardian Angel said.

"What did people do before the phone was invented?" I asked.

"Before I became a monk I was going to surprise a girlfriend. I bought flowers, a bottle of wine, and went to her house. There was a broom salesman making a house call, but he wasn't sweeping the floor," my Guardian Angel said.

I don't know what it is but it seems the only parking spot ever open at Linda's is next to the dumpster. They say a person always returns to the scene of a crime, but this was taking it a little too far.

Before I got to Linda's apartment I heard her talking. I stopped. There was a tree with a gas barbecue pit under it a short distance from Linda's and I hurried to it. I could see the front of Linda's apartment and I was partially hidden. Linda had her porch light on and was standing in the doorway. She was still wearing her work clothes. Kevin, the golf pro, was holding both of her hands. "We have to be careful," I heard him say.

Linda kissed him on the lips and then they embraced. When they stopped, Kevin patted her lovingly on the rear. He didn't notice me as he walked to the parking lot.

"Surprise, surprise," my Guardian Angel said.

I waited for at least fifteen minutes before knocking on Linda's door. I heard her approach the door and knew when she was looking through the peephole. When she opened the door she smiled at me like Cleopatra smiled at Caesar.

"I was in the neighborhood and thought I'd stop by," I said, "I hope I'm not disturbing you."

"No, come on in, I was just about to take a bath."

Linda was wearing a blue terry cloth bathrobe and like most people who are trying to keep something from someone she had her arms crossed in front of her.

"I bet she's naked under that robe," my Guardian Angel said.

"Do you want a beer?" Linda asked.

"No thanks...listen...you're about to take a bath, it's better if I go," I told her and started to walk to the door.

"I have a better idea," she said, letting her bathrobe fall open. "Why don't we take a bath together?"

I looked at her body. I looked into her eyes. I smiled. "I can't," I said like it was an apology.

"You idiot," my Guardian Angel said.

Linda smiled like she knew an inside joke and closed her bathrobe.

"Have you found out anything about the murder?" she asked calmly as she sat on the sofa.

I didn't sit down.

I've found out a few things that have surprised me," I said.

"What?" Linda asked a little too quickly.

"Nothing I want to talk about," I said.

"Do you think you will solve Gloria's murder?"

"I think there is more than murder involved, Linda," I told her. "A lot more, but, to answer your question. I'll solve the murder. After being shot at twice, dodged a ball bat and a knife attack, and being followed by two men in a car, I've started to take this case personally."

"You were shot at again?" she said, seemingly surprised.

"This afternoon somebody tried to shoot me through my front door. They must have thought a duck lived in my apartment."

"Roosevelt, you should load up your Volkswagen and get out of here," Linda said with what I took for genuine concern.

I went to the door. "Hon," I said. "If I had always done what I was supposed to, I'd be bored to death."

"Being bored is better than being dead," Linda told me with a crooked little smile on her face as I shut the door.

"Roosevelt," my Guardian Angel told me as I drove back to the apartment. "Where do you want to be buried if you get killed in Arizona?"

At times my Guardian Angel has as much faith in me as a late night radio evangelist who wants people to buy his book, THE PATH TO GODLINESS. The book is $99.95 and there is no shipping and handling charge if you buy two or more.

Back at the apartment I thought about Linda kissing Kevin.

"I don't think it was a love kiss," my Guardian Angel said.

"Me either," I said.

I went out to Matilda and got a screwdriver. I took the doorknob off my bedroom door, got the Q-tips with the blood sample on them out of the refrigerator and put them in the hole for the doorknob, and put the doorknob back on.

I then decided to organize my clues. Five hours later, after two beers, four cups of coffee, and sixteen sheets of paper, I'd organized my notebook by eliminating and combining clues.

"You can call it organizing, but it looks like a list of useless information to me," my Guardian Angel said.

I ignored him and went to bed. What does he know about writing?

CHAPTER NINE
ME AND WHOEVER KILLED GLORIA

Detective Richards was not a happy camper before his morning coffee. "Why didn't you call first?" were his first words as I walked into his office.

I felt like going into an old hippie spiel about how he was a servant of the people, and therefore worked for the people, but I know that had as much merit as B-52's dropping get well cards on Iraq. Politicians make laws not the people, and cops work for politicians, who, in most cases, could care less about the people, that is, unless the people are large corporations, so instead I said. "This was the only place I figured I could get a free cup of good coffee."

"I've told him to call," my Guardian Angel said. "But Roosevelt likes being rude."

Miss Stone clicked in with two cups of coffee, wearing a pair of high heels that would make most women dizzy. I smiled at her like a little boy in 8th grade who had fallen in love with his 26-year-old female math teacher.

Her return smile was brighter than the sunrise.

"Careful, careful, I've warned you about this one," my Guardian Angel said.

Richards inhaled half of his coffee and was immediately in a better mood. "It would be terrible to be English and have to drink tea in the morning," he said.

"It would be terrible to be English and have to say 'God save the Queen' and 'we could have won the war without you Americans', all the time," I said.

Richards laughed then asked. "So what brings you here?"

"Did you get the news about me getting shot at last night?"

Richards didn't look surprised or show even an intsy winsty bit of concern, but I could tell he didn't know and I wondered why Williams hadn't told him?

"Somebody put two shotgun blasts through my front door," I explained.

"You want to play with fire sometimes the fire burns," he said, trying to be the Dali Lama of detectives.

During my hippie days I was into philosophy, but trying to solve life's riddles with more riddles only made me more confused.

"You didn't come over here to tell me you'd been shot at. You've been shot at more times than Buddha has been on a diet," Richards said.

"That's a good one," my Guardian Angel said.

"I was wondering if you ever talked to Cecil Hoffman." I asked.

Richards gave me a look like ‘what do you think I am, a Boy Scout?' before answering. "Williams and I went over to his house the afternoon after you found the body. He has alibis stacked on top of alibis. In fact, he has so many he could sell a few to felons who need them?"

"I didn't know you knew where he lived?" I said.

"If you're suspected of bank robbery, we know where you throw your cigarette butts."

"How about the other men that Springer informed on. Do you know where they are?"

"Awalt and McVede live with Hoffman. Reid and Blackwell have dropped off the face of the earth."

I wanted to be snide and tell him since Reid and Blackwell were also suspected of bank robbery why didn't the police know where they were? But, older and wiser, I kept my mouth shut.

"Why don't you give me Hoffman's home address?" I asked.

Richards opened a drawer, fumbled around for a few seconds, and then wrote on a piece of paper and handed me the paper. His writing looked like a doctor's who wrote a prescription after eating a handful of diet pills.

9401 Paradise Valley Rd., I read. "That's the area where all the basketball and golf pros live."

"You live there, you have more money than a senator," Richards said. "But Hoffman doesn't own the house. His mother does."

"Peel me a grape," I commented, continuing, "I happened to be at Tony's Pizza one night and saw Hoffman and his two henchmen pick up the night deposit."

I couldn't tell Richards the only way I connected the two was through Gloria's phone book. "Do you have any idea the connection between Tony's and Hoffman?"

"We know that Tony's is owned by a company that we think is a front for Colombians to clean drug money."

"Colombians cutting in on Italian pizza, I like that," I said.

"The company headquarters is in L.A.," Richards informed me.

"How many Tony's Pizza's are there?"

"I don't know the exact number but I know there are over fifty."

"You can channel enough cash to buy Peru through that many stores," I commented.

"More cash than you and I will ever see," Richards frowned.

I changed the subject. I've never had enough money for it to be a problem. "There's a golf pro at Tatum named Kevin, I don't know his last name, I was wondering if you had checked up on him?"

"We ran a check on everybody at Tatum's from the bargirl to the guy who washes the carts." Richards rummaged around in his desk again, pulled out a file, sorted through it, pulled out a sheet of paper, and read. "His name is Kevin Brown and he hasn't always been the squeaky clean golf pro. When he was twenty he got busted with 40 pounds of pot in Illinois and instead of doing his time he squawked like a chicken and sent everybody else to jail."

"I take it that's what brought him to Arizona?"

"We get all the good citizens," Richards commented dryly.

"Has anything come up on the people who shot at Hoffman?"

"No, and I don't think anything will?"

"Did it ever cross your mind that the other two men involved in the bank robberies, Reid and Blackwell might be the shooters?"

"No," Richards said, a little surprised.

"Let's presume that Springer was telling the truth that the two million bucks was hidden and they were waiting for everything to cool down before they divided the money. Hoffman, being the brains, would have the money. But, what if he wanted to cut out a few guys? Maybe Reid and Blackwell? Maybe Springer wasn't killed because somebody found out he was a snitch? Maybe he was killed so Hoffman wouldn't have to pay him? If you and I stole two million bucks and I hid the money where you didn't know where it was, would you feel comfortable?"

"I wouldn't trust you to hide my dirty underwear," Richards said. "But, you've brought up an interesting point that has nothing to do with Gloria Simpson's murder, but a good point none-the-less."

I didn't tell him maybe it had everything to do with Gloria's murder.

He fidgeted with his coffee cup. "Let's say Reid and Blackwell were the guys who shot Hoffman. Then who shot at you at the golf course and your apartment?"

"I don't think they were the same people," I replied, "but I know whoever it was doesn't want me to solve Gloria's murder."

"Solving a murder that is not a murder of passion is tough work," Richards said.

"Not as tough for me," I replied. "I don't have to play by the rules, not insinuating that the police always play by the rules."

Richards gave me a wry grin.

I stood. "Thanks for all the information. I'll be in touch," I said.

"Next time call first."

I was about to open the door when Richards asked me. "Just out of curiosity, have you been doing more with Linda than asking questions?"

"I wish he was," my Guardian Angel said.

"Is Miss Stone single?" I asked.

"I think that is what Miss means," Richards said.

My Guardian Angel laughed at my stupidity.

Feeling brave I was going to ask Miss Stone out but she was not in the office. As I walked toward the lobby I ran into Detective Williams. Williams looked like he had been up all night eating

potato chips, drinking beer, and watching the triple X channel. He was also limping worse than he had yesterday.

"You were one lucky enchilada last night," he said, which in my opinion isn't very lucky. The only thing that happens to an enchilada is it gets eaten or tossed in the garbage.

"I have a Guardian Angel," I told him. "He's this little short guy who used to be a monk, not a good monk mind you, but still he was a monk. The first time I found out he existed was when he saved my life in Vietnam. He warned me last night or I would be, as you say, an unlucky enchilada."

"You've got one top drawer missing," Williams told me and limped away.

"See what happens when you tell someone the truth," my Guardian Angel said. "They think you're lying."

I drove toward Paradise Valley to take a look at Cecil Hoffman's house.

Paradise Valley borders Scottsdale. The homes range from spacious to so big they verge on being obscene. The Paradise Valley Country Club is so exclusive if you make ten million a year you can apply for a job as the cart boy.

There were only two houses on the block where Hoffman lives, both were surrounded by walls so massive Israel would be interested in them. The rock wall that surrounds Hoffman's property is over eight feet tall. There are large trees growing above the wall. There are monitoring cameras on top of the wall spaced about every twenty feet. Most disturbing of all there are signs on the wall in both English and Spanish stating - GUARD DOGS ON DUTY - NO TRESPASSING.

"I wonder if a Jamaican out to rob the house and getting all chewed up for his efforts could sue on the grounds he hadn't been able to read the sign?" my Guardian Angel asked.

"In California it would be a shoe-in case," I said.

Driving slowly I looked through an ornate wrought iron gate, but large palo verde trees bordering the winding driveway obscured a complete view of the house, which was at least 75 yards from the gate. All I could see were small sections of the red tile roof through the gnarled branches and leaves. I drove around the block and turned around. The trees were so thick along the back wall the cameras would almost be useless. I drove slowly back the way I had come, noticing a call box by the gate. I felt like stopping, picking up the phone, and saying. "Let me in, I want some of the bank money," but then I saw a monitoring camera on top of a gate pillar.

"Can you imagine living in a place like that?" my Guardian Angel asked.

"He's afraid of something," I commented.

"Oh to have such fear."

"What's life if you're afraid all the time? If you're so chained to your possessions you forget the true aspect of living is to give and help." I said, surprising myself - years ago I did

give Buddhism a try but I got tired of rice.

"You know, when you have used up all your luck and get killed, with an attitude like that you'd make a good guardian angel," my Guardian Angel said.

"I'd rather do a stint in purgatory," I replied.

"Not if you saw it, Roosevelt. Believe me."

I turned around at the corner and drove by the house one more time. "How can I get in to take a look at that house?" I muttered to myself.

"Don't ask me?" my Guardian Angel said. "It would be like breaking into jail." He laughed at his own joke, which, like most of his jokes I didn't think was funny.

I was hungry and stopped at a fast food restaurant where I could get two eggs, bacon, juice, and three rubber pancakes for $2.99, all to the serenading of thirty crying kids.

While I ate I tried to think of my next move. Richards told me Awalt and McVede lived with Hoffman, hopefully it wasn't a love triangle, but who knows. If my assumption was right, that Reid and Blackwell had tried to shoot Hoffman, they have to be in town. Since the police don't know where they are, how can I find them? I doubt Reid or Blackwell is into the arts and spend their free time going to the opera or plays. I also doubt they spend their evenings going to good restaurants and arguing what kind of wine went best with their meal. They might go to basketball games, but it would be almost impossible to spot them at a game packed with jumping people shouting sportsmen like things like: "The ref sucks," and lamenting how much they owed their bookie. Taking the last bite of my rubber pancake, smothered with artificial maple syrup made by Dow Chemical, I had a good idea.

"This could be dangerous," my Guardian Angel said.

Driving back to the apartment I didn't think about Gloria. I didn't think about Linda. I didn't think about Hoffman or any of his partners in crime. I thought about Miss Stone. Tall, blond, long-legged, with high heels so high she could get a nosebleed. "I should ask her out and pursue my feelings for her?" I told my Guardian Angel.

"Why won't you listen to me?" he said. "She is not the lady you are looking for."

"Do you think she will go out with me?" I asked.

"She'd go out with you the day Congress votes in a pay cut," he replied.

At the apartment I looked through the yellow pages and wrote down the addresses for all the topless clubs in the metro Phoenix area. I then wrote down the addresses for the gentlemen's clubs - which are still topless bars but a guy parks your car, the beer is more expensive and all the girls are reported to be coeds, which has always seemed strange to me. What is the difference between coed skin and non-coed skin? And why is coed skin more expensive than non-coed skin? To my surprise, there were only ten nude establishments in town. In most big cities there are twenty on each block.

It was a little past noon and too early to go to a dark, smoke-filled room and watch naked ladies dance to music so loud it would make the top of my head vibrate.

"Maybe for you, undersexed one, but not for me," my Guardian Angel said.

I started another list of clues.

"Call you clue man," my Guardian Angel said.

When I was finished I looked up ‘parks' in the phone book and found what I was looking for, the 50 acre Desert Botanical Center, located in the middle of Phoenix. There would be somebody there who could answer a question that has been burning in my mind since I found Gloria.

The Desert Botanical Center is located in Papago Park. It is a beautiful walk through saguaro cactus, barrel cactus, prickly pear cactus, and every other cactus that grows in the desert southwest and many parts of the world. The cacti are set off by palo verde trees, mesquite trees, Russian olives, all surrounded by desert flowers and the steady buzz of hummingbirds and bees. It is a desert Central Park without muggers, pick pockets, rapists, and panhandlers - all the things that make New York unique. In the center of the park is a futuristic adobe house designed to save water and rely more on the sun for both heating and cooling. Most modern people don't like the house because it doesn't waste enough money. What is the object of being rich if you can't prove to people how much money you can waste?

I walked through the park and enjoyed watching people from all over the world marvel at the stark beauty of the desert, and for a short time remembered the feeling when I was a hippie and there were really no cares in the world. Everything had a place, a purpose, life was to enjoy and learn and make better. God, it's hell to grow up. Or, maybe it's hell to have told myself I had to grow up. I saw a white haired, older man, with a long white beard, wearing a shirt with a park service emblem on the shoulder. He was watering a plot of yellow California poppies and I walked over to him. "They're gorgeous," I told him looking at the flowers.

"During a wet spring the desert will be covered with them," he informed me. "This year it's too dry."

"That's too bad," I said.

"It's no big deal," he said. "Mother Nature gives and takes."

"I was wondering if you could help me out." I asked.

"If you don't want me to baby-sit, loan you money for a cup of coffee, or paint your house, I might be able to."

"Funny guy," my Guardian Angel commented.

I laughed at the man's reply. "No," I said. "I have a question about ants."

"I can help you there. I took entomology in college."

"What is entomology?" my Guardian Angel asked.

"I don't know but it sounds impressive," I said.

"What type of ants are there in the desert?" I asked the man.

"To make it simple for you there are three main types of ants in the desert: red ants, black ants, and red and black ants. The red ants are small and it hurts when they bite you. The black ants are small and it hurts when they bite you. The red and black ants are a cross between the two and it hurts when they bite you. It's interesting, but when a red ant hill has a war with a black ant hill they fight until there are only a few survivors from each hill, then they will stop fighting and cross breed and form another colony."

"It's only man that is into total destruction," my Guardian Angel said. "I guess ants have no God."

"How about big black ants?" I asked the man.

"How big?"

"The ones I've seen are about 1/2 an inch long."

"Those aren't desert ants. Those are tree ants. If you saw a big black ant in the desert he got carried there by the wind. If a scout red ant sees a big black wood ant it would be like you seeing a twelve ounce medium rare sirloin."

"That's interesting," I said.

"Years ago, before the town had grown so much and all the people from the Midwest had moved here the only place you saw black wood ants was in cottonwood groves along the river. Now you can find them in people's backyards who have planted non-native shade trees and grasses."

I didn't comment, feeling like I was going to be tested and should be taking notes.

"You know why people from the Midwest come out here and plant grass and trees?" he asked me.

"I have no idea."

"So they can still have hay fever," he answered, laughing so loud people walking by turned and looked at us.

"Well thanks," I told him. "You've been a great help."

"No problem, you have any more questions, just look me up."

What a great life he has I thought as I walked away.

"Who cares about ants?" my Guardian Angel said. "Let's head for the topless bars."

"Me and whoever killed Gloria care about ants," I replied.

"Oh," is all my low class Guardian Angel could say.

I went back to the apartment and added one more clue to my new list. I have 38 organized clues and 8 new ones. I then decided to take a nap. "Boy, you are getting old," my Guardian Angel said.

"You never used to take naps."

"It's going to be a long night," I said.

"Why?"

"Tonight I'm going to visit as many topless bars as I can."

"Roosevelt, sometimes I love you," he beamed.

CHAPTER TEN
SILICON HEAVEN

It was 8 p.m. and I reread my descriptions of Chuck Reid and Randy Blackwell. Old hippie minds are not good on long-term memory. Their main characteristics are: Chuck Reid has a tattoo of an eagle with BORN TO DIE under it on his right forearm, weighs 250 pounds, and is about 5'8" with blond wavy hair. Randy Blackwell is 5'6", is about 210 lbs, with black hair, balding, and usually wears a gold loop in his left ear.

I took my list of topless bars and gentlemen's clubs, my pistol, and headed for the underbelly of life. My Guardian Angel was so happy all he could do was mumble something about dollar bills and lap dancing.

Years ago most topless bars were owned by biker gangs and their 'old ladies' were the dancers. While the bikers were selling dope, pulling off armed robberies, killing bikers from other gangs, or getting tattoos, the women were making an honest living by showing their charms to traveling salesmen and doing tricks. Gentlemen's Clubs are now owned by people who belong to the Rotary.

The Great Alaskan Bush Company is on Grand Ave. It's located in a seedy part of town - shattered beer and cheap wine bottles litter the gutters like so many lost dreams, homeless people stumble around carrying signs stating 'Will work for food but I really don't want to,' and cops drive around who are assigned the area because they don't have the verbal skills to work in a nice part of town. I parked Matilda as close to the club as I could and left my pistol under the seat. I weaved through six hookers on my way to the door. Once inside I had to let my eyes adjust from dark to darker and was surprised there was nobody named Bruno collecting a cover at the door. The place smelled of sweaty bodies, beer and smoke. There were chipped and dented tables scattered about with chairs placed haphazardly around them. A long bar that stretched down one wall had six men at it. A small-elevated stage protruded into the room. The stage had a backdrop of black velvet with silver sequins on it and white, blue, green, and yellow lights illuminating the stage. There were chairs around the edge of the stage. Five men were sitting by the stage. A girl, maybe 20, with a tattoo of a snake on her ankle and nothing else on was dancing. I sat at one of the tables. I didn't want to sit at the stage. Naked women dancing in front of me are not really my cup of instant coffee. I hadn't been at the table more than 15 seconds when a waitress, chewing gum and wearing nothing but six-inch high heels clicked over. She looked like the Hustler Magazine type. "What's it be hon?" she asked, as if speaking was a problem.

"Give me a draw," I ordered. I figured being polite in a place like this was as useful as saying please to a judge.

She set a napkin on the table, nice touch, and a laminated sheet of paper. I glanced at the paper: lap dance - $10.00. Table dance: $5.00. Back room body painting - $50.00. Private shower dance - $75.00.

I heard "Oh yea baby" and looked toward the stage. The girl was down on her knees with her more than ample bosoms about a 1/2 an inch from a man's face. "Come to papa," he hollered.

The men sitting at the bar had their backs to the stage and didn't bother to turn around. They had to be regulars and even naked women can become old hat if you see them all the time.

Ms. Hustler clicked back over with my beer. "Four bucks," she said, popping her gum. "Want a lap dance or anything?" she asked me as I took a five out of my billfold.

"I do," my Guardian Angel said.

"Keep the change, hon," I told her.

She smiled at me and clicked away.

The girl on the stage finished her number and disappeared behind the velvet curtain. "Come on back honey," one of the men hollered.

Drinking my beer, I looked closely at the men sitting around the stage. None of them resembled Reid or Blackwell. They looked like bookies that had forgotten to cover their bets and were now trying to figure out a way to draw unemployment. I finished my beer and went to the bar, taking my empty glass with me. I stood on the far end of the bar so I could see the men sitting at the bar. None of the men resembled Reid or Blackwell. The bartender, a short squat man with long brown hair came over. I slid the glass to him. He took the glass, filled it and brought it back. I laid a five on the bar. He took it and brought me back a one. "I'm looking for a big guy with a tattoo of an eagle on his right forearm and the words BORN TO DIE underneath. You haven't by chance seen him here?" I asked.

"What are you mister, a cop?" he smarted off.

"If I was a cop, I'd bust you for that gram of cheap crank in your pocket," I told him, and gave him a look that he was a pooper-scooper.

He started to say something but I butted in. "No, he owes the wrong people some serious cash and they hired me to get it back. In fact, they're paying me so much money if I find him I'll toss a little money to the person who helps me to him."

"How much money?"

"500 bucks."

"Mister, I wish I'd seen him," the bartender said, letting me know that for $500 he'd turn in his mother.

There is a large part of our society that looks up to gangsters. When I was younger, I called them lost souls. Now I call them scum.

I walked back to my table as another dancer came on the stage. She was tall, close to six feet, and no doubt a real blond. She started dancing to a fast rap tune. "No self- respecting bank robber would come here," my Guardian Angel told me.

"Who does come here?" I asked him.

"Minimum wage workers who are single or fighting with their wives and college kids with fake I.D.'s," he informed me.

I finished my beer and left. Two hookers were talking to a man in his car. Across the street a homeless man was trying to get some sleep on a bus stop bench.

"Let's go to one of those classy places," my Guardian Angel said. "You know, one of those places where attorneys and big drug dealers hang out."

I looked down my list and picked out Le Girls. It was advertised as having five continuous stages and a big screen TV.

"People who go to a topless bar to watch TV have a problem," my Guardian Angel said.

It also advertised food. I pictured the menu as I drove: Bare breast Chicken sandwich. Bun chops. Table Dance soup. Nipple Rueben.

The parking lot for Le Girls was packed but none of the cars were junkers. All the cars were new. When I pulled up to the well lit front a young man wearing dark slacks, white shirt, and a red tie opened the door for me, handed me a parking ticket, and parked my car. A pretty lady in a white teddy, white high heels, and white fish net stockings met me at the door and escorted me to a table. The tables had white starched tablecloths. The place had a stage in every direction I could look. Young women, none of who have tattoos, were dancing on each stage. There were no chairs around the stage. The waitresses working the large floor were all wearing teddies. The clientele was mostly suits, most with their ties loosened and cuffs rolled up to show off their gold bracelets and expensive watches. In my Levi's, western shirt, and boots, I felt like an Arab in Hong Kong. There were naked girls doing table dances at several tables. Across the room there was a glass-enclosed poolroom. The panels of glass had etched nudes on them. On the other side of the room was a glass-enclosed bar and I could see the large screen TV. I figured there was close to 100 men in the club and at least ten women. A waitress came to my table that was so pretty my Guardian Angel started to drool. If anybody else could see him I would be embarrassed to death. "What would you like, sir?" she asked, with a voice that could have melted half the North Pole.

"Ask her if the teddy she is wearing is edible?" my Guardian Angel slobbered.

"Bring me a draw and a shot of Jim Beam," I told her.

The drink was $9.50. I gave her a ten and told her to keep the change. She looked at me like a dog looks at a tree he was about to tinkle on.

I gulped the shot and chased it with a swallow of beer. It burnt all the way down the way whiskey is supposed to. If I drank three shots I would start feeling ornery. Jim Beam is good for getting your teeth knocked down your throat and not knowing they're missing until the next morning. I looked around the room. The only way I would be able to get a good look at everybody was to walk around. I got up, taking my beer with me, and went to the poolroom. I didn't see anybody that vaguely resembled Reid or Blackwell.

There were ten tables in the poolroom. Men with custom-made pool sticks played at all the tables, most were smoking cigars, not Swisher Sweets. By the looks of the men, they don't need to rob a bank - they own them.

I went to the bar. The bar itself was polished walnut, old style paintings of nudes in gilded frames hung on the wall. The large screen TV was turned to a basketball game. The tables had old-fashioned kerosene lamps on them that had been converted to electric. A hundred years ago the four bar maids working the floor would have ended up with every ounce of gold or silver a miner brought to town. There was nobody in the bar that vaguely resembled Reid or Blackwell. I started to leave. "Forget Reid and Blackwell," my Guardian Angel pleaded, "this place has the prettiest women I've ever seen in my death."

"It's not costing you close to 10 bucks for drinks either," I told him, heading for the front door.

The valet parking cost me another $5.00 and I tipped the guy $4.00. There has to be some compensation for having to stand outside and never get to look.

I read my list and told my Guardian Angel to pick out a club. He picked out Heartbreakers. "I chose the name because of you," he said, like I should feel sorry for him.

I feel sorry for him all right. The way I feel sorry for cattle as I eat a steak.

Heartbreakers is a few minutes from the airport. At least I got to park my own car and by the pickup trucks in the parking lot I knew it wasn't a suit club - which was too bad for the ladies - everyone knows cowboys don't tip, unless you count quarters as tips.

When I walked into the club it was obvious that a prerequisite for working at Heartbreakers was a girl had to have a boob job. They were too perfect, too perky, and too firm. It was a silicon heaven.

"I like silicon," my Guardian Angel said.

The place was decorated like an old time western saloon with swinging doors. Chaps, branding irons, and other old western memorabilia hung on the walls. Large wagon wheel chandeliers dangled from the ceilings, not emitting bright light but enough to make out people's faces. The three ladies working the floor had nothing on but white cowboy hats and white cowboy boots. There was a mechanical bull to ride and two stages opposite each other. The patrons ranged from cowboys to construction workers, unless white T-shirts have become a new fashion statement for the rich I looked over the heads of all the people to try and find a seat at one of the closely packed tables. There was a bar, but no chairs. There was a large sign over the bar that stated - 'LOOK BUT DON'T TOUCH'.

As I headed for the bar my Guardian Angel was over his bummer and singing, "Get along little doggies."

The bartender was a large man with a shaved head and enough tattoos on his arms I couldn't tell where skin left off and ink took over. "What it be partner?" he hollered as a girl came out on stage and Western music vibrated the rafters.

"You wouldn't by chance have any food?" I hollered back.

"Ham and cheese pizza, I cook it myself, tear a whole in the cellophane and pop it in the microwave," he hollered.

"Ham and cheese and a draw," I hollered.

The beer and sandwich came to $6.00. I ate the sandwich positive I wouldn't hurt my system by ingesting a few vitamins from the fake ham and imitation cheese. The sandwich was so good I ordered another one and another beer. Waiting for my other sandwich I looked over the crowd. With two stages and two gorgeous girls dancing the men's heads shifted from stage to stage. Some of them would have whiplash in the morning. The music ended and men tossed dollar bills up onto the stages. I had been wrong about broke cowboys. The girls came back onto the stages

and picked up the money. During the lull in the action some men ordered table and lap dances. I did notice bouncers placed strategically around that looked like breaking bones is there favorite thing to do.

My sandwich arrived and when I was on my second bite the music started up again. When the lady came out onto the stage closest to me I almost spit out my rubber ham. Miss Stone, alias Miss April, my maybe love, started dancing. "Bye, bye love," my Guardian Angel said.

Miss April had on a short blue jean skirt, a wrap around halter-top and her trademark high rise high heels. A few minutes later she was naked and making moves with her body she didn't learn from tip tapping away on her computer. I was startled, engrossed, amazed, impressed and depressed all at the same time. "You'll get over it, Roosevelt," my Guardian Angel said.

"I know," I said sadly.

I didn't look around as somebody jostled me to get to the bar. Ten minutes later, with the music over and Miss April picking up more money than most people make in a week I turned my head and looked directly into Detective Williams face. "Roosevelt, this isn't a place for a famous private eye," he said.

"After watching Richards' secretary, you are some kind of ugly," I told him.

"Don't I know it," he agreed then looked at Miss April. "I bet they are not real."

"Don't take that bet," my Guardian Angel said.

Williams pointed to a table and we went and sat down. His limp seemed to have improved. "The women in this place are the best," he informed me. "Plus it doesn't cost you an arm and a leg."

"I take it you're not on duty trying to bust people for doing more than lap dances in the parking lot?"

"Not me. I don't care what people do as long as they don't kill people."

A waitress came over and Williams ordered a rum and coke. I didn't want anything else. "So what are you doing here?" he asked me. "I figured you would be the type that hung out at a law library."

"I'm playing a hunch. I think I can find Reid and Blackwell by hanging out at topless bars."

For a brief instant Williams looked worried.

"Remember that guy that got shot in the parking lot at Linda's apartment. Did anything come up over that?" I asked.

"We know you shot that guy," Williams said, looking at me like I would admit it.

I didn't say anything.

"The guy that got shot," Williams went on, "is a street tough named Randy Fearless. His arrest record is longer than the Old Testament. Whoever shot him," Williams put emphasis on 'whoever', "did the city a favor."

"Do you know where he is now?" I asked.

"All we know is that after he got out of the hospital he left town. We couldn't arrest him for anything. Getting shot isn't against the law."

"How about the other guy?" I asked just as the music came back on and two girls walked out onto the stages.

"A Mexican national. The Border Patrol sent him back to Mexico to grow marijuana," Williams hollered over the music. "We figure they were trying to rob you," he bellowed.

I didn't reply but gave him a look like I am as innocent as a 10 year old girl going to Catholic school.

While the girls danced I looked over the room. If Reid and Blackwell were there they had had complete body and facial plastic surgery. When the ladies finished dancing I stood. "It's not that I don't like your company," I told Williams.

Williams could care if I stayed. By the look on his face he was getting ready to order a table dance.

I went outside and stood by the door. It was interesting that both men who had tried to ambush me at Linda's were now out of town, but I didn't think for a minute they were merely trying to rob me. I heard the door open behind me but didn't turn around and started toward Matilda. "Roosevelt," a female voice called.

I turned and it was Miss April. "I saw you inside," she said, sounding as good as real cream and strawberries. "Did you like my show?" she asked with a smile on her face that put a jack-o-lantern to shame.

I didn't know what to say. "Yes, you have a great body and I like the way the shadows curve around your rear end when you bend over and dance a few inches away from a man's face," didn't seem like the nice thing to say, so I said, "You have a lot of talent and put art into your show."

"You lie," she smiled.

"Even to his mother," my Guardian Angel said. "But I loved your show."

"What are you doing Roosevelt? Working on your murder case or out seeing how the lonely spend their time?" she asked.

"I'm trying to locate two men and I figured the best place to start looking would be topless bars."

"Are you going to another one?"

"That was my plan. The next place on my list is Babe's."

"Would you like some company? It's only eleven and I'm not the least bit tired."

How do you say no to a woman you have already seen naked? "Your car or mine?" I asked.

"My car is in the shop."

As I opened the door to Matilda for her I asked, "By the way, what is your first name?" which seemed like a strange question.

"Barbara."

"Nice to meet you," I said as I started Matilda.

I started to put Matilda into gear but Barbara put her hand on my knee. "You know ever since you came into the office the first time I have wanted to get you naked. Why don't we skip Babe's and go to my house?"

"She is not the love of your life but let's head for her house," my Guardian Angel hollered.

"I'll tell you what, after Babe's, we'll go to your house, but I only want a cup of coffee," I told Barbara. I don't see any need to tell her my moral views about men and women.

For a mere instant she seemed disturbed. Then she smiled. "Ok soldier boy," she said, "Babe's it is," and leaned over and kissed me on the neck. Barbara seems to have her feet planted firmly in reality although it might be the reality of Mars or Pluto.

My Guardian Angel was in the back seat gagging.

CHAPTER ELEVEN
LORD SAVE US

When Barbara and I went into Babe's Gentlemen's Club all the men looked at her like a woman with clothes on was the sexiest thing they had ever seen.

Babe's interior looked like a good French restaurant. The tables were large and the high-backed chairs were covered with red velvet. On the walls were gilt-framed paintings of nude women, ranging from Egyptian and Greek to the early 1900's. The floor was covered with a deep pile light beige carpet. People for sure don't toss their cigarette butts on the floor and grind them out with their heel. The ladies working the floor were dressed like French maids, not the type that clean the house, but the ones that polish the master. There were four large stages, one with a glass shower stall in the middle, but instead of chairs around the stages, there are booths. A French maid with a rear end a Rodeo Queen would die for showed us to a table in the corner. Barbara ordered a dry martini, which surprised me - she doesn't look like the Martini type. I ordered a Corona.

"You can take Barbara home and leave me here," my Guardian Angel said.

The patrons of Babe's didn't look like money is a problem. A French maid selling 20 dollar cigars was doing a brisk business. A card on the table had a price list - a table dance was $75.00. "Breasts have come a long way," I told Barbara.

"Roosevelt," she smiled, a smile that would make a donkey grin, "Boobs have always gotten a girl a long way if she knows how to use them."

"This one knew how to get off the farm," my Guardian Angel said.

"This one owns the farm," I informed him.

The French Maid brought our drinks. "I'll get these," Barbara said, handing the girl a gold Master Card.

I'm all for equal rights.

"To coffee," Barbara smiled over the top of her glass.

An announcer, dressed in a black tux with a red cummerbund, walked onto the stage that had the shower stall, "And now ladies and gentlemen Miss Rene Sharp for your entertainment."

"That is the best shower I have ever seen," my Guardian Angel said when she was done.

"I've been thinking of adding that to my act. What do you think?" Barbara asked.

"You and Roosevelt could have a rehearsal tonight," my Guardian Angel said.

"Showers are nice," I told Barbara.

"Roosevelt, when I'm done with you, you won't have the energy to turn on a water faucet," Barbara said, her remark sounding almost like a threat.

"Time to leave, time to leave, time to leave, time to leave," my Guardian Angel said in a cheap imitation of Big Ben ringing four o'clock.

Barbara waved at a French Maid as two men walked into the club. Both were heavy set men, not tall, one has dark hair and is balding and has a small gold loop in his left ear. The other has wavy blond hair and is wearing a short-sleeved shirt. I couldn't read the words under the eagle tattoo on his right forearm but I'll bet every dime I have wasted it says, 'Born To Die', and not, 'Mary had a little lamb.'

You look like you've seen your ex-mother-in-law," Barbara said, eyeing me suspiciously.

"I see who I've been looking for," I said, not taking my gaze off Reid and Blackwell.

"Roosevelt, sometimes you amaze me," my Guardian Angel

said.

Barbara turned and watched as the two men were escorted to a table on the other side of the room. "What are you going to do now?" Barbara asked.

"I don't know," I told Barbara truthfully. Finding the cat and catching the cat are two different things.

"I think we should follow them," she said, sounding like she was the smartest thing since twist off caps on beer. "Let's go outside and park around the corner and wait for them to come out."

"Barbara, people get hurt in this business."

"I like excitement, Roosevelt. It does something to my hormones."

"Ok, before long we'll go outside and wait. When they come out we'll follow them," I conceded, perhaps letting my desire to know where Reid and Blackwell live override my better judgment.

I could see Reid and Blackwell clearly from where Barbara and I sat. While we had two more drinks they had two table dances and I could tell by the smiles on the dancer's faces as they walked away they had been tipped well.

My Guardian Angel was admiring a red headed French Maid who was setting drinks down at a table close to us when Detective Williams walked into the club. He scanned the room as though he was looking for someone, saw us, looked surprised, hesitated for a moment as though unsure of himself and then limped over to our table. "Barbara, you'd better watch out for this guy," he said and looked at me like I was going to ask him to sit down.

Barbara smiled at him like he was a big time producer who had just signed her for her first movie role.

I noticed Reid and Blackwell talking but they didn't look over at our table.

"You definitely get around," Williams said to me in a sarcastic tone.

"This is a private party," I said.

"Don't call me the next time you need a cop," Williams replied gruffly and headed toward the bar.

Barbara didn't say anything about me not asking him to sit down, but I could feel tension in the air.

When the next stage show started I stood and took Barbara's

hand. "Time to get out of here," I told her. I was hoping Reid and Blackwell wouldn't notice me because of the show. If my assumptions are right I figure they know what I look like. Williams ignored us.

We walked out with Barbara on my right shielding me from Reid and Blackwell. I didn't see them glance in our direction. I moved Matilda to where I had a good view of the front door and directly in line with the parking lot exit. "Now we sit and wait," I told Barbara after I turned off the engine.

"This isn't too exciting," she said. "My hormones aren't fluttering."

"Being in this business is like being in the infantry during a war, most of the time it's boring, but when the frog hits the fan it's more excitement than you really want."

"I can't wait," Barbara commented in a tone that is almost scary.

While waiting Barbara and I talked about her. I've found the best way to get on the good side of a woman is to talk about them - of course for a woman to get close to a man it works the same way. We were talking about her first dancing job in Kansas City when Williams left the club. He walked as quickly as a man can with a limp to his unmarked squad car and sped out of the parking lot.

"He's a bad boy," Barbara said, "Using the company car for personal business."

Thirty minutes later Reid and Blackwell left the club. They got into a new four door light green Chevy. When they pulled out I was right behind them. I followed them down Thomas Street for several blocks, letting a car get between Matilda and the Chevy as a precaution, but with the heavy stream of headlights I wasn't too worried they'd discover they were being followed. A few blocks later they turned onto McDowell. We drove about ten blocks and they turned onto Shea. On Shea they drove all the way to Tatum and turned left into a strip mall, parking in front of a Denny's that was on the corner. As they got out of their car I kept driving. Barbara watched them go into the restaurant at which time I parked where I could see their car. While they ate we discussed the good points and bad points of dancing nude for a living. I found out that on a good night Barbara earned anywhere from $500 to $1000, which is one reason it's better to be a female in this modern world.

When Reid and Blackwell came out I followed them up Tatum and we drove past the apartments where I live. Three blocks away, on the corner of Bell and Tatum, was a large apartment complex called Tatum Place, they pulled in. I pulled in at another entrance. If their apartment was like most when somebody rents an apartment they are assigned a parking spot with the same number as their apartment. I circled the apartment complex and when I saw their parked car I got out and looked at the number that was painted on the curb - 304. Life is good.

"That's it," I told Barbara as we drove away.

"That's it," she said disappointed. "No fights, no shootouts, no nothing."

“Most of the time life is boring and then it gets dull. I can take you home now. Where do you live?"

"I live off of Pima," she replied sounding like a spoiled little rich high school girl who was sulking because her father bought her a new Honda and not a Porsche.

I parked in the driveway of a large adobe colored brick home on a corner double lot. The house was beautifully landscaped, with small lamps that illuminated the cactus in the sand and gravel yard. The windows have ornate wrought iron over them and there was an entryway to the front door with a wrought iron gate that matched the window coverings, giving the front of the house double protection. A red bougainvillea grew up each side of the wrought iron gate and draped over the top into a small entryway. I got out of Matilda and a motion light came on over the gate. I opened the car door for Barbara as she had made no attempt to open her door. I guess she expected men to open car doors for her. A beat up old Ford pickup slowly rounded the corner as Barbara and I walked toward her house. "Fighters at six o'clock," my Guardian Angel yelled as the pickup stopped.

I pushed Barbara away from me with such force she slammed into the ground like she was in a belly flop contest. I turned and ran in a crouch toward Matilda to get my pistol. A bullet sang by my head and hit the house. I dove to the ground and started low crawling to Matilda - who says infantry training doesn't help one in civilian life. Another bullet hit inches from my head, sand and grit cut into my face. Another bullet screeched off the ground. I reached Matilda, raised up and yanked open the door and fumbled for my pistol under the seat. I looked at the truck as a Mexican man with a rifle started to get out of the truck. My hand found the butt of the pistol. The Mexican started to raise the rifle toward me but the barrel hit the open door giving me an extra second to get control of the pistol. The rifle barrel pointing at me looked like the barrel of a 150 m.m. recoilless. I saw a wicked smile on the man's face. I fired four quick rounds, three of which hit the man in the chest. The rifle clattered to the pavement as the man fell to the ground with a look of utter disbelief on his face. The pickup engine revved but then slowed down, as if the driver planned to speed away but changed his mind. The driver got out of the truck, firing a shotgun over the bed of the truck more to keep me down than in my direction. He then crouched, keeping the truck bed between himself and me. I ran to the front tire of the truck, hid behind the tire, then peeked under the truck and saw his legs as he crept toward the rear of the truck. I fired twice, hitting him in at least one leg. He fell, exposing his body. I fired three more times - hearing the impact of each bullet. His body twitched, then was still. In the ensuing silence I heard Barbara groan. I stood, pointing my pistol at the first man and walked cautiously over to him. The man was laying face down on the pavement, which couldn't have been too comfortable. I rolled him over with my foot, pointing the pistol at his head. I was a better shot than I thought. There are four neat bullet holes in the center of his chest and it didn't matter if he was lying on a cactus - he would never feel anything again. I crouched in a shooting position and moved cautiously around the front of the pickup, stepped out into the open and pointed my pistol at the other man. Before I got to him I knew he was dead by the amount of blood on the pavement. One of my shots had shattered his skull. I looked down at the man. He had on leg braces. The last time I'd seen him he was doing a bad impression of Babe Ruth thinking my head was a baseball. He should have learned his lesson. I always figured once burned twice shy. I went back to the other man. I don't know for sure, but I would have bet all the hash in Afghanistan he was the Mexican man who had tried to knife me. The last time we met I had partially crushed his Adams apple. I ran over to Barbara. She was sitting up and looking at her scraped knee that wouldn't have rated a kiss from her mom if she were eight years old. "You're still alive," she exclaimed like it was a big surprise," then added, "Holy bazookas, Roosevelt, going out with you is more exciting than going to a hockey game,"

Her hormones must be bubbling.

As I helped her up we heard the approaching sirens. A neighbor must have called the police. I knew Richards would be in for a big surprise. As the first squad car turned the corner I asked Barbara. "Do you sleep with Richards or Williams?"

"Only in their dreams," she said. "I hate cops."

"I bet Williams tips good for a table dance," I said.

"What you're going to get tonight cowboy makes a table dance seem like taking a nap."

"O boy, Roosevelt," my Guardian Angel said.

"You have imported coffee," I asked Barbara.

The first policeman to arrive knew Barbara. I didn't ask if it was from her day job or her prowess at table dancing. She explained to him what happened. How we had been out for the evening, came home, and all hell broke loose. All the policeman did was ask for my pistol and tell the neighbors who had come out of their houses to stay back. Within five minutes four squad cars and an ambulance arrived. With all the red lights flashing it looked like a street party for hookers. Ten minutes later Detective Richards showed up. He looked at me. He looked at Barbara. He looked at me. He looked at Barbara. I could tell he wanted to say something like, "You lucky piece of concrete," but he didn't.

Barbara went inside the house and Richards and I looked at the two dead men. "They're the men from Linda's apartment that you didn't shoot and beat up," he said.

"They won't bother anybody else," I commented dryly.

They must have followed me. But I didn't want to tell Richards they had followed me while I was following Reid and Blackwell. It would only confuse the issue for Richards but to me it made some things quite clear. As the cops were making drawings on the pavement, like they were getting ready for a hopscotch tournament, a tow truck arrived. Richards had me sign a preliminary report and a few minutes later a policeman gave me my pistol back, commenting, "You're a good shot partner or you're one lucky guy,"

"Both," my Guardian Angel said.

Richards went in the house to ask Barbara a few more questions. While he was gone the ambulance loaded up the bodies, the tow truck pulled the pickup away, and the policemen got into their cars. The people who had come out of their homes to watch went back to watching some boring cop show.

I was putting my pistol back under the seat when Richards came back out. "You can't seem to do anything without getting shot at," he said.

"I told you my karma is the pits," I said.

"You know, I bet if you moved to the Arctic nobody would try to kill you."

"Polar bears would put a price on his head," my Guardian Angel said.

I didn't think either Richards or my Guardian Angel's pun was funny.

"Roosevelt, if you stay in town long enough you'll kill every bad guy in the area and I won't have a job," Richards said.

"If he stays in town long enough he might break his vow of chastity," my Guardian Angel said.

I didn't comment to either one of the snide, not so good comics.

"I want you to do me a favor," Richards told me as he opened the door to his car.

"What?" I replied, thinking he might want my autograph.

"I want you to take pictures of you and Barbara." He was laughing as he drove away.

"That's a good idea," my Guardian Angel said.

I knocked on the door and Barbara met me with a cup of coffee.

"The perfect little housewife," my Guardian Angel said. "Kiss her and do kinky things to her body. You owe me."

I followed Barbara into the living room. There was a sofa big enough for the Knicks basketball team to sit on. "Make yourself at home, I'll be back in a minute," she said.

I'd finished half my coffee and was sitting on the sofa when Barbara strutted in. She had on 8 inch black spiked high heels, black fish net stockings held up by a black leather garter belt, a black leather split bra, a black leather silver spiked collar with a black dog leash attached to it, her eyes have black mascara under them and she was wearing black lipstick and holding a black leather riding crop. "Roosevelt, you done messed up," my Guardian Angel said.

Barbara put her hands on her hips and stood with her feet apart looking like a Drill Sergeant in drag. She then slapped the riding crop in her palm. Her eyes looked like what I imagine the eyes of a Bolivian cop look like who was about to torture a drug dealer who hadn't paid his bribe.

"Does daddy need to be punished?" Barbara asked me like a little girl who enjoyed sticking needles in her pet puppy.

I didn't know what to say.

"Stand up you dirty rotten man," she ordered. "So I can spank the evil out of you."

"I'm not into this sort of thing," I told her. "Pain is something I try to avoid at all costs."

"You filthy man," she screamed as I stood and stepped backwards.

I retreated, bumping into the sofa as she followed me with slow menacing steps and a look on her face that would have made Alice Cooper fire his makeup man and hire her. I felt like I am a bit player in a bad scene from a Felini movie and she was Grace Kelly with a hormone imbalance.

She suddenly jumped at me, at the same time raising the riding crop to strike me. As the crop came down I hit her with a straight left smack dab in the center of her dominant forehead. She stood for one second, her black eyes pools of confusion, and then slumped to the floor like Dracula being caught by the sunrise. I was out the door, into Matilda, and driving down the road quicker than Bugs Bunny can eat a carrot.

"Lord save us," my Guardian Angel said in relief a few minutes later, adding dejectedly. "I can't judge women any better than you can."

"It has something to do with getting older," I said.

"Roosevelt, you are one hard man to work for," he replied. "But that was one good straight left."

I smiled. I couldn’t remember the last time my Guardian Angel complimented me.

CHAPTER TWELVE
CASH, GREEN, LETTUCE, BUCKS

It was 2 a.m. when I got back to the apartment but I was not tired. I don't know if it was from getting shot at, losing out on love before it even had a chance to bud, or being attacked by a leather clad man-hating woman. I felt like a truck driver who had washed down two black beauties with five cups of coffee. "I'll drive this rig non-stop from coast to coast and run over every slow driving little old lady in a four wheeler that I can. Whoopee damn."

I dug out everything I've collected concerning the case and set it on the dining room table. I looked at the note I'd found in the mesquite tree and wished I was a soothsayer and the image of the person who had typed it would miraculously appear on the paper. I looked at the photograph of Gloria. I read over my organized clues and added 4 clues to my new list, which now gives me 12 new clues. I also had several new questions to add to my list.

How did the Mexican and Randy Fearless follow me in an old beat up pickup? Maybe Reid and Blackwell had never shot at me? And, if so, who shot through my apartment door and who shot at me at the golf course? I felt like a ghost who had slept through Halloween.

Looking over my new questions I had another question? Why did the men who had followed me in the Nova drive away when I ran at them if they had intended to hurt or kill me? There were two of them and only one of me.

"Since you're in a question mood," my Guardian Angel said. “How many stars are there? Why does life go by so quickly? Why do the rich get richer and the poor poorer? Why do politicians always say, 'for the good of the people?' Why is a criminal never guilty? Why can't you get a real job? Why are women always right? Why does a clock move to the right and not to the left? Why do the French hate Americans? How does a Chinese restaurant make a living when their portions are so big? Will America ever have another good president? Why are French fries called French fries and not potato fries? Why is a hamburger a hamburger when there is no ham in it? Why do people who cheat normally win? Why do middle-aged men who are going bald grow a ponytail? How come the children of hippies never smoke pot? How come the most degenerate entertainers always become stars and then think they're prophets. Why does the word fly mean - an insect, zipper, and go through the air? Why does the phrase 'that's bad man', mean something that's good?" My Guardian Angel was still rattling on when I went to bed. He is enough to make an insomniac sleepy.

The last thing I heard before I fell asleep was, "Why doesn't the country legalize drugs, tax them, and get rid of the national debt? Then, we could sell dope to the Colombians and would care less if they were a most favored nation."

I woke up in the morning feeling like a rock star that had gone to bed without getting high or drinking a bottle of booze. Taking a shower I remembered I'd left my pistol in Matilda, not a good move. I dressed quickly and headed out the door. My Guardian Angel looked like he'd been on an acid for three days and had answered every question concerning life, God, and the cosmos, written a 600 page book in his mind that would make him millions, but now, that he was straight, he couldn't remember anything and he didn't have enough money to buy an Egg McMuffin.

My pistol was still under the seat, which made me feel good. If somebody had stolen it during the night, killed ten people, robbed four convenience stores, three banks, and a gas station, and then tossed the gun where it could be found, dumb me would have to do some quick explaining. Guns that are purchased legally can get one in trouble. You can shoot somebody with a stolen gun and toss it at their feet if you want - that is if you're smart enough to wear gloves - ask the Houston police.

I drove to a donut shop and bought two chocolate covered donuts and a large coffee and headed to the Tatum Ranch Golf Course. I want to talk to Linda. Driving into the parking lot I saw Linda's Mazda and parked next to it. Kevin, the golf pro, was giving a golf lesson on the driving range to a man that by the way he is swinging at the ball should forget golf and take up bowling. I watched people hitting balls for a while and then watched people practicing putting. I didn't see Linda in the area of the clubhouse but past the cart shed, I saw a large brown metal building with two fairway mowers parked in front of it. I headed for the building. The building has an electric garage door big enough tractors could be driven in and out. I looked inside. It was the maintenance shed. Two men were working on a greens mower. "These pieces of junk always break," I heard one man say.

"If they bought those Japanese mowers instead of these American made things we wouldn't be working on them all the time," his partner said.

"The unions got it all messed up now," the other man said.

I went inside. The men looked over at me but didn't say anything to me. With my boots and Levi's they must have figured I have something to do with the golf course. The shed was exceptionally clean. There were no greasy rags thrown everywhere, no grease spots on the concrete floor. The greens mowers were all in a line. The fairway mowers were all in a line. Rakes, shovels, spades, hung on the wall from hooks. Hoses were all coiled up in a neat row. There were six gas powered leaf blowers leaning against the wall next to four sidewalk trimmers and six gas powered weed eaters. All the equipment was spotless. Whoever used it had to have orders that when they were done with it they cleaned it and put it back in its place. There was a large bulletin board with the schedule posted on it for fertilizing the fairways and greens and chemical application schedules to kill weeds and fungus. The chemicals also cause cancer for everything that walks, swims, or breathes - perfection on a golf course has its price.

I walked over to the two men and overheard one say as he removed one of the bolts that held the mower reel in place. "If I would have stayed in the army in two years I'd be retiring."

"If you'd stayed in the army you'd be working off bad time for all the times you'd been in Leavenworth," his partner replied.

"You guys run a clean shop here," I told them.

They both looked at me like nobody in their lives had ever said anything nice to them and then smiled. "Me and Gary here try to keep things tidy," the man who obviously wasn't Gary said.

"Well, you sure do a good job," I said.

I then looked at Gary. "Listen, I've been sent out here to check out the course for some men who are thinking about buying it. Would you mind answering a few questions?"

"Didn't know the place was for sale," the man who wasn't Gary said with a worried look on his face.

"No need to worry, if they do buy this place, I'll see to it you two stay on and even get a raise. I've been to a lot of golf courses and never seen maintenance sheds this clean or organized."

Both men looked at me like I was an Aztec king and they were happy I was going to cut out their hearts.

"We got time, what are your questions?" Gary asked.

"I was wondering who keeps the keys to this place."

"Gary and I got keys and there is one at the pro shop. Sometimes they work later than we do and they might have to get something," the man who wasn't Gary said. "We also hide one out front," Gary said.

"Is there a night watchman for the course?"

"No, the housing development has a security squad that drives around. There's never been nothing stolen here," the man who wasn't Gary said.

"But a few days ago somebody cut the lock off to the shed. The door was wide open when I came to work but nothing was missing, strange, huh?" Gary said.

"What time do you guys usually get out of here?

"They don't pay me overtime, I'm out of here at five," Gary said and the man who wasn't Gary nodded his head.

"Well thanks for your time gentlemen," I said and walked away. As I got to the door I heard Gary say, "Damn American made mower."

"Obviously they didn't fight in World War II," my Guardian Angel said.

I stopped at the cart shed but nobody was there and I went back to the pro shop. Kevin had just finished his lesson on the driving range and was walking with his student toward the putting green. He was limping badly with his left leg. He saw me but didn't wave - my feelings were hurt.

I went to the pay phone and got Detective Richards' card out of my billfold and called his office. "Detective Richards' office," Barbara's voice came over the line like a spring breeze through the window after four months of a Minnesota winter.

"Little miss leather," I said. "Let me talk to your boss."

She didn't tell me how good I throw a straight left.

"Roosevelt," Richards' voice came over the line. "Have you killed anybody today?"

"No, my pistol jammed when I tried to shoot a guy who cut me off in traffic," I said.

"Better buy a revolver," he told me.

"I'd laugh," I replied. "But I have a sore throat."

"Why are you calling?"

"I was wondering if either the Mexican guy or Fearless had a gunshot wound on them that didn't happen last night."

Richards was quiet for a moment. "Hold the line."

I listened to three country and western songs while I was on hold. One was about a guy who had fallen off his riding lawn mower and would never be able to drive his truck again. One was about a woman who had caught her husband trying on ladies' cowboy boots. And one was about a cowboy who lost his wife to a rock star and dumbfounded by shame he was going to run away and join the Bulgarian army after he sold the pickup, burnt the trailer, and gave his dog to the neighbor.

"Roosevelt, you still there?"

"No, I decided to move to Nebraska," I said.

"The morgue says one man had a partially healed bullet hole in each leg but all the other wounds on the bodies happened last night."

"Thanks," I said.

Richards hung up without a comment.

Kevin was in the pro shop, doing what he does best, running the cash register. "I noticed you hurt your leg," I told him.

He looked at me like he wanted to rip my nose off but he knew before he could I would rearrange his lips and teeth. "Got hit with a golf ball," he told me. "Knocked me right down."

"Too bad it didn't hit you in the head," I told him and went back outside.

"That wasn't a nice thing to say," my Guardian Angel told me.

"For some reason I don't like that guy," I told him.

"That's no reason to be rude," he said.

I decided to walk the cart path backwards starting at 18th hole and circling back to 1.

It is a beautiful day. Birds were singing, rabbits scampered across the fairways and large coveys of quail darted from bush to bush in the rough.

I walked by the green to the tenth hole and watched my old buddies, the three lizard skins, putting. When they were done they walked by me without a jolly word, only a nod of their heads. Hustlers who get hustled carry grudges for a long time.

Linda was by the 10th tee box mixing four Bloody Mary's for a foursome that looked like the only reason they play golf is to get drunk. After they happily walked away with their drinks I approached Linda. Seeing me she smiled a smile at me that is so big I thought a rainbow would suddenly appear in the sky and she would start dancing with the Tin Man. "Roosevelt, what brings you to the hub of civilization?" she asked.

It wasn't until I was standing by her that I saw the large bandage wrapped around her upper arm. "What happened to you?" I asked, truly concerned.

She frowned and hesitated for a moment before saying. "A friend of mine has those old types of windows that open out and I walked into one."

"When I was a kid the house we lived in, in El Paso had those. I still have knots on my head from all the times I ran into them," I told her.

"Some people never learn to duck," she grinned.

"You know those two guys who tried to ambush me at your apartment?" I said, seeing no need to continue the polite chit-chat.

Linda gave me an inquisitive look as she nodded her head. I noticed she had on long dangling silver earrings that were clip on, her ears are not pierced.

"They tried again last night, only this time with some serious firepower. I was lucky though they missed and I ended up killing them both."

Linda's hand covered her mouth, she looked confused, or bewildered. She sat in the cart, took a deep breath and seemingly fought with her thoughts. She looked at me and her eyes darted from side to side like I was a man about to murder her and she knew there was nothing she could say or do that would stop me. After several more deep breaths she said, "I told you, you should leave here Roosevelt, somebody is going to kill you. Don't you care?"

"I care," I replied. "But it doesn't scare me. Fear and I parted ways a long time ago. I only want to find out who killed Gloria and then I'll leave."

"But why should you even care who killed Gloria?" Linda asked. "You didn't know her."

"People shouldn't get murdered, Linda, it's as simple as that."

"You are so full of hot air," my Guardian Angel said.

"Those two detectives that came to see you were they large men, one of them dark haired and balding, and the other one with blond wavy hair and wearing an earring?" I asked Linda.

"No, they both had brown hair and were around 160 lbs."

"Not the answer you wanted," my Guardian Angel said.

"Can I call you?" I asked Linda.

"Anytime Roosevelt, but call soon, before somebody kills you," Linda responded.

She drove off and I continued my walk around the golf course. It's amazing how tranquil a golf course can be when one isn't playing golf.

By the time I got to the clubhouse I was hungry, two donuts and coffee for breakfast was like feeding an elephant four peanuts and telling him to watch his weight. I drove to a Mexican restaurant and ordered Eggs Rancheros - eggs smothered in cheese, onions, and green chili sauce - and asked the waitress if they had the yellow pages to the Phoenix phone book. "Do you want chili on it," she joked before she brought me a phone book.

There is only one Mazda dealer in the Phoenix area. The chili on the eggs was so hot I drank three glasses of water while eating and knew the cooks in the kitchen were laughing at the gringo.

Driving into a car lot I always feel that ten thousand buzzards are looking at me wondering if I'm dead meat. I had no sooner parked Matilda when the first smiling buzzard approached me, his arm outstretched to shake hands, and smiling like I am his long lost Uncle who was about to die and leave him my house in Florida. "Looking for a new Mazda?" the buzzard asked.

"No, I came here to eat a hamburger," I told him.

I've always hated people that ask me obvious questions, even though I wasn't looking for a car. It's like the question when somebody walks into a room and the person they came to see is there. "You're here," they'll say in surprise. I always feel like saying, "No, I'm in Switzerland trying to recover money the honest Swiss bankers helped Hitler steal from the Jews." But I normally smile and keep my snide remarks to myself.

"Bob Roosevelt," I said, taking his hand and shaking it. "What I came here for is some information?"

I took out my billfold and took out a 50 dollar bill. "A certain person bought a car here and I want to know how it was paid for?"

The buzzard looked at the 50. "We're not supposed to divulge any information concerning our customers unless you're with the I.R.S. or the police."

"Both," I said taking out another fifty.

The buzzard looked at the money like a trout looks at a hook with a juicy worm on it in a river where people are only supposed to fish with artificial flies or lures. "What would the person's name be Mr. Police or I.R.S. agent?" he asked.

"Linda Adams, she bought a new gold Mazda."

He started to reach for the money. "No, no, when you come back. I'll look at the cars until you return."

My mother taught me to never, never, pay first.

"Your mom is one smart lady," my Guardian Angel said.

The salesman was back quicker than Porky Pig can say, "Tha, tha, tha, tha, that, that, that, that's all folks."

Before he said anything he held out his hand. I gave him the two fifties. He stuffed them in his pocket. "Linda Adams bought a new gold Mazda with everything, C.D. player, electric windows, rear window defrost," he was about to go on. "How did she pay for it?" I butted in.

"$23,000 in cash."

"Thanks," I said and started to walk away.

"Hey, Mr. Roosevelt, take my card, if you need anymore information you can get in touch with me."

I stopped and took his card. "I do need some more information," I told him.

He looked excited and smiled, probably figuring I am dumb enough to give him more money.

"Who killed Gloria Simpson?" I asked.

The word killed wiped the smile from his face.

I went back to the apartment and got my golf clubs. It was barely past noon and knowing that tonight I was going to break into the apartment of two dangerous characters I decided I had better play a round of golf, it might be my last, and before I die I want to make one three foot putt when it mattered.

"You might die but you won't make a three-foot putt," my Guardian Angel said.

CHAPTER THIRTEEN
LIKE A SALMON SPAWNING UP THE WRONG RIVER

If I am going to die tonight it is going to be without having made a three-foot putt.

"I told you so," my Guardian Angel said.

I sat at the dining room table cleaning my pistol and pondering why God so cursed some people they couldn't make short putts?

"If you place your head over the ball so your dominant eye is directly over the top of the ball you might make more putts," my Guardian Angel said.

"When did you ever play golf?" I snapped.

"There's no need to be snooty," he retorted.

A man who shoots a bad round of golf is not fun to be around. Ask any golfer's wife on a Saturday afternoon if this statement isn't true?

I put my pistol back together, loaded the clip with gloves on, and got my notes. I added seven more clues to my new list. I now have 19 new clues to go along with my 38 organized clues.

"Roosevelt," my Guardian Angel said. "Detective Richards might think you're smart. Detective Williams might think you're the bee's knees to the private detective industry. But you and I know you don't know diddly squat about this case and didn't know diddly squat about any case you have lucked out and solved. What do you think any of these clues are going to do for you?"

"Confuse me," I said.

I had to tell him the truth. It's hard to lie to my Guardian Angel.

He shook his head sadly.

I read and reread my clues until 9 p.m.. I went through my suitcase, which contains all my possessions besides the ones hanging in the closet, but I couldn't find my lock picking kit. "Where could I have lost it?" I asked my Guardian Angel.

"Where did you lose your mind?" he replied.

I stuck my pistol in the back of my pants, put my Levi jacket on and left the apartment. "I have a feeling we're not going bowling," my Guardian Angel said.

"Breaking and entering," I said. "You'd better be on your toes."

The Tatum Place Apartment complex sprawls over at least two acres. Two story units with eight apartments to each unit were located at various angels to each other.

I drove by parking spot 304, which was empty, but I drove all around the apartment complex looking for a light green new Chevy in case Reid and Blackwell had parked in another spot.

Not seeing their car, I parked in open parking and followed the building numbers until I found apartment 304. To my dismay, it was an upstairs apartment and a light was on over the door. The apartment had its own front porch, separated from the next-door apartment's patio by a wall, which stops one from conversing with his neighbor. All the interior lights were turned off. "The only person who would try to break into an upstairs apartment is an idiot," my Guardian Angel said.

"Call me Mr. Idiot," I replied as I went up the stairs.

There was a green plastic patio table and two chairs on the porch. The first thing I did was unscrew the light bulb over the door. I then tried the doorknob, who knew, there was one chance in a million they had forgotten to lock it, but not this time. The front windows were metal and were screened. I took off the screen but the windows were locked. I examined the door. The hinges were not on the outside and the door was metal. I don't want to break the window and take the chance the noise would alert somebody who would call the police, so I put the screen back on. I pulled a chair over to the dividing wall where nobody walking up the stairs could see me until they reached the middle of the patio.

"Roosevelt, what in the world are you doing?" my Guardian Angel asked with genuine concern as I sat.

"I'm going to bring this kettle to a boil," I said.

"All you're going to do is scald yourself," he replied, like I am dumber than a sixteen-year-old boy who is in love for the first time.

The sad thing about it is I know he is right.

Sitting on a porch, with a pistol in my hand, waiting for two men with arrest records longer than the constitution and suspected of six digit bank robbery should wear on my nerves - that is if I had any. Since my nerves went out the door the second time I got shot in Vietnam, in all truth, I felt bored. When I'm bored I think - which in modern life I have discovered is not a good thing to do. People who think make change and question life. Making change and questioning is not viewed as a good thing by governments - any government including our own. Of course, what I normally think about doesn't have enough depth to it to change a diaper. I thought about Barbara for a while wondering why love was so evasive for me? I thought about Linda and how weird it was both she and Kevin had been hurt at about the same time. I wondered if I would ever again meet a woman I would fall in love with. I thought about the time when I was a hippie and a group of us went to the mountains to spend the weekend. We ate synthetic mescaline and played softball. When I hit the softball it looked like a huge moon in slow motion as it went over the pitcher's head and how he had ducked because to him it looked like a surface to air missile with a rainbow colored fire ball behind it over fifty feet long. I thought about the day I flew out of Vietnam and how silent everyone in the plane was when there was only the ocean below us, and how I felt happy to be leaving but concerned for my friends left behind. An idle mind is a strange thing. I wondered where all my old war comrades were? I've never bothered to look any of them up. I remembered the first time I read a Kahill Gibran novel and how moved I was and then how shocked I was when I found out he had only lived to be 42. I thought about a girl in my sixth grade class that I had been so in love with I couldn't sleep, but was so shy I couldn't approach her - now I can't remember her name - but I can still see her face. I thought about the first time I saw a slum and couldn't believe it happened in America. I remembered the day I knew there were no solutions to war, only quick fixes, and that wars would follow wars until every country was brave enough to not need an army. I was trying not to remember anything else when I heard a man talking - hopefully not to himself. "I can't believe Dallas threw that one away," the man said.

"Dallas isn't worth a hoot this year. But you know if you'd bet Dallas every game they've covered the spread more than any team in football."

Footsteps thudded up the steps. "Cheap light bulb burnt out," Reid or Blackwell said.

"No need to tell you the kettle is boiling, Roosevelt," my Guardian Angel whispered.

Both men, unsuspecting, walked by me. Reid unlocked the door and started to open it. "Gentlemen, it's a good time to put your arms in the air," I said.

Both men spun around quickly, but even in the dim light they could see the pistol and didn't make an aggressive move, unless raising their arms like they were under arrest is an aggressive move. I figured it was second nature to them. "Put your hand inside the door slowly and turn on the living room light," I ordered Reid. "Don't be an idiot either. I don't miss from this range and I'm not a cop who has to read you your Miranda Rights."

He was a smart boy and turned on the light. I stepped toward them but not close enough they could turn and hit me. "Now both of you walk into the apartment and stop in the middle of the living room. Keep those arms up high."

"Who are you?" Blackwell snarled, not moving.

"If you don't get inside the house I'm going to be the one who sends you to your maker," I replied in a tone that left no doubt I meant what I said.

They stopped in the middle of the living room. I noticed neither one of them had a limp. I shut the door behind me but didn't lock it. The room was a mess, dirty clothes were strewn all over the furniture, ashtrays were overflowing with cigarette butts, beer bottles cluttered both the dining room table and a coffee table. A sofa was against a wall with a chair set at an angle so they both faced a TV that was on a table against the opposite wall. "Take your jackets off," I ordered.

The coats came off. "Now turn around in a circle slowly."

They turned. Neither of them had a pistol in their belt or wore a shoulder holster. "Pull up your pant legs."

They also didn't have a pistol strapped to their ankles.

"Pull all your pockets inside out."

Loose change fell to the floor. No knives or pocket pistols.

"Now take your shirts off."

Neither of them had any wounds on their upper body.

"Ok, now sit on the sofa and you can put your shirts back on."

"It's easy to be Mr. Bossy when you have the gun," my Guardian Angel said.

They both sat in the middle of the sofa but I waved the pistol so they knew to spread as far apart as possible. Never taking my eye off of them or lowering the pistol I moved the chair into the middle of the room and sat facing them. "Now it's a regular Boy Scout meeting," I smiled. "Did you bring your dues?"

"If you didn't have that pistol I'd rip your heart out," Reid swore at me.

"Chuck Reid," I said calmly, noticing his surprise that I knew his name. "If I didn't have this pistol and you tried to rip my heart out by the time I was finished with you an ant wouldn't bother to pick your bones."

For some reason Blackwell thought that was funny and started laughing. Reid gave him a dirty look.

"You guys wouldn't happen to have any beer?" I asked since they had been rude and hadn't offered.

"In the fridge," Blackwell said. "Bring me one while you're at it." He tried to sound like a smart guy, but stupid people never sound smart, they only sound stupider.

"No, Reid, you play maid and go get us three beers," I said.

I stood and moved to the side as Reid got up and went to the kitchen. He got three beers out of the refrigerator, opened them, and brought them back. "Set mine by the chair," I ordered. If I kept giving orders I was going to start feeling like a colonel in the army.

Reid bent down and set a beer by the chair, but as he straightened back up he lunged at me like an offensive tackle coming up out of his stance. I kicked him in the middle of the chest, sending the two beer bottles flying as he landed on his rear, the wind knocked out of him. Blackwell started to stand up but spinning, I kicked him on the side of the face with a roundhouse kick, knocking him back onto the sofa. Keeping the pistol on Blackwell I stepped over to Reid, jerked him up by his shirt and pushed him over the top of the coffee table and onto the sofa, knocking beer bottles and an ashtray on the floor in the process. I sat in the chair, picked up my beer and took a drink. "Now that we all know each other let's say we have a little pow wow," I said to them.

"An Indian you're not," my Guardian Angel said.

By the looks on the men's faces I knew they weren't happy Easter bunnies and if they got a chance they weren't going to give me chocolate eggs and jellybeans.

Reid rubbed his chest, looked at me, looked at the pistol, and said. "Listen buddy, we don't even know you, so what gives?"

I thought it strange that both Reid and Blackwell had made it clear they didn't know me.

"You guys have tried to kill me and you can sit there and tell a bold faced lie like you don't know me?" I said, feeling ridiculous, but getting my message across. Why would I think people who had tried to kill me are going to tell the truth?

"Only a jury in California," my Guardian Angel said.

"Listen buddy," Reid said. "We've never seen you in our lives."

"I'm not your buddy," I said, "You don't see any earring in my right ear."

"Honest mister, for all we know you're Hop Along Cassidy," Reid corrected himself.

"Your name is Chuck Reid isn't it?"

Reid nodded his head.

"And you're Randy Blackwell," I said, pointing the pistol at Blackwell.

Blackwell nodded his head while holding the side of his face.

"Now let me get this straight, you guys say you don't know me which means you didn't try to shoot me at Tatum Ranch Golf Course. You didn't try and shoot me through the door at my apartment and you didn't follow me in a Chevy Nova."

"You don't owe us any money," Blackwell said.

At least I know they only killed people over money.

"You guys didn't hire anybody to try and kill me?" I asked.

They looked at me wondering where I'd put my straight jacket.

"You really don't know me?"

"Roosevelt, the day you do something right the Muslims and Christians will stop killing each," my Guardian Angel said.

"I know you're not the president," Blackwell said, "but you do look familiar. You care if I smoke?”

Obviously my element of surprise and fear is wearing off.

"As long as you don't inhale, it's bad for you," I told him.

He picked a long cigarette butt off the floor and lit it with a book of matches from the table. He took a deep drag, inhaled deeply, blew the smoke out noisily and looked at me closely. He took another drag off the cigarette and an expression came over his face like he was in a spelling bee and had remembered how to spell fig. "I know you," he said. "You're that private dick that solved that kidnapping case in Florida. You were on TV. The rich family who got their kid back only gave you ten grand. Roosevelt, Bob Roosevelt. I'll be a son of a monkey."

"It is him," Reid said. "That was a good job buddy."

I waved my pistol at him. "Sorry, I mean Roosevelt," Reid apologized.

I've had a lot of friends, partners, cohorts, chums, but I'm not the buddy type.

"I watch all those cop shows," Blackwell said. "They teach criminals what not to do."

"Your hair has grown since then," Reid said.

"It looks better longer," Blackwell said, like he is a world famous hairdresser and not a crook.

"Don't let them snow you, Roosevelt," my Guardian Angel said. "You're ugly with or without long hair."

"You make ugly seem like a compliment," I said out loud.

"Who are you talking to?” Reid asked looking around.

"I have this Guardian Angel who keeps telling me how ugly I am," I said.

"I'd fire him," Reid said. "In your line of work the devil would be more help."

My Guardian Angel's feelings were hurt. "What does this scumbag know about anything?" he said.

"I know why you're here," Blackwell said, like besides

knowing how to spell fig he had figured out how to spell tree, to make a complete thought, fig tree. "Hoffman hired you to find us."

"Hoffman doesn't know I'm here. I'm trying to solve a murder and I know everything about him and you guys."

"Whose murder are you trying to solve?" Reid asked.

"Hoffman's ex-wife."

"Gloria?" Reid muttered in astonishment.

"You didn't know?" I asked, bewildered at his response.

"No, but I can tell you for sure Hoffman and Gloria were as chummy as two foxes in a chicken coop. They did get a divorce but it was only for income tax purposes and to divide up assets so the cops wouldn't get everything if he got busted. He wouldn't kill her."

"She was living with him in his big house over in Paradise Valley," Blackwell said.

"I was told he used to beat her," I said, not mentioning she had lived in the same apartment complex I did.

"He never hit a woman in his life. She's the demanding type and when he didn't go home on time she would destroy things and call the cops making it look like they had a fight," Blackwell said.

"Was she in on the bank jobs with all of you?" I asked.

"What bank jobs?" Reid asked, trying to do an imitation of an altar boy with red wine on his upper lip after he had denied getting into Father O'Malley's hidden stash.

"Listen, I don't care if you guys robbed fifty banks. All I'm interested in is finding out who killed Gloria. Now, I'll ask you again, was she in on the bank jobs with all of you?"

"She drove the getaway car disguised as a man," Blackwell said.

"Life is full of surprises," my Guardian Angel said.

"Who killed Randy Springer?"

They both looked surprised, as surprised as bank robbers can look. "We didn't know he was dead," Reid said haltingly.

I feel like a salmon that had made his spawning run up the wrong river. "Did you know Springer was a snitch?" I asked.

"Springer was no snitch," Reid said. "He was the most stand-up guy I've ever met."

"He got picked up in California and according to police

records agreed to set up everybody who had been involved in the bank robberies. They tried to make contact with Hoffman but couldn't and he called you, Blackwell, and set up a meeting at a bar. The cops followed him to the bar but Springer went out the back door."

Blackwell and Reid both smiled. "Must have been dumb cops to not watch the back door," Blackwell said.

I had to agree.

"Three days later Springer was found in a dumpster," I continued. "Somebody cut his throat. You guys don't know anything about that?"

Reid and Blackwell looked at each other. "Tell him, he ain't no cop, and he must know a lot more than he's letting on," Reid said.

"Reid, Springer and I have done a lot of things together," Blackwell said. "We're not exactly choirboys you know. After you've been on the wrong side of the fence as long as we have you start to learn things. One thing you have to accept is some day, no matter how good you are, you're going to get busted, and when you do, you have to look out for yourself and try and make a deal with the cops. What you do is when you make a deal with the cops is have a lawyer draw up a contract between you and the cops and in it, it has to say you will do your best to help them arrest certain people - the catch words are ‘do your best' and the people have to be specifically named. We all decided that if any of us got busted and the cops wanted us to snitch out the rest of us, we would agree to it but we had a code word. When Springer called me he said, “Hey Randy, meet me down at The Green Onion, I got to talk,” I knew it was a set up. He'd used the word ‘down'. So I didn't go."

I am impressed.

"If he would have called me again, I still wouldn't have gone. After a while, because of the agreement with the cops they'd have to cut him his deal, even without anybody being arrested because he had done ‘his best' and it wasn't his fault the cops couldn't pinch anybody. If they would try to use him to pinch people that hadn't been specifically named in the contract he would refuse. If they insisted the lawyer would take the contract to a judge and the cops would have to stand by it."

"We had a contingency plan that if anything ever happened we'd all meet at this apartment," Reid added. "We've had this place rented under a fake name for two years."

"I was wondering why he never showed," Blackwell said, not sounding greatly saddened by Springer's death.

"Live by the banana die by the banana," Reid said.

"For crooks these guys are very pragmatic," my Guardian Angel said.

"Do you think Hoffman killed Springer?" I asked.

"There was no way he could contact Hoffman. You can't call him, he never answers the phone. If you went to his house, Awalt or McVede wouldn't let you in. The only way we made contact was when Awalt or McVede contacted us. Then we went with them, drove all over for a few hours and then met Hoffman."

"That's when you figured out Hoffman didn't plan on paying you," I said.

"Dirty thieving jerk," Reid swore letting me know it is true that Hoffman had kept the money.

"There is no honor anymore," Blackwell said. "Used to be when a man gave his word it was written in stone."

My arm was getting tired from pointing the pistol at them but I didn't lower it. "How would you ever agree that Hoffman could keep all the money and not divide it up after each job?" I asked, if for no other reason than my own curiosity.

"How could you do something that stupid?" my Guardian Angel asked.

"We made a deal," Reid said. "Hoffman knew some big time coke dealers. If we put in all the money we'd make a small fortune. We all decided we'd do enough jobs to raise two million. Two mill divided six ways is only a little over three hundred grand each. That is nothing in this modern world. But if we put up two million on blow we'd make about a mill and a half each. Also, we didn't know if the bank money was marked. If it was we couldn't have spent it without leaving a trail a basset hound without a nose could follow. A dope deal would change the money."

"In other words, you got greedy and were stupid," I said.

They nodded their heads sadly.

"Stupid is what stupid does," my Guardian Angel said.

"Who do you think killed Springer?" I asked.

"Springer had more enemies than there are stars," Reid said. "I do know if anybody we know killed him they wouldn't have found the body. Tossing a body in a dumpster is something some street punk would do."

"So, after the last job you haven't seen or heard from Hoffman in over two months."

"I've seen him since," Reid said. "I shot the two timing punk and plugged Awalt and McVede. I didn't kill them though. If I killed them there's no chance of getting our money. I just wanted them to know we want our money and if it takes until the day I die they'd better be looking over their shoulders."

"How come you used a black Volkswagen bug?"

"A guy owed us a favor and we used his car," Reid said.

"You told me you know where Hoffman lives. Why haven't you gone over?"

"You mean little Fort Knox in Paradise Valley. We've left a few notes on his gate."

"What if he doesn't have the money?" I asked. "Let's say the coke got busted, or the Colombians stole the money."

"If it would have got busted he would have told us. And if Colombians would have stolen the money we'd be killing Columbians," Reid said. "No, he planned on keeping everything from the beginning."

"You're sure about that?" I asked.

"Nobody stole the money," Blackwell said.

I finished my beer, which was now luke warm. "You guys want a beer, since I made you spill your last ones?"

Reid started to get up. "I'll get it," I told him.

I kept them in sight as I got the beers. Sitting back down everyone took a long drink. "I have a deal for you two," I said. "This has all been a mistake and I apologize. The only reason I came over here was I thought you guys had killed Gloria and have also been trying to kill me because you knew I was on the case. I'll tell you what I'll do, I'll help you guys get your share of the money, if you help me find the person or persons responsible for killing Gloria? And, I promise you I won't contact the cops."

"How can you help us?" Reid asked suspiciously.

"I think I can get close to Hoffman, you two for sure can't, especially since you gave him a bullet love bite."

"If we get our money how much of a cut do you want?" Blackwell asked.

"Ten percent" I said. If you tell a crook you don't want anything he knows you're lying.

"A guy with the gun always makes a good deal," Reid said looking at the pistol.

I stuck the pistol in my belt.

"You are one dumb idiot," my Guardian Angel said.

Reid stood up cautiously. I watched him and did not see Blackwell reach under the cushion of the sofa. Although it was hard to miss the nickel-plated 357 he pulled out and pointed at my head. It looked like a shiny bazooka. Blackwell stood and grinning at me like he is Graybeard and I am about to walk the plank he pulled back the hammer. Reid was grinning like Sylvester the Cat after finally eating Tweety Bird.

"Pack your bag," I told my Guardian Angel.

"Maybe God will assign me to Miss April," he said.

Blackwell started laughing.

Reid started laughing. I am about to die so I started laughing. I have learned how to laugh when the joke is on me.

"You know, you're one brave monkey," Blackwell said as he lowered the pistol and stuck out his hand to shake. "It's going to be fun working with a guy that was on TV."

"Your luck will one day run out," my Guardian Angel said while visions of Miss April darted out of his head.

CHAPTER FOURTEEN
HUNCHES

Reid and Blackwell and I had drunk six or seven beers each. It was strange but I was having a good time with the two bank robbers. There isn't much difference between them and cops: They think the same way. They know the law. They keep weird hours. They have the same sick sense of humor and they hang out at topless bars.

I knew Reid or Blackwell would try and kill me if they thought I was going to double cross them.

"They'll also try to kill you if you recover the money," my Guardian Angel said.

I told them everything Detective Richards had told me about Hoffman and them - they didn't show any concern - they knew the heat was on. And I told them how I had found them. They were impressed and said it was a good thing I wasn't a cop. "With the organized crime laws and all the conspiracy laws, it's tough enough to make a good living being a crook as it is," Blackwell commented.

"That's a weird way you found Gloria," Reid said. "Leaving her body on a golf course, what kind of move is that?"

"Do you think Hoffman thinks you might have killed her to get back at him?" I asked.

"We don't kill women," Blackwell said with a scowl. "He knows that."

"Now that you know it wasn't us who tried to kill you, who do you think it was?" Reid asked.

"When I came over tonight I thought I had a handle on about

everything. I only needed a few more breaks and I would have busted this case open like a Hawaiian cracking a coconut. But now I realize I don't know much."

"Face it Roosevelt," my Guardian Angel said, "You didn't know anything in the first place."

"How do you figure on getting close to Hoffman?" Blackwell asked.

"Easy, I'm going to call him."

"Once you get close to Hoffman how are you going to get us our money?" Reid asked, probably thinking I was joking about the phone, simple ideas are normally ignored in life, modern reasoning being if it isn't complicated it normally isn't feasible.

"If I told you my plan, you wouldn't need me," I said, trying to be cagey, but knowing it was true. Crooks, like everybody else in life, except nuns, look out for themselves. The main difference between crooks and normal people is crooks kill you when they don't need you. Normal people steal your money, your home, your car, or your wife.

"How are we going to help you find Gloria's killer?" Reid asked trying to sound like he cared.

"I don't know yet, but I feel confident something will happen."

"You don't know now, you won't know tomorrow, three days from now you won't know, or next year," my Guardian Angel said. "Nothing will fall into place."

At times I wish he wasn't an angel so I could punch him.

"Is there anything about Gloria you guys might know that would help me?" I asked Reid or Blackwell.

Reid tried to give the impression he was thinking, which he wasn't very good at. Blackwell looked perplexed. "I know something," Reid said. "Gloria would get depressed and would start babbling how nobody loved her, or appreciated her. Hoffman sent her to some fancy doctor and he put her on some pills that controlled her depression."

"Do either of you guys play golf?" I asked.

They both gave me a dirty look. "Golf is for sissies," Reid said puckering up his face like he had just eaten a dill pickle. "I go to the horse races or the casinos. Blackwell, he likes boxing or wrestling."

"Do you know Linda Adams?" I asked quickly, hoping to catch them off guard. There was no need to ask them if they wanted to play golf.

"Does she work at a topless bar?" Reid asked.

"No. But she could."

"Don't know her then. But I wouldn't mind meeting her."

"When you guys left California after not getting paid how did you find out where Hoffman lives?"

"We might look stupid and act stupid," Blackwell said. "But we're not always stupid. We know about his house in Florida too."

"We got connections," Reid said.

I couldn't think of anything else I wanted to ask them and I was tired. I can only take so much of a good time until people start to bore me - even bank robbers. "Listen guys. It's been entertaining but I have to leave. Do you have a phone so I can get hold of you?"

"No," Reid answered. "People with phones make mistakes. They get lazy. When you want to get hold of us come by the apartment. If we're not here leave a newspaper by the front door and come back in the morning before ten."

I opened the door then turned to face them again. "Don't do anything against Hoffman. It's not time to scare him."

They looked at me like they were Hindus and wouldn't step on an ant, but they might sneak out and kill a cow every once in a while.

As I walked down the stairs I didn't hear Blackwell tell Reid. "After he helps us get our money I'll kill him although I kind of like the guy."

"I'll flip you for the pleasure," Reid said. "But you're right, he's an ok kind of guy."

"He'd make a good crook," Blackwell said. "Too bad he got off on the wrong foot."

As I drove I figured Reid and Blackwell figured I know more than I had let on. I only hoped they didn't try and kill me before I accomplished what I wanted.

"Roosevelt, all the years I have known you. All the times I have saved your hide. I have never, I repeat never, seen you put yourself in such a precarious situation," my Guardian Angel said.

"Why thank you," I said. "That's the second nicest thing

you've said to me in two days.

Back at my apartment I felt like a football player who had warmed the bench all year. With one minute to go in the last game of the season the coach signaled for me to go in, but I got so excited that while running onto the field I fell over the first down chain and sprained my ankle.

I got all my organized clues and all my new clues and set them on the table. I made a cup of instant coffee. All I have to do is wade through the lies and pick out the truth, which has always been difficult for me - I always think everybody is telling me the truth.

The evening with Reid and Blackwell had been more informative than they thought, in fact, it had made one thing clear to me. I carefully read my organized clues. I read them from the front to the back and then from back to front.

I read my new clues and added six more. I have 25 new clues. I looked at the organized clues again and was about to cross many of them off but changed my mind. I read my list of 36 questions and added four more: If Reid and Blackwell didn't know Linda, who posed as the detectives who talked to her? If Gloria and Hoffman got a divorce only to save money, why was she afraid when I first met her? If Reid and Blackwell didn't shoot at me then who did? Who did I wound through my door? I now have 40 questions. The sad thing is I can’t answer any of them.

The coffee was cold so I made another cup. "You should read over your new clues again and organize them and then you would only have organized clues and not organized and new clues," my Guardian Angel said.

"I was going to," I replied tersely. I hate being told what to do when I really don't know what to do. I'm the type of man who will drive around a city for six days, more lost than Moses was in the desert, before, by God, I'll stop and ask some idiot how to get where I'm going, but six days is my limit.

I reread my new clues, crossing out many and combining some until I had them organized. I'd taken 25 new clues and reduced them to 17 new and organized clues. I now have 50 combined clues. "If you were in the first grade Roosevelt," my Guardian Angel said. "I'd put a little gold star on your paper, but since you didn't graduate from college I'll give your clues a C for effort and an F for what they mean. You wouldn't know a real clue if it hit you in the face."

"Well then help me if you know so much," I said.

He didn't say anything, proving he was only running his head.

First thing in the morning I went to see Detective Richards. I took my pistol and notebook with me. If I had time I'd read over my clues and questions a few times during the day. I know Richards had told me to always call first but I thought I'd surprise him - what are friends for?

Miss May, at the reception desk, smiled at me as I walked by. I felt like stopping and telling her Babe's would hire her in a heartbeat, and if she did the shower act men would toss so much money at her feet she could move to Brazil and open up a Tango Bar.

Much to my surprise, Barbara, after telling me Richards was on the phone and to take a seat, brought me a cup of coffee. "You should have spanked me after knocking me out the other night," she said. "I was a bad girl."

"I'm glad you're not hurt," I said, noticing she didn't have a bruise on her forehead and she is wearing pumps not high-rise high heels.

"How about we get together again? I promise I'll be nice," she said, insinuating that nice meant more than a free table dance.

I was about to answer when Richards came out of his office. "I thought I told you to call," he said like he should be angry but it was too early.

"I don't have a quarter," I replied.

"Come on in, but make it quick. I have to testify at a trial in an hour."

I walked by Richards and he shut the door behind me. "I want you to know anything I've said about Barbara is all in jest," he said as he sat down. "I don't two time my wife."

"I didn't think you did," I told him. “You're one of the few cops I've met that I think is honest," adding, "do you lie on the witness stand?"

"If I know the guy is guilty," he replied angrily. "Now what is it?"

"Don't take this wrong, but I was wondering how long

Williams has been a detective in Scottsdale?"

"He came here six months ago from L.A. The department needed a detective. He applied for the job and got it. His credentials are excellent. Why?"

"No reason, really, I was merely wondering. What did he do in L.A.?"

"He was a detective in the robbery division. Is the only reason you came over to ask me stupid questions?"

"No, I really came over to tell you I talked to Reid and Blackwell last night."

"You found them?" he sputtered.

"I suppose I did if I talked to them."

"Roosevelt, part of the time I like you, but most of the time you get on my nerves. Now tell me what happened with Reid and Blackwell."

I told him everything, Gloria's sham divorce, the fact Reid and Blackwell swore they didn't know me, Blackwell had shot Hoffman, Hoffman hadn't paid them, the plan to roll the money over on a coke deal, including the fact I'd made a pact with them to help them recover their money if they helped me find out who killed Gloria. I also told him about several hunches I had.

Richards whistled softly when I finished. "You've been a busy boy. Now what are you going to do besides get killed?"

I wonder why everyone thinks I'm going to get killed.

I told him my plan which revolved around my hunches. When I was done I didn't know if Richards was impressed by my idea or thought it was dumber than ketchup on steak. He sat for over a minute and didn't say a word before smiling. "It might work. It's better than one of my men getting killed."

His reasoning was sound but I didn’t like it. "You'll have to give me your home phone number so I can get hold of you anytime day or night," I told him. "When the skunk walks into the trap, you're going to have to come running or all I'll have is a big stink."

Richards wrote his home phone number on one of his cards and handed it to me.

"When are you going to get started?" he asked.

"As soon as I can, but I have a few things I have to check out."

Barbara was tip tapping away on her computer when I walked

out of Richards' office. She looked up. "Will you come over tonight?" she asked, looking as sweet and innocent as Elizabeth Taylor before her breasts developed and she started to hang out with Richard Burton.

"Give her a chance," my Guardian Angel said, this from the mouth of an angel that's on the kinky side. But then I've always been up to a challenge.

"I'll call around 6," I told her.

She looked happier than Porky the Pig eating a pesky wabbit.

There were two pay phones in front of Police Headquarters. I suppose so cops could call their bookies or buy a lid for the weekend. I dialed Hoffman's number. "You know what to do, leave a message."

"I called you before and left a message that wasn't very nice. I've had a change of heart, nice guy that I am, and can help you get back what you are missing. I'll be at the Subway on Bell Rd. next to Dunkin' Donuts at 5 this afternoon. Be there or be square. I'll only wait ten minutes. Leave Awalt and McVede in the car."

"You're making a big assumption," my Guardian Angel warned me.

"I've always been good at hunches," I informed him.

"Roosevelt don't try and lie I'm not a woman," he replied.

Phoenix in the winter has gorgeous weather. The 17 million cars, green air, 46 robberies, 10 murders, 53 car wrecks, 4 car jackings, and 3,000 drug deals a day dampen the overall effect of nice weather, but what the heck, no place is perfect.

I went to the Orange Tree Golf Course where a bucket of range balls is seven bucks and green fees are more than a man spends on a girl he hasn't gotten naked yet. I played with three men from Alberta who wore enough gold Fort Knox is trying to make a deal with them and whose golf clubs cost more than Matilda, my clubs, my pistol, and the house I wished I owned put together. They were fun to play with though, they bought me beer all the way around and lunch when we were done. I have a feeling they thought I was a pauper, which, after a few more weeks in Scottsdale I would be - my money was running out faster than Drano wipes out a hairball.

We finished eating at 3 o'clock and I had nothing to do. I didn't want to practice putting, it wouldn't help. I didn't want to hit a bucket of balls and improve the snap hook I've perfected. I decided to drive to Tatum Ranch Golf Course and look around the housing area once again.

I drove up and down every street within a mile radius of the Golf Course. There wasn't one tree over three feet tall or a single blade of grass. I was perplexed, but at least I'd killed two hours, and headed for my meeting with Hoffman.

The Subway was located in a strip mall. Phoenix has more strip malls than houses. In the mall, besides a Subway, were a dry cleaner, a dress shop, a car parts store, furniture store, card shop, pet shop, bicycle shop, a grocery store, a head shop, and a Walmart. I could have pitched a tent in the parking lot and never had to walk more than 100 yards for anything I needed the rest of my life. The age of Daniel Boone this isn't.

Parking in front of Walmart I stuck my pistol in the back of my pants, covered by my jacket, and took my time walking to the Subway. I didn't see a silver Jaguar, a black four door Mercedes, or a black B.M.W.

A young couple with two kids was eating when I walked in. The kids were both under five or six and crying about what they wanted their parents to buy them at Walmart. The young couple did not look at each other while they ate, both probably wondering whose idea it was to have kids.

I've always had a hard time at Subway shops, something about eating a sandwich in a shop painted orange and yellow bothers me. I ordered a large coffee and sat at a table facing the front. The entire front of the shop was glass including the door.

At five till five a silver Jaguar with gray tinted windows slowly drove by. At exactly 5 o'clock Cecil Hoffman walked in and without hesitating walked over and sat down opposite me.

"Roosevelt," he said. "You have to be the stupidest person I have ever met in my life."

"I've been told that before," I replied.

My hunches were right. He knew me. When I called and told him to meet me I didn't say what I looked like or who I was. And, for sure, Hoffman doesn't have the money. He didn't come to meet me just to say hello. Somebody has stolen the money from him.

"I'll be ex-communicated," my Guardian Angel said.

CHAPTER FIFTEEN
THE GLEEN GLEEN GLASS OF HOME

Hoffman stared at me looking as cool as the latest Hollywood hunk star that was in Sheboygan, Wisconsin on a goose hunting trip. He was in bed with a 19-year-old waitress from Joe's Corner Cafe who was telling him, "You can do anything you want with my body. I'll be your sex slave, but take me from this place, the fried cheese balls are driving me crazy, and I don't like the Packers."

I scrutinized Hoffman. His hair was perfect. He was wearing a black silk shirt - the kind actors wear that are portraying rich South American gangsters but in truth are only worn by gamblers in Vegas who haven't won a hand in 15 years. He had gold-rimmed sunglasses with lenses so dark they would make a Highway Patrolmen from Oklahoma ashamed. He had a Rolex on one wrist, a gold bracelet on the other, a large diamond pinky ring, and a gold chain around his neck a rap singer would think is gaudy. His moustache looked like it had been trimmed one hair at a time. He was the kind of guy who doesn't wrinkle his sheets when he sleeps.

In the old days some of my hippie friends became pot smugglers. They went from Levi's and boots to sports cars and gold jewelry. They are now doing forty years at various government hotels around the country where they have learned to carry a bible around and say "they framed me." I'd bet Matilda's spare tire Hoffman is headed in that direction. I hope to speed him on his way.

"Where's my money?" Hoffman demanded in a lousy James Cagney impression. Like I am going to jump up and write him a check for 2 million.

"Why did you kill Gloria?" I asked calmly, demands and I get along about as well as wolves and sheep.

"Why you," he snarled coming half out of his seat and swinging at me.

I blocked his punch, noticing the look of shock on the faces of the young couple eating with their sniveling kids, grabbed his gold chained decorated throat and squeezed his wind pipe. His glasses fell on the table as he struggled to breathe. "You listen to me," I said in a cool, collected voice. "You ever try and hurt me I'll stuff every piece of your lousy gold jewelry down your throat and then beat you so badly you'll poop gold coins for a month. Do you understand me?"

He didn't answer so I squeezed harder. "Yes, yes," he croaked like a tree frog with a cold.

I released the pressure on his throat and pushed him back into the seat. He rubbed his throat and scowled at me.

"I like that line, poop gold coins for a month," my Guardian Angel said. "It shows good abstract thinking."

"Hoffman, you might be the biggest gangster in the world," I told him. "But to me gangsters are nothing but punks, cheats, and cowards, who live off honest people's fears. But since the only thing that scares me is AIDS and since I'm about broke, we can do a little business. I think I can get your money back. If I could do it alone I wouldn't have contacted you. So, for doing you a favor, and the use of you and your two goons, I only want 20 percent."

He looked at me like I am one blade of grass lower than a cow pie. I slapped him on his upper right arm like he was my golfing partner who had made a good putt. He winced in pain. "Blackwell told me the next time he won't miss and to tell Awalt and McVede hello," I smiled at him like we were long lost brothers and sipped on my coffee.

The young couple quickly finished eating and carried their two whining kids out the door. The mother saying, "Ok, Ok, hon, we'll buy you Walmart."

Hoffman put his glasses back on either because he is a coward and couldn't look me in the eyes without them as a shield or to stop the glare from the orange and yellow paint in the Subway. "I didn't kill Gloria," he said. "I loved her. It had to be Reid and Blackwell."

"You think they killed her because you didn't pay them? I doubt it. They might kidnap her and hold her for ransom, but killing her wouldn't get them their money, in fact, it would ensure they wouldn't get paid."

"Who else would kill her?" Hoffman asked.

I ignored his question and asked instead. "When the money was stolen, why didn't you tell them?"

"You think they'd believe me?" Hoffman said.

He had a good point. A crook thinking another crook is telling the truth when two million dollars went missing would be hard to believe.

"If the money hadn't been stolen were you going to pay Reid and Blackwell?" I asked.

"Does it matter?" he replied, which, in truth, it didn't.

"Hoffman, I know almost everything about you. I know why you got a divorce. I know Gloria lived at your house in Paradise Valley. I know she drove the get away car. I know you wanted to roll the money over on a coke deal. I know you killed Springer."

"You're a regular walking encyclopedia," he said. "But I don't give a hoot about what you know. I'm only interested in getting my money back. Besides, how do I know you're not working for Reid and Blackwell and they're paying you to set me up?"

"If I was you'd be bleeding to death in the parking lot along with your two ignorant sidekicks. I don't work for anybody. You guys can kill each other for all I care. I recover the money, I give it to you, you don't want to pay them, that's your business."

"You're one brave guy, Roosevelt," he said.

"No, I'm a guy who happens to need some money and about the only honest job I'm qualified to do is bag groceries."

"After you nabbed that guy on the kidnapping case in Florida you'd think it would have given you such a reputation as a private eye you'd be making the big bucks."

"Life is fickle," I replied.

"Some people don't know what to do when opportunity knocks," my Guardian Angel said.

"So what else do you need from me besides muscle?" Hoffman asked.

"Right now just answer a few questions?" I told him.

He looked at me apprehensively before saying, "Shoot."

I felt like pulling out my pistol and following his orders. It would save the state a lot of problems. But, even killing gangsters is murder and doing 20 for killing somebody that should be killed doesn't really appeal to me. I've heard the food is bad in prison and they don't change the sheets everyday. If I was a contract killer, and not an honest person, I could kill Hoffman and then make a deal with the Feds and they'd let me go. I could then write a book, make about 19 million big ones, and be a guest on all the talk shows telling people ways to kill people and get away with it. But, being honest, I couldn't offer the Feds anything and would have to do my time.

"Why did Gloria move out of your house?" I asked, mystified over the American judicial system.

"You know how it is, we had a fight, she left, that's all."

I was disappointed, even a gangster can't control his wife, what is life coming to?

"Who did you trust with your money so it could get stolen?" I asked.

Hoffman looked at me like I was a cop who thought he would sign a confession. "If you know where the money is, get it. How it got stolen is none of your business," he said.

In a weird sort of way he was right.

"Did Awalt and McVede ever pose as detective's?" I asked. I didn't want to mention Linda's name.

Hoffman looked confused before answering, "No."

"Why did Awalt and McVede try to kill me?"

"Why would we want to kill you, Roosevelt? You're about the only one who might find out who killed Gloria. The cops in this state can barely scratch their head."

I wanted to tell him he might be surprised how smart the cops were, but a cocky crook will meet his end quicker than a crook who respects the police.

"It was Awalt and McVede that followed me in the Nova, though, wasn't it?"

"Roosevelt, your brain is up in the clouds. Why would we want to follow you? I know where you live."

"Who told you who I am and where I live?"

Hoffman smiled. "I can't tell you that. A guy has to have some secrets."

"If you don't there's no deal," I threatened.

"Answer a few questions for me and I'll answer yours," he said, calling my bluff.

I nodded apprehensively. We were playing a cat and mouse game and I didn't know if I was the cat or the mouse. I might have caught him off guard when I grabbed his throat but I don't think there are too many things Hoffman is afraid off. People who rob banks normally don't have a paranoid problem.

"Who do you think took my money?" he asked.

"I can't answer that," I said. "If I did, you wouldn't need me, but nice try."

Hoffman smiled. "How did you find out my phone number?"

"I can't answer that," I said.

"Tell me where Reid and Blackwell are."

"I can't answer that," I said.

I was beginning to sound like a stuck record.

"How do I know you won't turn me over to the cops if you find the money?"

"You don't," I said. "You have to hope I'm like you and my greed will override my civic duty."

We scrutinized each other for a moment. He knew I wouldn't back out of the deal just as I knew he wouldn't - big money has a way of overriding caution.

"We're even," he replied. "You don't answer my questions. I don't tell you how I know where you live."

I saw Awalt and McVede walk by the front of the shop. "Ok, here it is in a nutshell," I said. "I'm going to make a move on the people who have the money. When everything is right, I'll need your help for the muscle. It shouldn't be more than a few days."

"When you're ready, call," Hoffman said. "But don't say anything over the phone. Every police agency in the United States is listening to my conversations. When you call I'll meet you at Seafood Central on Shea."

"You like that place," my Guardian Angel said. "That's where you took Linda."

"Not that I don't trust you but you go outside and bring Awalt and McVede in here," I ordered more than told Hoffman.

Hoffman left and came back with Awalt and McVede. When they sat down, all three of them looked at me like they were a three man tag team but they weren't going to make a tag and let one man stomp me into the mat - they were all going to stomp me into the mat.

"Wait ten minutes until you leave," I told them as I stood and then said to Awalt and McVede, "Reid and Blackwell send love and kisses."

"Tell them to eat raw eggs," Awalt said.

I started to leave but stopped again. "Hoffman, do you play golf?" I asked.

"Golf is for punks," he said. "I wouldn't play that stupid game if people paid me."

I walked as fast as my booted feet would carry me to Matilda and drove away wishing Matilda had a Porsche engine in her. I did several U-turns in a residential area but then felt stupid as Hoffman knows where I live. "I'll say one thing for you, Roosevelt," my Guardian Angel said. "You are one brave man. A stupid brave man, but brave none the less. When you get buried, I'll have engraved on your headstone - HERE LIES ONE BRAVE STUPID MAN or HERE LIES ONE STUPID BRAVE MAN, which ever you like the best."

"You do your job over the next few days and I won't need a stone for a while. But if I do need a stone I want it to say - HERE LIES THE SMARTEST, BRAVEST, MOST HANDSOME, CLEVEREST MAN THAT WAS FAMOUS FOR FIFTEEN MINUTES AND TWO RERUNS."

"There is only so much a Guardian Angel can do," he told me in a tone that verged on being sarcastic.

I drove to a gas station, Matilda needed food, and after giving her a tank of premium for being such a good girl I called Barbara. "I'm so glad you called, it is after six and I thought you'd forgotten me."

"Barbara," I said. "Nobody who has ever seen you naked could forget you," which included me and about 10,000 other guys.

"Roosevelt, you know just the right things to say," she gushed.

"Are you coming over?"

"Do you have any cheap beer?"

"No, I have two six packs of an expensive import?"

How could I say no?

Driving to Barbara's I felt I had enough information to solve Gloria's murder, but there is something I am not seeing, and whatever the something is, it has to be obvious.

"I don't think you should go see Barbara," my Guardian Angel said, which surprised me. "I think you should go back to the apartment?"

"She might be able to answer a few questions for me," I said.

"I think you should go back to your apartment."

"Are you feeling Ok?" I asked, concerned that my lecherous, shameless, Guardian Angel might be getting morals.

He was silent for a moment, trying to pretend he was thinking. "Well, maybe if you leave on the lights and don't stay long," he said.

That was more like him. "You had me worried," I said.

Barbara answered the door wearing a white lace teddy and high heels that would make a normal person dizzy. She is holding a silver tray with one beer on it. "Enter kind sir," she said sweetly.

"I only came over to talk," I stammered.

"You can talk all you want," she said.

I followed her but we didn't go to the living room. We went to her bedroom. She has a round waterbed King Arthur's court could have frolicked on. The walls and ceiling are mirrored and candles burned on nightstands on either side of the bed. She held out the tray and I took the beer and she sat the tray on the nightstand. She pushed a button on the wall and low seductive music filled the room. She swayed to the music and slowly removed the teddy and then sprawled out on the bed with her arms above her head.

"I'm glad you didn't go to your apartment," my Guardian Angel commented hoarsely.

"Roosevelt, are you going to stand there with your tongue on the floor or are you going to join me?" Barbara asked.

I guzzled the beer. I hate wasting good beer.

The shadows dancing on her naked body are the best shadows I have ever seen.

"No, no, Roosevelt," my Guardian Angel pleaded. "Don't say what I know you are going to say."

I smiled at Barbara and shook my head. "I'm sorry, but I don't think this is right," I said.

To my surprise Barbara put her teddy back on and smiled. I wasn't in the mood anyway," she said. "Want some coffee and an omelet?"

Barbara made an omelet and ground coffee beans in an electric grinder for coffee. The omelet was delicious and the coffee so good it verged on being sinful. "What do you think of Detective Williams?" I asked while she poured me another cup of coffee.

"I don't like him. I can't really tell you why but there's something about him that gives me the shivers."

"Does he go watch you dance a lot?"

"The other night was only the second time I've seen him."

"We'd had almost had cheap meaningless sex, eaten, and drank a cup of coffee, the only thing missing was smoking a cigarette, but since I'd quit when cigarettes started costing more than pot, it was time for me to leave. But, after such a shallow evening, how does one say goodbye with class. "Goodbye with class," doesn't sound right as you walk out the door. So I looked at my watch like I had something to do, kissed Barbara on the forehead, which is the universal sign of goodbye between men and women when the party is over. She walked with me to the door, obviously not bothered I was leaving so soon, which at my age doesn't hurt my ego one bit.

As I drove back to my apartment I remembered a bar in Thailand several of us had gone to during my R & R from Vietnam. An enterprising cab driver who specialized in girls, cheap silk suits, fake diamonds and rubies, told us about a bar that played country and western music. As we walked into the bar it was a strange sight seeing oriental women dressed in Levi's, western shirts and boots. The oriental members of the band were singing, "The Gleen Gleen Glass of Home." It's one of those strange memories that have never gone away. "The Gleen Gleen Glass of Home."

When I reached the top of the stairs I knew something was wrong. All the lights were on in my apartment and the front door was open. I pulled out my pistol and walked cautiously into the apartment. The door had been pried open. My apartment had been ransacked, sofa cushions were cut open, the refrigerator door was open, the cupboards were open, all the drawers had been emptied onto the floor and the mattress and pillows cut open. My clothes from the closet were thrown on the floor and all the pockets turned inside out. My notebook of clues had been thumbed through and tossed on the floor. I stood in the middle of the living room looking at the mess when I saw the note on the dining room table. It was another typed love note. ROSES ARE RED, VIOLETS ARE PURPLE, YOU HAD BETTER GET YOUR OLD HIPPIE REAR OUT OF TOWN BECAUSE THE NEXT TIME I WON'T MISS.

It was obvious my visitor wasn’t a poet.

"I told you, you should have come home," my Guardian Angel said.

"You didn't put up a strong argument," I replied.

"That's because your art of persuasion is better than most peoples," he said, trying to put the blame on me.

"Don't patronize me," I warned him.

I learned the phrase from an old girlfriend of mine, but I really don't know what she meant when she said it. "You look nice.” Is that patronizing? "I like your dress.” Is that patronizing?"

Before I called Wang I checked to see if my bedroom doorknob had been removed. It hadn't. Wang was at the apartment in two minutes. Looking at the mess he said in his normal oriental casualness, "Mr. Roosevelt. I have a strong feeling somebody in this town doesn't like you."

"I'd like the furniture replaced with something in a Southwestern print," I told him. "Earth tones, soothing, subtle, but bold at the same time, something that makes a statement without being overbearing."

"Would you like a machine gun set up on your porch painted a matching Mesquite brown and a triple steel thickness bulletproof front door?"

The only question the cops asked me when they came was if I was hiding drugs. I didn't tell them about the note and they didn't bother to dust for prints. Even my Guardian Angel would have known whoever did it was smart enough to wear gloves - smarter than I was when I broke into Gloria's apartment.

When the cops were gone and Wang had left to order the machine gun for the front porch. I stood by the open door and wasn't thinking about anything when the maintenance man started up the steps with another door. "As often as I come here I should move in," he joked.

People need less humor on their job. I went back into the apartment and for no particular reason was looking down at the carpet - a tiny object, no larger than 1/4 of an inch caught my attention. I picked it up carefully. It was a fingernail. As I examined it I noticed there was no trace of either clear or colored finger nail polish. Life has a way of giving people small surprises.

Looking at the mess around me it had been a hasty search. I know it was not a pro as the switch plates were still on - they would have been removed.

The maintenance man finished mounting the door as I finished cleaning up the apartment. "It's a lousy world we live in," he told me as I looked at his work. "People stealing all the time, killing each other, breaking into houses, rapes, people kidnapping kids. What are we going to do?"

"Maybe try and be good and help those who can't help themselves," I said, but feeling as helpless as he sounded.

"Mr. Roosevelt, nobody's Superman," he told me as he left.

I sat in the living room and sipped on a beer as I read over my clues. I have the two notes, the photograph of Gloria, her phone book, and the bit of fingernail on the table. The maintenance man's words kept bouncing around in my head, "Nobody's Superman. Nobody's Superman. Nobody's Superman."

He was right. I sat down my notes and picked up the piece of fingernail. "There is no Superman," I said. "But there is a Mighty Mouse,"

CHAPTER SIXTEEN
FOREPLAY WENT OUT WITH WOMEN'S RIGHTS

I stayed up until 1 in the morning reading and rereading my clues and questions. I felt like a college student who had eaten three bennies and tried to learn in one night what he hadn't studied for in eight weeks. "There's one big difference," my Guardian Angel said. "You flunked out of college."

I took a shower and went to bed feeling not exactly confidant but knowing I was on the verge of shaking up the entire situation. I was almost asleep when my Guardian Angel whispered. "Roosevelt, are you going to be the shaker or the shook?"

"Ask me that in three days," I grumbled. "But, since you were planning on waking me, why did you bother to whisper?" I didn't give him time to answer, continuing, "Besides it's not shook it's shaken."

I got up at 5 a.m. and with my trusty 9 m.m., was out the door by 5:15. The traffic was already heavy, even though it was dark, and I felt sorry for the people who are slaves to their jobs. Those people who think that nine to five and car pools are the road to salvation and not understanding why they have high blood pressure and ulcers. I also wondered why my stomach has been bothering me lately.

I rang Barbara's doorbell about twelve times. The porch light came on and she opened the house door, looked at me standing behind the wrought iron gate like I was a freak in a side show, grunted something that sounded like what a bear would say to its mate after sleeping for six months, and went back inside the house without asking me in. I was hurt. I am not her morning cup of tea, the spice that would make her day, the ray of sunshine that would make her life a merry dance through the flowers of life. She came out of the house wearing a pink terry cloth bathrobe and slippers that matched and unlocked the gate. "What do you want?" she asked, motioning for me to come in, obviously not the little bird who gives a feather about catching the early worm.

We sat in the kitchen drinking instant coffee. I know for sure the thrill is gone - she hadn't ground coffee beans. "I need your help, Barbara," I told her.

"How much is it worth to you?" she asked.

I didn't know she was such a materialistic girl.

"I need your help as a friend."

"How much is it worth to you, friend?" she asked.

"I'll pay for ten minutes to the Dominate Dementrious 900 number for you if you help me."

She thought it over. I thought she was going to make a counter offer for fifteen minutes but she didn't. "What do you need before I make a decision?"

"Do you know where Detective Williams lives? I can't find his address in the phone book."

"No, but I can find out. I have access to everyone's records."

"I'll stop by at work and get his address from you."

"You mean you came by here at dark thirty to tell me you want me to get Williams' address for you?"

"Plus, I want you to ask Williams to take you out tonight."

"What are you up to Roosevelt?" she asked.

"Nothing your pretty little sleepy head needs to know about," I told her.

"Twenty minutes of Dominate Demetrius," she said, knowing she had the upper hand, "but I won't sleep with Williams, at the most, some heavy petting."

I like Barbara, she has her head screwed on, it might be screwed on backwards but it's still screwed on.

By the time I got to the Tatum Ranch Golf Course the sun was about to clear the horizon. A man was mowing the putting green and cart boys were driving carts from the cart shed to the front of the pro shop. Inside the pro shop was a line of golfers waiting anxiously to pay their green fees. Kevin looked like a harried clerk at Walmart when toilet paper is on sale. I went to the rack where the putters were on display. There was a Zing, a Flop, a Dead Eye, Bullseye, Mallet, Blade, one that looks like a horseshoe, an Even My Mother Can't Miss, a center shafted, a heel shafted, a soft insert, a Bass Ackwards, one that stands up by itself so when a golfer gets drunk it would help him walk back to the clubhouse. The cheapest putter was $122.00. For that kind of money I'd hire somebody to putt my three footers for me and fire him when he missed.

When all the golfers had paid their green fees and were outside happily telling each other lies I approached Kevin. Kevin was as happy to see me as a convict out on parole who is smoking a joint in his living room when his parole officer makes a surprise visit. "Kevin, I want to apologize for talking to you so badly," I told him. "At first I thought you might have had something to do with Gloria's murder but now I know I was wrong. There's been a break in the case."

Kevin smiled like he was no longer a club pro, but was walking down the last fairway of a major tournament with the TV cameras on him while 55,000 people clapped. He was going over in his mind what he was going to say, "Yes, I am a god. Throw money at me and give me a gaudy trophy and I will write ten instructional articles for Golf Digest giving away all my secrets so you too can bask in glory. See what a kind and generous god I am."

"That's ok, Mr. Roosevelt," he replied. "Everybody makes mistakes."

"There's no doubt about that," I said, shaking hands.

"Can you tell me what the break is?" he asked timidly.

"No, but I guarantee you it will be in the paper soon."

He looked disappointed. "When does Linda come to work?" I asked.

"She'll be here in thirty minutes."

I was almost to the door when Kevin stopped me. "Here, Mr. Roosevelt," Kevin said. "Here's a pass to play a free round, cart included."

I noticed as Kevin walked away, he no longer had a limp.

I went to the Walmart at the end of the strip mall where I'd met Hoffman. Even early in the morning Walmart is filled with people, mostly returning things that have broken. I went to the toy department and found what I wanted. A toy police set complete with a silver plastic badge. The clerk who checked me out was chewing gum so furiously in a few years her teeth would be worn down to nubs.

Outside I opened the toy police set and gave the pistol to a little boy who was with his mother. He looked at me like I was some kind of idiot because the pistol didn't have real bullets and he couldn't shoot out car windows or kill a few pedestrians. When I was in Matilda I pinned the plastic badge in my billfold.

"I know what you are about to do and it isn't smart," my Guardian Angel said.

"When did smart ever get in the way of anything I've done?" I asked.

"Knowing you are doing something stupid is not wisdom," my Guardian Angel said.

The parking lot at Linda's apartments was almost empty - working to pay bills is such a joy. I parked in my reserved spot by the dumpster. If a person walks around an apartment complex long enough they will run into a manager, an assistant manager, an assistant to the assistant manager, or the assistant to the assistant manager's assistant. You always know who they are because they will have on a weird colored shirt with the apartment complex's name on it. I was lucky, I ran into the assistant to the assistant manager's assistant - a girl, maybe 18, most probably a high school dropout whose greatest accomplishment in life was hanging rental notices on people's doors while they are working their third job so they can pay the rent a week late. I looked at her with cold beady eyes like I was Tonto and had finally gotten fed up with The Long Ranger and was going to sue him on four different counts: I am a minority and don't get equal billing. My horse is smaller than The Lone Rangers. I have never been able to ride in front of the Lone Ranger and, last but not least, I have never been allowed to say anything more than "ke mo sa be."

Pulling out my billfold I flipped it open so she could see the plastic badge and quickly flipped it shut. "F.B.I.," I said. "I need you to let me into Linda Adam's apartment."

The word F.B.I. scared her speechless. She didn't say a word as I followed her to the apartment. After she opened the door I told her, "Don't tell anybody about this. This is an ongoing investigation." I glared at her like if she didn't do what I told her little men in dark suits and yellow ties and wearing hushpuppies would follow her until she was 85 years old and bust her every time she parked illegally in a handicapped parking spot. She scampered away quicker than a drug runner can holler, "BORDER PATROL" or "I CAN DO FIFTEEN YEARS STANDING ON MY EAR."

I shut the door behind me. The unicorns on the table ignored me. The Save the Whales, Save the Wolves, Save the Spotted Owl posters beckoned to me for a donation. I examined all the unicorns in the living room, picking up each one and carefully setting it back exactly where it had been. I looked at the plants like I was a spider mite inspector and would fine their owner if they were being abused. I looked under the sofa, under the cushions. I went through all the cupboards in the kitchen - picking up and replacing every cup, saucer, plate, and Tupperware dish. I looked under the sink. I examined the toaster. I opened the stove and the broiler drawer. I shook the boxes of cereal in the pantry and picked up each can of vegetables and soup. I went through the hall closet, checking all the pockets of her clothes in the closet, shook out her shoes, and went through the empty shoeboxes. I looked under the bed and picked up and examined all the unicorns on the bookshelf and the stuffed toys. I went through the first of her two dressers, there was nothing unusual. I looked through the jewelry box on top of it. The box was not lined and contained costume jewelry - the kind people at flea markets sell, telling you they are collector items. I held up the box and examined the bottom - it was solid wood. I went through the second dresser, each drawer was filled with sweaters. I opened the jewelry box that was on top of it - it was lined in red felt. There were six sets of diamond earrings for pierced ears, three gold bracelets, four gold necklaces, and a ladies Rolex watch. I picked up the jewelry box and looked at the bottom - it was solid wood. I went back to the bookcase. There was a row of books ranging from TRIM THAT TUMMY to THE GRAPES OF WRATH. I fanned through each book and found nothing.

“What are you looking for?" my Guardian Angel asked.

"I don't know," I answered truthfully.

I went back to the living room. I was missing something, part of my brain I know, but also something in the apartment. I looked at the posters on the walls. They are unframed and tacked to the walls with a tack in each corner, the tacks match. I un-tacked the Save the Whales poster and looked at the back - tacked it back to the wall being careful to put the tacks exactly back in the holes in the poster and the wall. I took down the Save the Wolves poster and looked behind it. "It's like your life," my Guardian Angel commented. "You're always looking behind not forward."

"When you walk through life backwards you have to," I explained to him.

I took down the Save the Spotted Owl poster and looked behind it. Taped to the back was a receipt. Using the paper and pen by the phone I wrote down the information on the receipt, making a special note of the date and place. I returned the poster to the wall.

The assistant to the assistant manager's assistant was standing outside when I left. "She is under investigation for mail fraud," I told her as I walked by.

I drove to Police Headquarters. I tapped on the glass at Barbara who got up and came out to the hall. She handed me a slip of paper. "Here's Williams's address. He's going to pick me up at seven, take me to work, and then we're going out to eat."

"I bet he's so excited he can hardly sit down."

Barbara laughed, blew me a kiss and went back into the office.

On the way to Reid and Blackwell's apartment I stopped at an oriental fast food restaurant and had three California rolls. Sometimes I need food that at least tries to sound healthy.

It was almost eleven and Reid and Blackwell still hadn't shaven or gotten fully dressed. The apartment had more beer bottles scattered around it to add to the ambiance. "The topless bars are going to kill you guys," I told them, not bothering to sit down.

They both grunted which in late night topless bar language means, good morning. "I only came by to tell you guys I made contact with Hoffman and I'm going to see him again soon. Things look good. Everything is going to jell within a few days."

They grunted again, which I took for, "You're doing a great job Roosevelt."

"You guys better stay home a few nights," I told them.

They didn't bother to grunt until I was gone. Then they each grunted three or four times arguing over who was going to get the privilege of killing me.

I went back to my apartment and got my golf clubs. I had a free pass and a person who passes up a free round of golf is one step dumber than I am.

"You should take up bowling. You don't have to chase the ball," my Guardian Angel said.

While waiting to see if there would be an opening for me to play I putted. An old man, who I would guess, was in his early 80's walked slowly by. He had a long walking stick with a pointed brass tip. I didn't recognize the type of wood. I went over to him. "That walking stick is a beauty. What type of wood is that?" I asked, looking closely at the stick and noticing large diamond protrusions that weren't carvings but actual parts of the wood.

"Diamond Willow," he said. "My grandfather cut this. It used to grow all along the Missouri River, but now it's all been bulldozed down."

"That's too bad," I said.

"More than that son, it's sad," he said.

After a moment thinking about extinct trees I asked. "Do you walk here a lot?"

"Walk around the course every morning at 7:30, start at number 1 and end here. Wife drops me off and picks me up. Used to play a lot of golf but I can't do it now, bodies all worn out, but I like looking at the course."

An elderly lady waved at him from in front of the pro shop and he left, not bothering to say goodbye.

I was put in with a man and his wife from France. They couldn't believe how friendly Americans were, cab drivers weren't over charging them, and they got meals at restaurants that are more than four bites served by a waiter who wasn't rude.

"When eez the time you last played golf, monsieur?" the man asked.

"A few days ago," I told him.

"Me too," he said. "Would you like to plaze for a small wager, let's say two francs a hole?"

"Only if the francs are all beef," I said with a grin.

He smiled.

Linda drove up to us at the 5th hole. The Frenchman ordered red wine and Linda told him he'd have to go to California and play golf. The bandage was off her arm. There was only a small cut. Maybe she had told me the truth about the open window.

"How come you haven't called me?" she asked. "Nobody's tried to kill you lately or what."

I pondered how women can ask three questions within two seconds and expect a man to answer them in one second. "Not lately, but I have a feeling that within a few days there's going to be a bunch of people who will want to kill me," I replied.

She gave me a quizzical look. "How about dinner?" she asked.

"It would have to be late, after nine," I said.

"That's OK. I've missed you Roosevelt."

Women who tell me they miss me have always worried me.

It was a worthwhile round of golf. I learned how to say five cuss words in French.

After the round I put, in good old American money, the equivalent of sixteen francs in my pocket. If the French would stop being the number one producer of plastic explosives I might have given him a break.

I headed back to my apartment, stopping to eat deep-fried cardboard dipped in fish flavored batter.

"I love Americans," my Guardian Angel said. "You will eat anything as long as it says, 'bad for you, guaranteed to cause hardening of the arteries, and fried'."

The furniture had been replaced and the maintenance man had just finished painting my wall. "Don't let anybody shoot at you for a few weeks," he told me. "I'm behind on a lot of little projects around here and won't have time to get to you."

I had three hours to kill so I did what most modern people do. I didn't read a book. I didn't meditate. I didn't try and mentally solve any of my personal problems. I didn't call home.

I didn't reread my clues. I turned on the TV and became a vegetable, ah....welcome to earth.

I watched a show about a woman whose sister is pregnant by her sister's ex-boyfriend, but the sister is trying to steal her sister's very, very, very wealthy husband by telling him the child is his, although it wasn't true because her sister's husband had never slept with his wife's sister, but he had been in a car wreck, had amnesia, and woke up in his wife's sister's bed with her naked beside him, not knowing how he got there, but liking it just the same. And now the woman, who is having an affair with her sister's ex-boyfriend, who is really the father of her sister's child, and still loves her sister, and had only slept with the sister of the sister who was pregnant out of revenge, is trying to get her husband back even if he had slept with her sister.

With only ten minutes remaining in the show I fell asleep not waking up until 6:20 and the end of the news. A middle-aged man, with perfect hair, obviously dyed, was smiling through perfect teeth and telling those of us who love fragmented news about some small country in the Middle East, who we could smash like a bug, was telling the world they would defeat the American pigs. If I was the President, I'd load up 95 bombers with 55-gallon canisters of pig manure, which would be about 1000 tons of manure, and drop them on their capital. When the manure was all over their dirty little streets I'd call them and tell them to straighten up their act or the next plane that came over would really make the manure hit the fan.

"Not nice," my Guardian Angel said.

I guzzled down a beer, stuck my pistol in my belt, made sure I had Williams' address in my wallet, turned off the TV and left the apartment as fast as I could. I had to get away from the TV before my brain dripped out of my ear and I started to have cold sweats on Monday morning thinking I might have to work late and miss Monday night football - but still, feeling like an ant as I drove in the endless stream of headlights, I wondered if the sister's sister went back to her ex-boyfriend who had been her sister's lover and if her sister got her husband back.

Williams lived at 1411 Rio Rico St. The neighborhood was an older, established, well-kept neighborhood. Street lamps are at the end of each block and in the middle - keeping the area well lit at night. The homes are brick, have nice grass front yards, many with flowers, walled backyards, and carports, not garages. Orange and grapefruit trees lined the street. A few bicycles were in front yards. It wasn't a neighborhood I could pull into the driveway, get out and snoop around for too long without a neighbor calling the police. Some neighborhoods I've lived in a robber could ask a neighbor to help load up his van. I found Williams' house. It is white brick. There are three orange trees and a lemon tree in the grassed front yard. Strangely, the house doesn't have either a garage or carport. A towering Weeping Willow grows next to the driveway, so big it shades the entire area. Some of its branches were trimmed back so they would not touch a parked car but others are so long they touch the ground and drape over the side of the house. There wasn't a car in the driveway. Ringing the doorbell I waited. I rang the bell again. I walked to the side of the house and parted the Willow branches to reach the gate to the backyard. I went through the gate. There are several fruit trees and another large Weeping Willow in the backyard. The grass was lush. There was a small back patio complete with barbecue pit and table and chairs. I looked at the willow tree. It is lovely. The long drooping branches touch the ground. I started to walk to the willow tree and almost walked into a roll out window. Going around the window I went to the willow, inched through the long flowing branches and touched the rough bark of the tree. I remembered a Willow that had been in my grandmother's backyard in Iowa when I was a boy. When I visited her, I would sleep in the upstairs bedroom. At night, the cool breeze would drift through the window and in the moonlight I could see the tree. It was a friend, filled with whisper dreams and childhood longings. The tree and the house are now gone. "I didn't know you were sentimental," my Guardian Angel said.

Sometimes it's better if people or Guardian Angels keep their mouths shut.

As I was about to get into Matilda several kids rode by on their bicycles followed by a couple out for an evening walk. They stopped. "Detective Williams isn't home," the man said. "He left about an hour ago. Tell me your name and I'll tell him you stopped by."

"No, that's Ok. I'll see him at work tomorrow. I was in the area and thought I'd stop in for a beer was all."

The man nodded and waved and he and his wife - or girlfriend - or mistress - walked off.

As I drove away, he watched me. I should have been paying more attention. I didn't think anything about the car that pulled in behind me as I turned off of Rio Rico. It was almost 8 o'clock and I drove until I spotted a pay phone. I was an hour early but I called Linda anyway.

"You're early," Linda said, women have a way of always stating the obvious.

"I'm so excited about coming over I couldn't wait," I said.

"Lie to me some more, I like it."

"Do you want to go out to eat?" I asked.

"I have beer. Why don't you stop and get a pizza?"

"If she wants to seduce you please don't say no," my Guardian Angel said.

"I have to," I said.

"Then why go over?"

"There's more to life than sex," I said.

"What?" he asked.

"Murder," I said.

"Party pooper," he said.

CHAPTER SEVENTEEN
IT HELPS YOUR LOOKS

Linda and I were sitting on the sofa sharing the last slice of pizza. "I talked to Kevin today," I mentioned to her casually. "For a long time I thought he was somehow involved in Gloria's murder, but I've stumbled onto some new information and there is no way he could be involved."

"What have you found out?" Linda asked a little too enthused. I have no doubt Kevin had told Linda about my conversation with him.

"I told Detective Richards about it and he told me not to say anything to anybody while he checked out a few more facts."

"Oh come on, Roosevelt, you can tell me," she said reminding me in a weird way of Hanoi Hanna.

"I'd like to tell you, believe me, but I can't," I told her, eating the last bite of pizza.

Linda frowned. Women aren't very nice when they don't get what they want, and they normally don't want the simple things in life like tools and golf clubs. Years ago I had a girlfriend who wanted New Mexico. "What is it, don't you trust me?" she asked, with the beginning of a pout on her pretty little pizza stained face.

"I only trust my mother," I said.

"And me," my Guardian Angel said.

"I have to trust you," I said.

"Please, Roosevelt, tell me," Linda said. "I'll be oh so nice."

"Tell her," my Guardian Angel said.

"No, Linda, I can't tell you, sorry," I replied like it broke my heart.

What had been a little pout on her face turned into a big pout. I did what all men do when this happens. I left as quickly as I could. If she could have squeezed out a few tears before I hit the door I might have told her everything.

Walking around the corner of the apartment building I had nothing on my mind except drinking a cold beer when I got home. "Duck," my Guardian Angel yelled.

He didn't mean a mallard because a fist crashed into my left temple. I started falling in what seemed slow motion - everything was a deep gray with outlines of black. Seeing a shadowed form, another fist slammed into my head. I hit the ground and the shadow crouched over me. I felt fingers circle my neck but I couldn't move my arms. The fingers grew tighter around my neck and the gray turned darker. Words came from the shadow that was choking me. "You've messed it all up. It would have been so easy. So easy."

The words hung in the air like mist, before falling slowly to my ears. My ears started to ring. I felt warm and then peaceful. My body seemed to float. The shadows were lifting. A white light, so brilliant it was brighter than anything I had ever seen, sparkled before my eyes. I had a strange thought. "This dieing isn't so bad, after all the worry, this isn't so bad."

Far off, like words shouted from a distant mountaintop, I heard. "What is going on here?"

The light began to fade, slowly, ever so slowly, then it was gray, black. My head started to hurt, a deep pounding throb. My throat hurt. I coughed, choked. I could move my arms and I sat up. A man was helping me to my feet. I opened my eyes. Another man helped support me. "What the heaven?" I stammered.

"You ok?" one of the men holding me asked.

"I've been better," I replied. "What is going on?"

"Some guy was choking you when we walked up," he said. "When he saw us he ran away."

"I can stand," I told them.

They let go of me and I mumbled, "Thanks," and then weaved toward Matilda. "You want us to call the cops?" one of the men called to me.

I didn't answer.

"I met duck, as dodge, move, bend down from the waist, not

bird," my Guardian Angel told me as I drove.

"English is a weird language," I told him.

Back at the apartment I checked out my face in the mirror. Below my left temple was a little red but it wouldn't bruise. However, I did have bruises on my neck from my assailant's fingers.

Sitting on the back porch and drinking a beer could have been tranquil if I could have seen the stars and not heard the incessant buzz of traffic. "I know what you're up to, Roosevelt," my Guardian Angel said. "You're trying to set a trap."

"Trying to keep something from you is like trying to hide Christmas presents from kids," I commented, more interested in my beer than the muses of my Guardian Angel.

"You had better be careful the trap doesn't snare you," he warned. He sounded like Sister Ann my sixth grade teacher.

I got up to go to bed. I would need all my rest and strength to do what I was planning on doing in the morning. If it didn't work, I wouldn't have to worry about getting caught in my own trap. I'd be dead meat, a cooked goose, a chicken with its head cut off, and last but not least, a beached whale.

In the morning, feeling weak from my duck experience, I headed out the door without my trusty 9 m.m.. I went to the friendly neighborhood grocery store where everything is overpriced because they know we have to eat and they make us pay out the nose. I bought a large package of stew meat, two day-old donuts, and a cup of coffee. Before I got to Matilda I ate the donuts and slurped down the coffee. I felt like a new man, caffeine and sugar do something for my system.

When I was a hippie in New Mexico I had a girlfriend named, Blue Sun Filled Sky of Glorious Summer Afternoon. She fed me bean sprouts, alfalfa sprouts, veggie burgers, carrot sticks, whole grain rice, some white stuff that comes from the orient and tastes like Elmer's glue, blue corn tortillas, natural fruit juices with crud floating around in it, and organic vitamin pills that tasted like grass clippings. She wouldn't allow anything with sugar in it, on it, or close to it, in the house. I never felt so bad in my life. I would sneak into town and eat French fries, hamburgers, chilidogs, and candy bars until they ran out of my ears. When I went back home I always

chewed gum because if I didn't, Blue Sun Filled Sky of Glorious Summer Afternoon, could smell the grease and become, Dark Cloud Filled With Lightening Who Will Never Give It Up To A Carnivore. The last time I heard about her she was Mrs. Ralph Jones, married to a dentist, has three kids that love Snickers, and owns four pizza parlors.

I drove around until I found a pay phone that still had a phone book and looked through the yellow pages for gun stores - there were at least 6,753 in the immediate area.

I drove to the nearest one called, KILL THY LOUSY NEIGHBOR, which was sandwiched between FRANK'S CHRISTIAN BOOK STORE and TEDDY BEAR DAY CARE CENTER. From the outside, the gun store looked like a Mexican prison except there wasn't a guard standing by the door wearing a pearl-handled 45 and taking bribes. There were no windows and the door was barred with steel thick enough it would take 16 hours to cut through it with a torch. Inside was a utopia for anyone who likes to kill things. There were pistols that can fire 2,184 rounds a minute that were advertised as target pistols, rifles with bayonets, folding gun stocks, and clips that hold 5,000 rounds were advertised as the latest necessary item for a deer rifle. There were camouflage clothes and grease paint so people could hide from man killing rabbits. I picked out a camouflaged pull over knit hat that left only my eyes exposed. I didn't need the cap for my plan but it brings out the green in my eyes. There was a large selection of knives, most of which wouldn't fit in a car trunk and were made for skinning dinosaurs. Clerks were walking around happily, each wearing a different pistol and talking about bullet penetration, exit holes, and bullet fragmentation. A lady clerk walked up to me wearing a T-shirt that read, "PEOPLE THAT SHOOT TOGETHER DON'T FIGHT FOR LONG." She had a pistol on her hip that could blow a hole through a concrete wall a herd of Texas Longhorns could stampede through. "May I help you find a means of destruction that will go with that stocking cap?" she asked with a smile.

"I need a tank, a 50-caliber machine gun with 100,000 rounds of ammunition, a 105 recoilless, 6 Chinese antitank rockets, and 3 claymores," I said.

"We don't sell those here," she smiled. "There's a place on the next block that does."

"What I really want is a stun gun," I told her.

"We have a company right here in Phoenix that makes them," she told me. "There's a special on them now."

Stun guns are not really guns. They don't fire a bullet but shoot a small dart that is connected to 15 feet of wire. When the dart hits the man, women, child, pig, cow, or whatever the target is, 100,000 volts of electricity run through their body knocking them down like they had been run over by a Mac truck. The stun guns are guaranteed not to kill but will give the object that has been darted Excedrin headache number 321. Two darts can be fired before having to reload. The nice thing about them is they are not classified as pistols so a murderer, who has done his two years and is out on parole, can buy 37 of them. The stun pistol was first developed in Canada, where it is illegal to carry a gun, but soon fell out of favor as people found out it is a great toy for robbing banks and little old ladies who won't give up their purses without a fight.

I bought two of the new models with four extra dart cartridges for each one. The darts come in a small plastic square that snap into the gun and snap out after being fired. The guns themselves look like flashlights and come with a simulated leather holster that clips to your belt. As I drove away I told my Guardian Angel. "If you weren't an incarnate being I'd test these babies on you."

"If I wasn't an incarnate being, you would have been dead in the mid-60's," he said.

Most of the time the truth is truly hard to swallow.

I drove to the discount home building store close to my apartment and bought two cans of glossy black spray paint - the kind you paint metal outdoor furniture with but can never keep the runs out of. I also bought twenty feet of sturdy manila rope.

"What are you going to do, Roosevelt, make them a pot of stew, paint them, teach them how to make cowboy knots, and then stun them?" my Guardian Angel asked.

"No, oh wise one," I said. "I'm going to break into Hoffman's house this afternoon."

"You're going to try and break into a house in daylight with surveillance cameras and guard dogs? What for Roosevelt? I might not be able to help you and you've already talked to Hoffman. Why not just knock on the door and snoop around while you talk to him?"

"That's too easy. When one has spent his life like I have, always doing things the hard way, it's hard to change, plus a daring, broad daylight raid has more class."

It was almost eleven. I found a pay phone and called Barbara at work. "Detective Richards' office, this is Barbara," she said, sounding as clean cut as a Girl Scout den mother making a batch of brownies.

"I want you to meet me for lunch at the Denny's by the Scottsdale Mall."

"Big spender," my Guardian Angel said.

"You're so romantic," Barbara said, "About as romantic as a pig eating corn. But, I will meet you for lunch. How about 30 minutes?"

I sat in Matilda waiting for Barbara during which time I braided a loop in the end of the rope that I could feed the other end of the rope through. I spent many hours when I worked on a ranch braiding rope and making splices. I figured it was something that might come in handy if I ever became a pirate.

"Williams is a pig, one of the vilest men I have ever met in my life," Barbara said as she picked at her Caesar salad. She didn't even notice the bruise on my face.

"You mean he wouldn't let you tie him up and beat him half to death with your riding crop?"

"I wouldn't let him in my house," she replied, plopping a cherry tomato in her mouth. "As soon as he picked me up he started telling lousy off color jokes. Besides, I only abuse people I like."

That made sense to me. "Did you notice during your lovely evening if Williams still has a limp?" I asked.

"His left leg must really hurt. It's hard for him to get up once he's sits down," Barbara replied.

"I really do want to thank you," I told Barbara.

"The Dominate Demetrius number is $4.00 a minute, you said 20 minutes, that will be $80.00, please kind sir," she replied, holding out her hand.

I gave her four twenties.

After Barbara headed back to the halls of justice I had two more cups of coffee. I figured the best time to go to Hoffman's was a little after one o'clock - any respected crook should be out and about by then and I was counting on the element of surprise.

When I turned the corner onto Hoffman's street I knew my plan was doomed. There was a large backhoe in the middle of the street ripping up asphalt. A half dozen men were standing around with hard hats on looking at a blueprint while two other guys were setting out road barriers. Obviously a water line had broken. "Your plan was lousy anyway," my Guardian Angel said. "You have to hit the place at night, and even then it's stupid."

"I thought maybe the direct approach was best."

"Did you stand up to charge North Vietnamese Regulars manning machine guns?" he asked me.

"That would have been suicide."

"Need I say more?"

I called Barbara. "How would you like to earn twenty more minutes with Dominate Demetrius?" I asked her.

"You don't have many friends, do you?" she said.

"It could be dangerous," I countered.

"How dangerous?"

"I could get shot, beaten up, or pulverized by two guard dogs."

"Oh boy, Roosevelt, I'll call in and tell them I can't work tonight. What time will you be by?"

"It gets dark around 6. I'll be by between 6:30 and 7:00."

When she said goodbye, she sounded happier than Cher when she finally got rid of Sony.

Now that my original plan was thankfully blown, looking back on it I wondered how I could have been so stupid. "Easy, you are always stupid," my Guardian Angel said.

I now have five hours to waste away until dark. I have wasted most of my life away but I really didn't want to waste the next five hours. I went back to the apartment and got my golf clubs and went to a driving range I had seen on Pima Rd. Golf is never a waste, it's merely futile. The driving range was one of those new places called ‘practice centers'. There was a driving range, a putting green, a sand trap, a machine you can rent that will tell you your swing plane, and 10 young men and women who will give you lessons and guarantee that if you keep practicing and spending thousands of dollars on lessons, someday it will all be worth it. I don't believe a word of it - it's never all worth it for the lousy player, the average player, or the above average player. Golf, unless you're a pro, is only an excuse to drink, lose at gin or poker, cuss, and get away from the wife and kids or the husband and kids, which ever the case may be. It is not a game you get better at with practice. I have found the best way to be a golfer is never to practice. Then, when you go play, you have an automatic excuse you can tell your friends - "the reason I play so badly is I don't practice."

The strange thing about this excuse is everyone believes it.

I hit two large buckets of balls and putted for an hour. All the practice did for me was make my hands sore. I went back to the apartment and read my clues.

"As many times as you have read them, you'd think you would have them memorized," my Guardian Angel said.

I got tired of reading and practiced drawing my new stun guns out of their holsters - a modern Wild Bill I'm not. I drank two beers. I turned on the TV and discovered to my delight the Golf Channel had been hooked up. Some pro senior player who has made 4 zillion dollars during his career, and looks like he has spent 2 zillion of it on Wild Turkey, is explaining how to hit the ball out of a sand trap when you're sober. He assured the audience it is much easier when you are drunk. Even the Golf Channel didn't interest me and I turned off the TV and read my clues again.

"You know what?" I told my Guardian Angel. "I'm going to solve this case."

"That would be a first," he said.

"This case has a definite order to it now. I would tell you what I know to be true but you'd only laugh. So I'm going to surprise you."

"You surprise me when you wake up every morning," he said.

At 6:00. I put on a dark shirt and my Levi jacket, loaded my two stun guns and put them on using the two simulated leather holsters. I put the extra darts in my breast pocket, put the two cans of spray paint in my jacket pockets, emptied the stew meat into a plastic sack and tied it to my belt, and took my rope and camouflaged knit hat. I felt like I am about to raid the great China wall and paint American graffiti all over it - CHINA SUCKS, CHINESE FOOD HAS TOO MUCH RICE, WHO SAYS WONG CAN COOK, EAT MORE BEEF NOT DUCK.

I drove to Barbara's. "What do you want me to do that could get you killed?" Barbara asked as I shook up the cans of spray paint while we sat in the kitchen.

"I want you to drive me to a certain part of town and let me out and once an hour for four hours come back to pick me up."

Barbara gave me a soul-penetrating look. "You're not some thief posing as a private detective are you? And are tricking me into being your get away driver?"

"No. I might have a lead on who killed Gloria and I have to break into a house that is guarded with surveillance cameras and guard dogs, not to mention two men who are meaner than Jack the Ripper."

"I've always liked stupid men," Barbara said.

Barbara has a brand new Dodge Van - the super duper model, leather seats, wood trim, state of the art stereo system, and 24 fold out cup holders. I disconnected the light over the back license plate.

"Let me get this straight," she said as she drove. "I let you out, go kill time for an hour, and come back to pick you up. If you're not there I come back in another hour. If, after coming back four times, you're still not there I call the dog pound to come find your pieces."

We turned onto Hoffman's block. The two-way street was reduced to one lane and marked by yellow flashing road signs - the type college kids like to steal to put in their rooms. There was a pile of asphalt over fifteen feet tall and a hole in the road deep enough to bury Matilda. As we past Hoffman's gate I could see lights at the end of the driveway. At the end of the block Barbara turned around and we drove back by the gate. At the corner I got out. "Right here in an hour," I told her, restating what we had gone over ten times, I don't trust her memory.

"This is exciting," she giggled.

It might be exciting but I didn't see anything funny about it.

I started to shut the door. "Aren't we forgetting something?"

she asked.

She couldn't want a goodbye kiss. "What?" I asked.

"We have to synchronize our watches, silly. It is exactly 8:30."

I set my watch - Barbara has watched too many low budget World War II movies.

I walked quickly to the front wall, making sure nobody was out walking their dog or jogging. But, normally, people don't live in walled houses to run outside of the walls - if they do why have a wall? When I came to the first camera on the wall I took the rope, tossed it around the base of the camera, loop end first, pushed the other end through the loop, tugged on it to make sure it would hold my weight, then pulled myself up the wall, holding on with one hand while I sprayed the lens of the camera with black paint. I hoped Hoffman didn't have a full time person watching the monitors. I repeated this with every camera on this wall until I got close to the gate. I backtracked, crossed the street, and walked until I reached the end of the other wall, crossed back and painted all the cameras until I again reached the gate. Since nobody had come out to investigate, I know nobody manned a surveillance room. During the entire time I hadn't heard a dog running around. I figured the dogs were of the highest quality and were trained not to bark, but to attack quietly, or they were kept in the house and only let out occasionally to do their rounds, either by themselves or with a handler. I then painted all the cameras on the side and back wall.

Taking a guess as to where the front of the house might be, using the driveway gate as my center point, I looped the rope over a camera and climbed up the wall. I let myself down on the other side as quietly as possible and crouching down, put on my knit cap, and left the rope hanging from the camera. The ground was sandy, lights from the house illuminated Mesquite and Palo Verde trees and various cactus. I removed a stun gun from its holster and moved slowly from cactus to tree, tree to cactus, inching closer to the house. After about ten minutes I crouched behind a large Mesquite tree and could see the front of the house. A porch light illuminated the front. The house was brown brick, at least five bedrooms, ranch style, and had a red tile roof. The driveway circled through the trees and cactus and ended at a three-car garage connected to the house. There was a floodlight on either end of the garage and a basketball hoop in the center. All the garage doors were shut, had no windows, and there were no cars in the driveway. I could see a tennis court about fifty yards from the house. Although there were a few lights on inside the house, I couldn't see inside since the curtains were closed, but I don't think anybody is home. "If you had waited until midnight, you would know for sure nobody is home," my Guardian Angel whispered.

"Why?" I whispered back.

"They'd be picking up the receipts at Tony's."

"If I want advice, I'll write Dear Abby," I said even though he was right.

"You can be such a snot," he retorted.

Having a Guardian Angel, more times than not, is like taking a city girl camping. It's ok until the first bug bite.

I circled to my right, trying to get into position so I could get to the side of the garage and not be illuminated by the light, discovering it was impossible. I would have to circle around behind the house, which is ok since the trees are thick. Moving away from the house and walking in a large circle I reached the tennis court and went to the far side of it, which shielded me from the house. At the corner of the tennis court I moved from tree to tree until I was behind the house. There was a large patio, a swimming pool and a Jacuzzi so large most people would call it a swimming pool. The patio doors were closed and curtained, but there was a light on. I kept moving until I was about fifty yards behind the garage and took a direct route to the side of the garage. There was no window on the side. All I wanted to do was look in the garage, but since I don't have X-ray vision, it was impossible.

There was nothing else to do but make my way back to the rope and boot scoot boogie for home. "Oh, he who never wants advice," my Guardian Angel said. "You are about to have company."

Company had barely cleared his smart mouthed lips when I heard a car approaching. I crept up to the edge of the garage, peaked around the corner, and saw headlights coming toward the house. I took the other stun gun out of the holster and glanced at my watch. It was 9:43. I had to make a quick decision, which is tough for me - normally it takes me three weeks to make a quick decision. As the car pulled into the driveway I heard a garage door opening. A five million dollar home without automatic garage doors with automatic inside lights would be like a luxury liner without a swimming pool and little umbrellas for the drinks. Hearing the engine shut off I ran around the corner, darted under the descending garage door, directly behind a four door black Mercedes. Awalt and McVede were already out of the car, holding cartons of Chinese food in their hands, and in the process of shutting the car doors with their feet. Startled, they momentarily froze. A dart fired from the gun in my left hand hit Awalt in the chest. The second dart fired from the gun in my right hand hit McVede in the stomach. They hit the ground like their bodies forgot they had legs and started flopping around like they were at Billy Joe Jones's tent revival and Jesus had entered their body and was making them jerk around like fish out of water. Sweet and sour pork, fried rice, won ton soup, lemon chicken, and fortune cookies splattered all over the floor. I released the two spent darts and reloaded. I quickly scanned the garage. There was a new silver Jaguar with Arizona plates, a black B.M.W. with Florida plates, and the black Mercedes. I noticed two bags of golf clubs in the corner. One bag was baby blue and had matching head covers.

Awalt had stopped flopping around and started to sit up holding his head and looking around like he didn't remember drinking a fifth of Jim Beam. I darted him again and sent him back to Jesus. McVede was still flopping around and didn't need any more religion. I extracted the spent dart while at the same time looking for the garage door button to open the door. I saw it by the door leading into the house. I was almost to the door when it opened. I don't know who jumped more, Hoffman or me. I do know the two Dobermans, one on either side of him, weren't scared at all, unless low guttural growls are dog language for fear. Luckily, I recovered first. A dart hit Hoffman in the arm. I figured a little religion wouldn't hurt him. He fell back into the house and flopped around more than Awalt and McVede. For some strange reason the dogs didn't attack me but only stood their ground and kept growling. I was impressed by their large shiny white teeth and how far back they could curl their jowls. "Good doggies," I said like I was talking to a baby holding a machine gun. "Very, very good doggies."

They must not like the word doggie because they crouched down and started to move slowly toward me. I didn't want to move quickly and I didn't think I could shoot them both with a dart before discovering how good of a chew toy I am. I kept talking and inching backwards. "You guys want some meat?" I tossed a handful of stew meat at them.

They didn't take their beady little eyes off me. They reminded me of lions inching through tall grass to get in exactly the right position before they charged and ripped out the throat of an 800-pound water buffalo. I tossed more meat. They were the first dogs I have ever met that were vegetarians. "Roosevelt, these bowsers don't like you," my Guardian Angel said, "or they don't like cheap cuts of meat."

I did what the dogs never expected. I suddenly stopped moving backwards, took a quick step toward them and yelled, "You flea bags", darted the dog on the right before he could lunge at me, giving the other dog a chance to lunge, which he did. The dart caught him in the middle of the chest when his pearly white teeth were about four inches from my throat. He hit the ground with a look in his eyes like the Big Bad Wolf discovering the hard way that Little Red Riding Hood had a twelve-gauge shotgun. Leaping over the dogs I pushed the garage door opener button and did my best to run the one-minute mile toward the wall, holstering my stun guns as I ran. I grabbed the rope and hoisted myself up and was about to go over the top of the wall when somebody grabbed my leg and yanked me back down. Landing hard I rolled quickly to my left and jumped up. McVede lunged at me. I ducked, stepped sideways and hit him in the side of the rib cage with a left hook, he grunted. I stepped back and chop kicked him in the left knee before he hit the ground. I kicked him in the face, snapping his head back violently. I grabbed the rope again and was almost over the wall when I was yanked back down again. This time I was able to keep my balance. Awalt circled me, holding a large knife in his right hand. He lunged, slashing out with the knife. I barely got out of the way but in doing so, stumbled backwards and landed on my rear. He plunged the knife down at me, I rolled to the left, barely missing his thrust, which left the knife sticking in the ground where I had been. I jumped to my feet and before Awalt could recover, kicked him in the ribs, spun, kicked him on the side of the head, and as he was going down, kicked him once more in the face. Just as I grabbed the rope I heard the dogs running toward me. I started up the rope when they were within ten yards of me. As I reached the top, they lunged, their snapping jaws missing my legs by mere inches. I landed hard on the sidewalk, left the rope, and took off running. "Please be there Barbara, please," I begged in the closest thing to a prayer I had said in years.

Behind me I heard a loud voice, "Attack!! Attack!!" I didn't look back. I saw Barbara's van parked on the corner. I only had twenty yards to go. I heard the dogs gaining on me. I heard Barbara start the car. Her lights came on. She was going to leave. "Wait," I hollered, she didn't hear me and started to drive away. I ran as hard as I could and reached the door as she started to accelerate. I pounded on the door. She slammed on the brakes and I opened the door just as the dogs reached the back end of the van. I jumped into the van and started to slam the door as one of the dogs lunged at me. The closing door caught him in the neck. His jaws were snapping inches from my face as I held the door shut. Barbara didn't have to be told and stomped on the gas pedal. When she was doing around fifty I opened the door. The dog bounced down the road doing a bad impression of a beach ball.

Barbara didn't say anything for a few minutes and then she started to laugh. First it was a giggle, then a few snickers, and then she was laughing so hard you'd think she had a date with Steve Martin. I took off the knit ski mask. "Leave it on," she laughed. "It helps your looks."

I would once in my life like to meet a woman I understood.

"Do as Barbara said and put the mask back on," my Guardian Angel said.

CHAPTER EIGHTEEN

A LITTLE OFF CENTER FROM BEING STUCK UP IN BETWEEN

It was 9 in the morning and I was sitting on the back porch finishing my fourth cup of coffee. I felt like I was at a bus station in Georgia and, because I was a Yankee, the ticket clerk wouldn't sell me a ticket even though I kept telling him it wasn't my fault I wasn't born in the south.

Wang walked by below, saw me, and waved. I felt like marching down and complaining. He had promised me a 50-caliber machine gun for the front porch and hadn't delivered. I hate it when people say they're going to do something then don't.

"What's wrong?" my Guardian Angel asked. "You look like you have lost your only friend if you had one."

"Funny, very funny," I said.

"I think you should go and read your clues and add any information, which of course is useless, to your list," my Guardian Angel said. "It might cheer you up."

"If it's useless, why add it?" I asked. "And how would it cheer me up?"

"Because, when you finally are man enough to admit you can't possibly solve Gloria's murder, we can get out of here, which will take a great load off your mind. Plus, I'm sick to death of rocks, cactus, Mesquite trees, and listening to people tell each other how good the weather is all the time."

My Guardian Angel must be reminiscing about his childhood in medieval Europe and missing cold, drizzly, foggy days that were so miserable frogs had to put on their woolies. But, none-the-less

I took his advice, useless endeavors do have a way of cheering me up and I went inside to read my clues.

When I was finished I had added 15 new clues to my 17 already organized new clues, making 65 clues altogether, counting my 38 previous organized clues.

Looking at Gloria's photograph I wondered how such a lovely lady could have fallen in with Hoffman. Looking at the two notes I had received I wondered how somebody could love me so much but not sign their name? I looked at the copy of the receipt I had found at Linda's. I looked at the fingernail and thought how gross. "You know you're right," I told my Guardian Angel dejectedly. "I feel like a complete failure."

"You've been addicted to failure your whole life. The first step toward recovery is admitting your addiction."

I ignored his remark. I wanted sympathy not a shrink. "I know who robbed the banks," I said. "I know who shot at me through the door. I know who shot at me at the golf course. I don't know who followed me from Detective Richards' office. I know who left me the love notes. I know who has the money and how they got it. I might know who broke into my apartment. I know who tried to strangle me. But, I only think I know who killed Gloria and if I did know more than think I know who killed Gloria, I couldn't prove it. What can I do?" I pleaded to God, Buddha, Confucius, Reverend Moon and The Rolling Stones.

"You could go back to being a hippie," my Guardian Angel said. "Eat three buttons of peyote, take two hits of acid, smoke four joints, bathe in hash oil, and then all the mysteries in the known and unknown universe will unfold themselves to you in all their truthful brilliance, of course, after seeing the truth in flashes of swirling colors and geometric designs beyond explanation, you would probably throw up for two days and then die."

"You're as much help as a golfer with a 25 handicap telling Phil Mickelson how to correct his putting problems," I told him.

"When I try to give you advice Roosevelt you never listen to me anyway," he sulked.

At least he can't call me a male chauvinist pig.

I didn't want to put up with him sulking all day because he doesn't feel appreciated and besides, there are so many people in

Phoenix who want to kill me I will probably need his help so I asked. "What do you think I should do?"

He didn't answer me.

"Pretty please with sugar on it," I coaxed.

He still didn't answer me.

"Turn that frown upside down," I cajoled.

He still didn't answer me.

"I'll take you to a porn movie," I offered.

He still didn't answer me.

"Answer me, you hard headed, fickle, low life," I demanded.

"That's more like you," he said. "I think you should find out where Kevin lives," he answered, never one to hold grudges.

"That's a good idea. Thanks," I said, having no idea why knowing where Kevin lived would help me at all. In all my calculations Kevin is only a bit player, but the number one rule of being a private detective is, ‘leave no stone unturned', and concerning Kevin, I haven't even turned over a pebble.

"You're like most people of your generation," my Guardian Angel said. "You don't respect your elders and you think older people are shriveled up nin-come-poops who don't know anything at all and all we do is sit around drooling and passing gas."

I have no idea what brought on his outburst. It had nothing to do with anything we had been talking about. "You're not people," I said, "and you can't get any older."

"It doesn't matter, it's the idea of it all."

"Have you been taking angel dust?" I asked.

I decided to call Detective Richards instead of dropping in unannounced, besides, I didn't feel like seeing Barbara. Her laughing when I had almost been chewed up by an attack dog and saying I look better with my face covered with a camouflaged ski mask had hurt my feelings.

"Detective Richards' office, Barbara speaking," Barbara answered.

I tried to disguise my voice. "Is Detective Richards in?” I asked while pinching my nose.

"Roosevelt, do you still have on your mask," she laughed. "You sound like you're holding your nose."

"No, I took it off to brush my teeth."

She was still laughing as she put my call through.

“Roosevelt, I thought you'd dropped off the face of the earth," Richards greeted me like I am his oldest son, whom he would just as soon never talk to again.

"I don't think my feet have ever touched earth," I replied.

"I can believe that."

It's sad when you try and make a funny and people take you seriously. "What do you need?" he asked, sounding like he was in the middle of something important, like practicing his baseball swing.

"I need Kevin Browne's address."

I heard him rustling around in a drawer. "Got a pencil?

"No, I have a pen."

"He lives at 1620 Isabella in Mesa."

"That has to be at least an hour drive each way for him to get to work," I commented.

"We spend most of our lives sitting on our butt in a car driving our lives away," Richards said.

I wondered if he was an old hippie who ate some cheap acid one-day and decided he should be a cop or just a bad philosopher. I dismissed both thoughts as being absurd. "Thanks," I told him.

"Call me before you get killed," he chided, which is a ridiculous thing to say. How could I call him after I got killed?

"Ok, I know where Kevin lives, now what do I do?" I asked my Guardian Angel.

"Are you patronizing me?" he asked.

"Don't push your luck," I warned him. "I've already been through that bit."

"You could drive over and see what type of house he has, who knows, you might discover something that will get you out of your funk, something that will break this case wide open. At least it will get you out of the house since you don't have the faintest idea what to do next. I don't want to watch you play golf again. Golf is more boring than boring."

I really didn't want to drive to Mesa. What good would it do to look at Kevin's house? But, my Guardian Angel is right, I don't want to sit around the house all day and feel worthless. I don’t want to play golf, although to me golf isn't boring. I don’t want to watch golf on TV, which is boring. I had quit doing drugs so I couldn't get high and sit around rationalizing how lazy is beautiful.

It took me an hour to drive to Mesa. There were 3,000 stoplights on the way and none of them were set in sequence. Mesa is more down to earth than Scottsdale. In Scottsdale, problems take on a different nature. One must decide what car they want to take to the golf course or beauty parlor - either the Jag or the Mercedes. They have to bother themselves pondering if five bedrooms are enough room for two people. Sometimes the water temperature to the Jacuzzi is a problem or the maid forgot to clean the bathroom in the garage. Uneven tan lines can cause depression. In Mesa, people hope they have enough gas in their car to make it to work and worry if they can save enough change to be able to buy a twelve pack for the weekend.

I found Isabella Street. It was an older neighborhood that had seen better days. A few houses were still neat and tidy but most had broken down cars parked beside the driveway and the paint on the house trim was peeling and cracking. Kevin's house was small, probably two bedroom, and made from cinder block that had been painted something between gray and brown. At one time the front yard had been red rock with a few cacti for decoration. The rock yard is now a patch of desert weeds, all with stickers, and the cactus are shriveled up and gone to wherever cactuses go when they die from neglect. The house has a one-car carport and under it there is a car with a car cover over it. The car cover was tied to the car with clothesline that is crisscrossed in so many different directions it looks like a spider web that had been made by a spider that doesn't have a clue. An unpainted cinder block fence enclosed the backyard. I rang the doorbell several times and, as I expected, there was no answer. I couldn't look through the living room window because it was covered with tin foil on the inside - a poor man's sun reflector - or he had an indoor pot crop - which wouldn't surprise me what with the wages golf courses pay their assistant pro's. I walked around and peaked over the fence. The backyard was filled with tumbleweeds and looked like a great place to breed rattle snakes and Gila monsters. A window was open, one of those old roll out types.

I went to the covered car and without untying any of the cord forced the cover up over the rear bumper. There was a decal for Avis rent a car on the bumper and it had Arizona plates. I quickly untied the clothesline and removed the car cover. The taillight of the white Chevy Nova was knocked out and there was red paint from another vehicle on the bumper and above the taillight. "I'll be," I muttered.

My Guardian Angel was strutting around like a tom turkey during breeding season with ten hens around him going gobble, gobble, gobble, gobble, which means in female turkey talk, "You've got the best drumstick we've ever seen, let's get it on big boy."

"Memorize this plate number for me," I told him.

My memorizing skills went out with the 60's.

I put the cover back on the car and retied the cord using a diamond hitch. There was no doubt Kevin would notice it and there is a slim chance him wondering who had looked at the car will play into my hands.

I drove back to Scottsdale feeling better. Don't get me wrong - I never feel normal - nor do I want to, but I did feel better, just a little off center from being stuck up in between.

Back at the apartment it was time to put my plan into motion. "I feel so good I think I'll have a party," I told my Guardian Angel.

"How can you have a party you don't have any friends in Arizona?"

"Who needs friends?" I said happily, "I'm only inviting people who want to kill me."

CHAPTER NINETEEN
PARTY POOPER

The last party I hosted was a peyote party in the late 60's. An artist friend of mine, who specialized in stained glass, drove from New Mexico to a ranch in Valentine, Texas and picked two gunnysacks of peyote buttons. The actual party is a blank, but when it was over I had a pierced ear with a chicken feather stuck in it, five girls informed me I had asked them to marry me on the conditions they knew how to make moccasins, pitch a T.P., butcher a buffalo and cure the hide, chop wood, fish, and give birth behind the T.P. while it was snowing. Needless to say all the ladies told me no - hippies were more materialistic than they like to put on.

"What kind of party are you going to have?" my Guardian Angel asked. "Sit down or mingling?"

"A surprise party. A real big surprise party," I replied. "With the emphasis on surprise not party."

I went to Tatum Ranch Golf Course. Kevin was giving a putting lesson so I walked around the cart path until I found Linda. "Roosevelt," she smiled at me like I was the best thing that's happened to her since bras came back into fashion, obviously not angry with me for running out on her.

"I to ask you over to my apartment tomorrow night at 8:30. Some friends are coming in from out of town and I thought you might like to meet them."

"I'd love to come over, but you have to tell me where you live?"

I gave her my address and was going to apologize for running out but decided what for - some things are better left unspoken.

Kevin was done with his putting lesson when I got back to the clubhouse. "I want you to come by my apartment tomorrow night," I told him seriously.

He looked at me apprehensively.

"I have word a few friends of one of the guys you sent to prison are in town and they didn't come to bake you a cake."

"Oh God," he muttered nervously. "I didn't think they'd ever find me. But how did you find out about my past?"

"It's my job, but don't worry, I'll be able to help you out, but I have to check out a few things first." I told him where I lived and to come by at 8:45.

"I don't have much money to pay you," he told me and looked around like at any second two men would jump out of nowhere and rip his snitching carcass into tiny bite-sized shreds.

"We'll work something out," I told him reassuringly.

Reid and Blackwell still hadn't cleaned their apartment. I guess cleanliness is against the honor code of true criminals. "We thought you'd skipped out," Reid said, handing me a beer like I was his long lost cousin who owes him 50 bucks.

"I never quit," I said and chugged the beer

"We don't either," Blackwell said. "But what's up? I know you didn't come here to drink beer and watch the ball game."

"Come to my apartment tomorrow night at 9 o'clock. It's party time," I said handing him my empty beer bottle. "How about another one."

He brought me another beer so fast he left spin out marks on the rug from his shoes. "You know where the money is?" he asked excitedly as he handed me a beer.

"Is Miami in Florida?" I replied nonchalantly.

"There's a Miami in Texas, too," Reid said.

I didn't know he knew his geography. "How come we have to wait until tomorrow night?" Blackwell asked, looking at me like if I didn't tell him what he wanted to hear he would take the beer back.

"Just show up. Not before and not after. Understand?" I told him firmly while looking straight into his eyes.

"9 o'clock tomorrow night," Reid said.

"I don't get it," Blackwell said. "You've found the money but you've never asked us to help you solve Gloria's murder."

"Everything will get solved tomorrow night," I promised him, finished my beer and handed him the bottle.

"There's a Miami in either Colorado or Wyoming also," Reid said.

When I left Reid and Blackwell were arguing. Blackwell argued there was no Miami in Texas and Reid insisted there was. If I was lucky, it would escalate into a gunfight and they would kill each other. People have been killed for less.

I'd been neglecting Matilda lately and pulled into a gas station to check her oil and top off the tank. Her oil was fine and she purred as I filled her belly. I called Hoffman from a pay phone in front of the gas station, listened to the answering machine, waited for the beep, beep, beep, and said, "This is Manuel Noriega. How would you like to donate for my appeal? I'm offering for those who donate..." I didn't get to finish. "Roosevelt, it's about time you called," Hoffman grouched.

"Seven this evening?" I informed him.

"See you then," he answered and hung up.

I had plenty of time and drove to police headquarters as leisurely as one can in bumper to bumper traffic doing 75 miles an hour on the side streets.

"Hey Roosevelt, where's the mask?" Barbara said from behind her desk, but didn't laugh, giving me a cute little smile instead. "You know I'm just kidding you, don't you. I didn't hurt your feelings did I?

"No," I lied.

"Yes I did. Come over here and let Barbara give poor little Roosevelt a big hug."

I went over and Barbara stood up, but instead of a hug she punched me on the shoulder as hard as she could, which was hard enough to smart a little. "Get over it crybaby," she said and started laughing. "You really were cute wearing that ski cap. I'd like you to come over one evening and jump my bones wearing nothing but that cap."

"You're twisted," I told her.

"At least I know it," Barbara replied sitting back down. "If you came to see Richards he's not here. His baseball team has practice this afternoon."

"No, I came to see you. I was wondering if you want to come over to my place tomorrow evening. I'm having a small party, just a few people I've met in town, and I thought you might enjoy the company."

"I'd love to," Barbara said, genuinely pleased. "I don't have to work tomorrow night. I pulled a double for a girl a few weeks ago and she owes me."

I told Barbara where I lived and to be there around 8:15.

"Is it dress up or casual?" she wanted to know.

"Hon, whatever rings your bell," I told her, adding. "Is Williams around?"

"I saw him walk by about an hour ago. He doesn't talk to me much since you told me to ask him out and I wouldn't get naked."

"I take it his office is down the hall."

"Three doors down."

Williams's desk was the only one in the small office so I figured he didn't have a secretary. "I thought you'd be out of here by now," he said, not bothering to stand. Some people use a desk as a sign of power, especially the ones who can't afford a Rolex watch or a pinky ring or a secretary.

His desk looked like it had been rifled through by a squad of D.E.A. agents who had kicked in his door, ransacked the desk in pursuit of 4 grams of illegal marijuana, thinking that if they found it they would rid the country of crime and put America back on the path of truth and justice - the heck with the constitution - who gives a hoot about search warrants?

"I have to talk to you, Williams," I said, trying to sound like he was the only person in the world who can help me.

"Talk then," he said. "This is a free country."

"I can't here. But you come by tomorrow night at 9:15. You might be able to help me and if you do, I can keep you from going to jail."

Williams stood up and I noticed him wince. His leg must still hurt. "What kind of game are you playing?" he demanded angrily.

"You'd better come by," was all I answered and left.

"You are playing a dangerous game," my Guardian Angel told me.

"Tell me something I don't know," I said.

"It would take three days," he said.

It was almost five and I still have two hours before my meeting with Hoffman at Seafood Central. I decided to hit a happy hour.

"Can you punch a happy hour?" my Guardian Angel asked.

Several blocks from Seafood Central was a bar called the Dubliner - an Irish bar, all sad songs and lack of potatoes. Green Irish clovers were painted on the windows. Most of the cars parked out front were shiny and new. An upward mobile, give me the money crowd. I needed a taste of what the majority of humanity really strives to be and went in although Matilda felt sorry for the new Volvo I parked next to.

All the men in the bar were wearing dark slacks, belts to match, loafers with little tassels on them, white shirts, ties, gold watches, gold bracelets, gold rings and cell phones on their belts. All the ladies were wearing nice dresses, not too long but not too short, just enough neck line to be seductive without being cheap and were wearing enough gold jewelry to float a loan to the Vatican. The chit chat centered on mergers and downsizing to expand profit.

I sat at the bar and ordered a pint of Guinness. I was halfway done with the pint when a lady in her mid to late 30's sat down next to me - I could tell she had more money than the Teamsters Union and hadn't gotten it by stealing from the pension fund. She was so pretty men begged her to take their money. "You an old hippie?" she asked me.

"At one time, now I don't really know what I am," I said.

"Join the party, let me buy you a beer," she said.

"I wish I had met you 25 years ago," I commented.

She laughed.

It was an enjoyable hour and a half. Mrs. Alexander, whose husband owns half of every major corporation in the West, was witty, smart, and bought all the beer. We talked about the West and how corporations, many of them foreign, own most of the big ranches and about the only thing that was country in the United States is music. It was a nice interlude, a chance meeting with no expectations. When I told her I had to leave, she smiled sadly and said. "The only thing bad about being an old hippie is you all had to get jobs."

Awalt, McVede, and Hoffman were already sitting at a table when I walked into Seafood Central. Awalt had a black eye and the right side of his face was swollen. McVede had two black eyes and his entire face was swollen. They were both feeling so badly they didn't bother to look mean at me. Hoffman looked like he had been on a whiskey drunk for two years and decided he would go straight and only drink beer. "You guys look like you lost the battle and the war," I said as I sat down.

"Don't talk loud," Hoffman said, rubbing his temples. "We all have bad headaches."

Stun guns might not knock an adversary down for long but they do have long lasting effects.

The waitress came over. "We waited until you got here to order drinks," Hoffman said.

I was impressed. I must be a very important person but anybody with the knowledge of where two million dollars is - is a very important person - money has a way of establishing shallow relationships. I ordered a gin and tonic with a wedge of lime. Hoffman and his crew of very much in pain flunkies ordered beers.

"What happened to you guys?" I asked, as we waited for the drinks.

Awalt grunted. McVede grunted. "Some smart guy tried to break into the house the other night," Hoffman said. "We cleaned his plow."

"With what, your faces?" I said, trying not to gloat.

My Guardian Angel laughed.

The waitress brought the drinks and after she left, I toasted. "To the recovery of your money."

They didn't clink my glass with theirs. It's a big problem with our modern world, no social graces. "You guys come over to my apartment tomorrow night at 9:30 and we'll go get your money."

"You found it," Hoffman said, playing the cool and debonair criminal who never gets excited.

"Did you ever have a doubt?" I asked, as smug as a 78-year-old Frenchman with a 22-year-old mistress.

I finished my gin and tonic and stood. "Tomorrow night," I said.

As I was getting into Matilda my Guardian Angel said, "It's going to be one wang bang party Roosevelt. I hope it doesn't wang bang you."

"You're not the only one," I confessed, adding, "I wonder what kind of wine I should serve, red or white."

When I got to the apartment complex I was immediately peeved. Somebody had parked in my parking spot. I drove to the far side of the apartments before I found an open parking spot. I took my 9 m.m. out from under the seat and wedged it in my back pocket. I was so angry I wasn't paying any attention to anything as I stomped towards my apartment. I was going to call a tow truck and have the car in my parking spot towed. I was rounding the corner of the swimming pool fence in back of my apartment when my Guardian Angel warned me. "Roosevelt, I don't know exactly what, but something is wrong."

I stopped walking, took my pistol out of my pocket and backtracked to the parking lot. The parking lot circles the apartments and I followed it toward my apartment, walking in front of all the parked cars and as close to the buildings as I could. Peeking around the corner of my apartment building I can see my parking spot, now empty. "False alarm," my Guardian Angel said.

I stuck the pistol back in my back pocket and went back to get Matilda and moved her to my parking spot before another inconsiderate jerk parked there. I parked Matilda, locked the door, and was halfway to my apartment when a car screeched around the corner. The headlights locked on me like a riflescope. I didn't have time to grab my pistol or time to jump out of the way. "Bye Roosevelt, it's been fun," my Guardian Angel said quickly.

I closed my eyes. The driver stomped on the breaks and the car squealed to a stop six inches from me. I opened my eyes. Two longhaired teenage boys stared over the dash at me. I ran around to the driver's door. Yanked open the door, grabbed the kid by his hair, pulled him out of the car, slammed him up against it and was about to punch him in the face. "I'm sorry mister, please," the kid whimpered. "I didn't mean anything, really."

The boy couldn't be more than 16. I didn't hit him.

Bending down I looked in the car. "Get out of the car and get your rear over here," I ordered the other boy.

The boy walked tentatively around the car. "Stand by your friend."

The boys still had pimples. I glared at them. They couldn't look me in the face. I wanted to smack them a few times, lecture them, but what good would it do? I took three deep breaths. "You were lucky," I said.

"Please, sir," the driver said.

"Get in the car and get out of here," I told them. "And slow down."

They were in the car faster than I could say, "Jack jumped over the candlestick."

The kid put the car in gear, stuck his hand out the window, tossed me the finger, and peeled out. See what life gives you when you give somebody a break?

In the apartment I got a beer and made a phone call.

"It would have been a lousy deal getting killed just before your party," my Guardian Angel said after I hung up.

"It would be taking the phrase, 'party pooper', to the extreme," I replied.

CHAPTER TWENTY
DON'T TELL ME IT REMINDS YOU OF THE ISLANDS

It was 3 p.m. and I was in a frantic state of mind. I have five gangsters coming to my party, two of which want to kill the other three for the trivial reason that the three owe each of them over $300,000. The three want to kill the other two they owe the money to for the mundane reason that one of the other two had shot them and might have killed one of their wives. I've also invited a homicide detective, a golf pro, a golf course refreshment cart driver, and a secretary who moonlights at a totally nude club. I was in a quandary over what I should serve for drinks to such a totally diverse group? Root beer is out. Champagne, to most of the group, would be considered a sissy drink. If I served beer it could get around I was cheap and affect my social standing. Bloody Marys don't seem chic enough. Tea and coffee are definitely out.

"If you had been thinking, you would have told everybody to bring their own refreshments," my Guardian Angel said, "and no guns, knives, or fist loads allowed."

"I'm not a good organizer," I said, plopping down on the sofa exasperated.

"You could have an island theme, everybody likes the islands, except those who live on them of course," my Guardian Angel said. "Serve a feisty rum punch with a little paper umbrella in each glass."

I jumped up. My dilemma was over. "If I could touch you I'd kiss you," I happily told my Guardian Angel.

"If I was alive I wouldn't let you kiss me. I was never the type that had to be hugged or cry to prove I was a real man."

I went to the friendly neighborhood liquor store which was about the size of Rhode Island. There were twenty-two rows of wine, eight rows of gin, twelve rows of rum, enough vodka to get Moscow drunk for a week, and thirty rows of booze made from orange pits to World War II combat boots. A clerk was helping a man pick out a wine. They were discussing ambiance, vintage, body, fruitiness, texture, and aroma. I wondered if the customer was going to drink the wine or dab it behind his ears. I bought a plastic punch bowl that came with a ladle, a box of little paper multi-colored umbrella's to put in each drink, a punch mix and four fifths of cheap rum. A nice thing about punch is one can't taste the rum - putting good rum in punch is like buying a sexy teddy for your mother.

I was carrying the booze to my apartment when Wang walked by. "Where's the machine gun for my porch?" I asked him.

"There's a shortage of machine guns right now," he said. "They told me it would take a few more weeks. Some guy in Florida bought them all and is taking them to the Arctic and selling them to Penguins who plan on killing tourists who take their photographs and say, "They are so cute, they look like they have tuxedos on."

I walked away disgusted. What is the world coming to when an honest man can't buy a machine gun and an apartment manager thinks he's a reincarnated Robin Williams?

I washed and dried the punch bowl and put it by the sink, made sure the ice trays were full, and read the instructions for the punch. Half punch and half booze even I can understand. I got out enough glasses for everybody and opened up a dozen colored umbrellas. I straightened up the apartment, which didn't take long as I've always been clean and tidy.

I put my pistol underneath the cushion in my chair. Took one stun gun, as I only had two darts left, loaded it, and placed it under a cushion on the sofa. I should go buy two more darts. Four darts are better than two darts has always been a saying of mine. I cleaned the bathroom and the toilet bowl. When I go to a party I always inspect the persons' bathroom - a dirty toilet bowl has always disgusted me - somebody who goes to the bathroom in a dirty toilet has something terribly wrong with them. Once, satisfied everything was in order I only have eight hours to wait until party time. Now is as good as any to go to the gun shop and buy darts.

The KILL THY NEIGHBOR gun shop was doing a brisk business. They were having a sale on a new 22 rifle that was imported from Italy and modeled after the old 45 caliber Tommy gun Al Capone used so efficiently. The 22 gun is a semi-automatic, which makes it legal, but for a mere $12.95 you could buy a file that was guaranteed to be perfect for filing down the sear pin. The round clip holds 15,000 bullets. People, dreaming about slaughtering rabbits, were buying the rifles two at a time. There was also a special on 22 bullets in crates of 100,000, buy one get one free, with a limit of two to a customer.

Buying two darts that wouldn't kill anything made me feel like a hippie in Marine Boot Camp.

When I got back to the apartment I loaded the other stun gun and put it under the pillow in the bedroom. I now have six hours before the party.

Waiting to go to a party or waiting for people to come to my house was like getting to the airport early only to find out my flight has been delayed for three hours. I had several choices: I could get drunk. I could walk around. I could get some cheap paperback bestseller with no plot, lousy dialog, frivolous sex, misplaced and unneeded violence and read it while trying to convince myself I was learning something. I did the latter and got out my questions and clues. "Roosevelt, your clues wouldn't make a decent outline for a cheap paperback," my Guardian Angel said.

He was right and after ten minutes I quit reading them and for some reason wondered how China could get away with not complying with the United Nations Mandate on human rights and at the same time have open trade with us.

I decided to go play golf - politics only makes me angry - in part because I'm not smart enough to be a politician and get all that easy money. I went to a muni-course several blocks away. I like muni-courses. The hamburgers are always inexpensive and good. The beer is cold. You don't serve a hot beer to some guy who has been working in a factory all week and his only recreation is four hours of beating a golf ball around that he pretends is his foreman.

Of course muni-courses aren't the best in the world - city fathers normally don't allot public courses much money - they want people working not playing. The parking lot is always in need of repaving. The putting green looks like a piece of dirt with a few holes in it and the range balls are so old they fly through the air like a duck missing several tail feathers. The fairway grass is always tall - a special mixture of crabgrass and bunch weed. The greens are so rough and trampled nobody is a good putter. If a sand trap is raked, it was purely by accident. But - they are great courses - the boys that went to war courses, not the boys that stayed home and learned how to sleep with other people's girlfriends courses.

I teed it up with a man in his early 70's, who was half-blind, and his 16-year-old grandson. The old man would hit the ball and couldn't see where it went, but his grandson would tell him. Then he'd hit it again. I could tell that at one time the old man had been a good player. The grandson is a stick. He shot one over par. The old man shot in the 90's. We were sitting in the bar after the round. The old man and I were drinking a beer and the kid a coke. "I bet you were a good player when you were younger," I told the old man.

"He's a great player now," the boy told me with pride. "He taught me everything I know."

I was feeling good when I left the course. If my party tonight turns out to be a fizzle and I get killed at least I'd learned something the day I died.

It was six when I got back to the apartment. I took a shower, trimmed my beard, put on clean clothes and my stepping out boots.

I made a batch of punch using two bottles of cheap rum and poured myself a glass - of course sticking in a paper umbrella. "They are so cute," my Guardian Angel said.

The cheap rum running down my throat masqueraded by imitation orange flavoring, imitation mango flavoring, imitation pineapple flavoring, imitation papaya flavoring, all held together by sugar water dyed red, was delicious and made me wish I was wearing an eye patch, had a parrot on my shoulder who could spew out cuss words, and was about to plunder one of Her Majesty's treasure ships so I could move to an island with my jolly men and spread disease to all the naked Polynesian women.

At 7 o'clock I went outside to take a walk. Halfway down the stairs my Guardian Angel said, "You didn't lock the door."

"I'm only walking around the apartment complex a few times. No need to worry."

Apartments are strange things. Little identical boxes set off in units and stacked on top of each other - each with an identical floor plan and each with their private parking space. They remind me of space ships without engines. Dream machines that go nowhere, slowly becoming the next slum. I walked around the complex six times. I passed many people as they got into their cars, not one person said hello or asked how my day was going. Back at my apartment I stood on the porch and looked at the night sky, the illuminated parking lot, listened to the steady hum of traffic. "You're getting melancholy," my Guardian Angel said.

"At times I feel I'm going through life on a big treadmill. I walk or run or crawl or push my way through life looking at all the things I pass but in reality I haven't moved, life has merely passed me by, an illusion, something I only thought I lived and saw."

"Roosevelt, you should never have stopped being a hippie. You could have grown enough pot each year to support yourself and then one day doing a synthetic drug that was supposed to make you one with the universe you would have turned into molecules of color and nobody would have ever seen you again. You would have forever spun through the cosmos full of trivial unanswerable questions while wondering what happened to your body or if you ever had one."

"Maybe that's what happened," I said seriously.

At exactly 8:15 Barbara knocked on the door. "Danger, Danger," my Guardian Angel warned.

He must think I'm an idiot. I know women are dangerous.

Barbara was wearing a black leather mini skirt so short it makes the word mini mean long. Her high heels would give most ladies altitude poisoning. She had on gray fish net hose and a gray leather top that was more cleavage than top. She also has a black leather purse hanging from her shoulder that was so big she could have hidden a Harley Roadster in it. "I must look a fright," Barbara said to me, "A girl got sick and I had to go do one dance and to get here on time I had to wear my work clothes."

"Some of the people coming to the party will think you're dressed for church," I told her.

I poured Barbara and me a glass of punch and put a paper umbrella in her glass. "These are so cute," she said, looking at the umbrella. "They always make me think of the islands."

I decided to get right to the point. "If you don't tell me the truth Barbara, the only island you'll ever see will be in a travel magazine you're reading in your cell."

"What are you insinuating, Roosevelt? You think I had something to do with Gloria's murder?"

"You said it, not me."

She stomped into the living room and sat down on the sofa.

"If you help me, I promise I'll do everything I can to get you a reduced sentence," I told her.

"I'd like another drink," she informed me coldly, holding out her empty glass.

Taking her glass I went to the kitchen. Going back into the living room my party had turned into a surprise party for me. Barbara was pointing a chrome plated Colt 357 with a four-inch ribbed barrel directly at my stomach. By the look in her eyes I knew she would use it and I have no doubt she wouldn't miss. "I take it you really don't like the punch," I said. "I'll go buy some beer if you like."

"Set the glass on the coffee table," she ordered me.

I did what I was told. "Now tell me what you know Roosevelt before I blow you in two."

"I know you have great legs."

She pointed the pistol at my head. She didn't like my attempt at being funny. "Tell me."

I was about to spill my guts when the doorbell rang.

"Saved by the bell," my Guardian Angel said. "But how can a live person spill their guts?"

I gave Barbara an, 'I'm sorry' look. "Answer it, but don't try anything," Barbara told me, sticking her hand with the pistol in her purse and keeping the pistol pointed at me. I don't think the leather would slow down the bullet. She stood several yards behind me as I answered the door.

"Danger, danger," my Guardian Angel said.

"Right on time," Linda said and walked in. She was wearing a light beige pant suit with a cream blouse and had a small strapless purse that matched her outfit. She saw Barbara and gave her a puzzled look as I shut the door. "Linda, this is Barbara. Barbara, this is Linda," I said.

"I suppose you think whoever this Linda is was involved also," Barbara said, saving me the trouble.

"Involved with what?" Linda asked, looking at me like she had no idea what the word involved meant.

"Would you like some rum punch?" I asked Linda.

"Yes, but involved with what?"

They followed me to the kitchen, Barbara keeping her purse trained on me as I ladled out Linda a rum punch and picked out a pink paper umbrella. I handed it to Linda. She picked the umbrella out of her glass. "These always remind me of the islands," she said.

"Let's go to the living room, it's more comfortable and I'll explain everything," I said.

Linda sat on one side of the sofa and Barbara on the other side with her well-aimed purse. I stood as a good host should. "All right, Roosevelt, involved with what?" Linda demanded.

"I know you're involved with Gloria's murder," I said.

"He thinks I am too," Barbara said.

"Roosevelt, you're too smart for your own good," Linda commented dryly and quicker than Popeye can eat a can of spinach she opened her purse and pulled out a 32 Beretta and pointed it at my head.

"You think that's a pistol," Barbara said disdainfully, pointing the 357 at my stomach. They smiled at each other, but it wasn't a smile I liked.

"You are a lousy party planner," my Guardian Angel said.

"Ok, what's going on?" Linda demanded.

"Dallas got beat by Chicago. Green Bay defeated Minnesota. Miami's best guard is on the injured list."

"Cut it," Linda ordered, pulling the hammer back on the pistol. Barbara followed suit pulling the hammer back on the 357.

If there was ever a time to talk, it was now, but I was saved by the doorbell.

"Twice saved by the bell. You must feel like a not very good boxer," my Guardian Angel said.

Barbara stood by the sofa hiding the pistol behind her back. Linda followed me to the door with her pistol stuck in the middle of my back.

"Danger, danger, danger," my Guardian Angel said.

Kevin had on slacks and a sports coat. I felt honored. But, I noticed he didn't look nervous as he came in, although he was surprised to see Linda. Linda stepped back, hiding the pistol behind her back. "You two have met," I said to Kevin, and then pointed at Barbara. "Barbara this is Kevin."

"Nice to met you," Kevin told Barbara.

"The same," Barbara replied in a tone like meeting another man was the last thing she wanted to do in her life.

"Take a seat in the living room I'll get you some punch," I told Kevin.

Kevin sat in the chair. I ladled Kevin some punch under the watchful eye of Linda.

Barbara remained standing. Linda kept a few yards behind me as I handed Kevin a glass of punch. He looked at the umbrella. "These always remind me of the islands," he said.

"I suppose you think Kevin is involved also," Linda said to me.

Kevin gave her an inquisitive look. "I know he is," I said.

"Involved with what?" Kevin asked me.

"With Gloria's murder," Barbara replied, which wasn't polite. I'm the host and Kevin wasn't talking to her.

Kevin looked at Linda and stood, at the same time pulling a Smith and Wesson 38 with a two-inch barrel out of his waistband and pointing it at me. Linda pointed the 32 Beretta at me and Barbara pointed her Colt 357 at me. "I figured you knew something," Kevin said forcefully - people with guns pointed at people always speak forcefully.

"Shut up," Linda snapped at him.

"No, you shut up," Kevin snapped back. "I'm sick of listening to you. You haven't done anything right since Roosevelt showed up."

Linda was the obedient little woman and shut up - maybe because Kevin's pistol was bigger. Kevin walked over and punched me in the stomach. It wasn't much of a punch but it still made me double over. "Tell me what you know," he demanded.

"I know you're a snitching punk," I told him straightening back up. "I know you crawl on your belly to eat."

He punched me in the stomach again, this time a much better punch. If I wanted to I could have hurled the rum punch I've been drinking all over him but it would have stained the carpet. He grabbed my shirt collar and shoved me onto the middle of the sofa. Then he punched me in the face. He was starting to make me angry.

"It's about time," my Guardian Angel said.

I shook the cobwebs out of my head, which wasn't a great thing to do, when my eyes cleared, Barbara was pointing her pistol at me. Linda was pointing her pistol at me and Kevin's pistol was about three inches from my nose. Barbara might miss, Linda might miss, but there was no way Kevin would miss. "Tell me what you know," Kevin demanded again.

"I bet you don't talk like that to people you are giving golf lessons to," I said.

He started to punch me again when the doorbell rang. It is the third time in my life I had been saved by the bell. "We have to answer it," Linda said.

Why? I don't know, but I am not going to be the one to argue.

"Quadruple danger," my Guardian Angel said.

Linda put her pistol back in her purse as she went to answer the door. Barbara hid hers behind her back. Kevin put his in his coat pocket and sat in the chair, glaring at me like glares bothered me.

Linda opened the door and Reid and Blackwell walked by her without bothering to say hello. They both were wearing suits and ties. I imagined after the party they were planning on going to go to a gentlemen's club and spending some of the money they thought they were getting back. "Get yourselves some punch, it's in the kitchen," I called to them. "And don't forget a little umbrella."

"I don't like punch," Blackwell said. "Got a beer?"

"In the fridge."

They came into the living room. Reid had a glass of punch. "The umbrella reminds me of an island," Reid said.

"I thought they closed Alcatraz," I told him.

He laughed. He was the only one at the party with a sense of humor.

"Reid and Blackwell, this is Linda, Barbara, and Kevin," I introduced. "I think they know where you're money is."

As soon as money was out of my mouth Blackwell hit Kevin on top of the head with the beer bottle and Kevin went out colder than ice brewed beer. Barbara had her pistol almost out from behind her back when I punched her in the forehead. She joined Kevin in da da land. As Linda started to pull her pistol out of her purse Reid grabbed her wrist with his left hand and twisted it until she dropped the pistol, all without spilling his punch.

I picked up Barbara and sat her on the sofa, then moved Kevin from the chair to the sofa, and told Linda to join them. I picked up the 357 and the 32 and took the 38 out of Kevin's pocket. I put all the pistols in the hall closet. "You want some more punch?" I asked Reid.

"Don't forget the umbrella," Reid told me.

I ladled Reid a glass of punch and myself one, not forgetting the umbrellas. Reid took his drink. "These little umbrellas really add something to a drink," he said.

Barbara came to and jumped up. Blackwell pushed her back down. "Don't move," he ordered her.

Kevin came to. "Good morning sleepy eyes," I said. "Reid and Blackwell are the bank robbers the money really belongs to," which was a funny thing to say when you think about it.

Linda turned two shades of white. Kevin turned three shades of white. "You don't look like bank robbers to me," Barbara sneered.

"This must be the lady you were telling us about that works in the topless bar," Blackwell said.

"That's her."

"If I don't have to kill you I'd like to take you out," Blackwell told Barbara.

Barbara stuck her tongue out at him.

Reid looked at me menacingly. "What is going on here?" he demanded, apparently over his infatuation with the paper umbrellas.

"It's recover the money and find out who killed Gloria night,"

I told him.

While answering Reid, Blackwell pulled a P.P.K. 380 out of his pocket and stuck the barrel against my temple. "You know," I said. "I'm tired of people pointing guns at me."

"You won't have time to be tired if I pull the trigger," Blackwell said. "Now tell us what is going on?"

Something in Blackwell's voice really teed me off. I moved my head quickly backward, grabbed his hand that was holding the pistol and banged it down onto my knee, making him drop the pistol, and then slammed my elbow twice into his forehead. Blackwell hit the floor like a featherweight who had been punched by a heavyweight. Reid was momentarily caught off guard and had his pistol only halfway out of his belt when I kicked him in the stomach. He doubled over, spilled his drink, his face turned red, his eyes bulged out, and then fell to his knees gasping for breath. Out of the corner of my eye, I saw Kevin, Linda, and Barbara leap to their feet and start toward me. They were too slow, I picked up Reid's 9 m.m. Browning - the weapon of choice for people who really know pistols, and pointed it at them. They all sat back down like the three monkeys that could do no evil.

Blackwell moaned and opened his eyes. "In the chair," I ordered. He didn't argue.

I half shoved Reid onto the sofa. It was a cozy fit with four people sitting on the sofa.

"You needed more chairs for the party," my Guardian Angel said.

I picked up Blackwell's P.P.K. 380 and put it in the closet while still pointing the 9 m.m. towards my guests. "More punch,?" I asked, "While we wait for the other people to show up."

Nobody said anything. I guess I should have served beer.

The doorbell rang. "Super duper danger," my Guardian Angel said.

Detective Williams entered in a huff. But I took the wind immediately out of his sales when I pointed the pistol at his beer belly. "Take your pistol out of your holster, slowly, and hand it to me and don't try any Dirty Harry tricks," I told him.

Williams handed me a nickel plated snub-nosed 38. "You pull this on a real crook, he'd laugh," I told him. "Now go into the living

room and join the party."

As Williams walked to the living room I put the 38 in the closet. "I don't think I have to introduce any of you to Detective Williams," I said. "I think you all know each other."

Williams looked at everybody like they were one step lower than a cat box that hadn't been cleaned in three weeks. "Sit in the middle of the floor," I ordered Williams. "This is a casual affair," adding, "would you like some punch?"

"Stick your punch up your nose," Williams replied rudely, which hurt my feelings after all the work I'd gone through to make everything just right. But, I let it slide, guests are guests after all and a host should always be gracious.

"Are you all sure you don't want any punch?" I asked again. "We have a few more minutes before the honored guest arrives."

"I will," Reid answered, obviously over being kicked and not one to carry a grudge. At least somebody appreciated the time and energy I took in getting my party ready.

Reid and I drank punch while the rest of the party sat and glared at me. I didn't know there are six distinctive glares. There is a glare with the eyes only. A glare with the lips slightly curled. A glare with the eyes half shut. A glare with the nose bent up. A glare with the mouth open, the eyes wide open, and the tip of the tongue showing, and a glare with the eyes only while sipping on punch.

The minutes ticked by slowly. A party is really a dud when nobody is talking. At exactly 9:30 the doorbell rang. "More danger than should be allowed," my Guardian Angel said.

I barely had the door open when the door was shoved into me, knocking me up against the wall and making me drop the pistol. Before I could react, Awalt had a sawed off double barrel twelve gauge stuck in my chest. McVede darted into the living room with a M-16, "Nobody move," he commanded acting like a D.E.A. agent.

Hoffman walked in casually, shut the door, locked it and picked up the 9 m.m. I'd dropped. McVede prodded me into the living room with his shotgun, which is better than a stick for making somebody move. Hoffman looked at everybody and grinned like he was Ponce de Leon and had just found the fountain of youth. "Thanks for coming to my party," he said.

"There's punch in the kitchen with little paper umbrellas for each glass," I told him. "But don't tell me it reminds you of the islands."

CHAPTER TWENTY-ONE
DON'T FORGET THE UMBRELLAS

Barbara, Linda, Kevin, and Reid were sitting on the sofa. Blackwell was sitting in my chair and Detective Williams was sitting on the floor. Awalt moved to the side of the room so he could cover everybody with his M-16, which I doubted was a sports model, but army issue and set on full automatic. I was standing in front of the group, facing the back patio, with McVede standing several feet behind me pointing his shotgun at my back. Hoffman moved several yards to my right and stuck the 9 m.m. in his belt I had dropped when the door hit me. He pulled a four-inch Smith and Wesson 22 pistol out of a shoulder holster, took a silencer out of his other pocket and screwed it on the barrel. The M-16, the shotgun and the silencer equipped 22 was a gross statement of potential overkill.

"Ok, Roosevelt, no more fun and games, tell me where the money is," Hoffman said pointing the pistol at my head.

"You need about ten guardian angels to get you out of this mess," my Guardian Angel said.

"A marine commando team would do better," I said.

"If you kill me you won't know where the money is," I told Hoffman, which sounded feeble even to me.

"Like I've always said. You're one brave stupid guy," my Guardian Angel said.

"If I kill you and then threaten to shoot somebody else, I bet I'll find out where the money is," Hoffman replied as confident as the United States invading Greece.

"But then you won't know who killed Gloria," I said.

Hoffman hesitated a moment before saying, "At this point do you think I really care?"

McVede snickered at the statement like only a gangster would. "I thought you loved her," I said.

"If you had your choice between two million big ones or the best looking woman in the world which would you take?" Hoffman asked.

It was a tough question but not that tough - romanticism went out of vogue about 300 years ago.

"I'm sure glad you're here," Detective Williams said to Hoffman and started to stand up. I noticed Reid, Blackwell and Linda give Williams a questioning look.

Hoffman pointed his pistol at Detective Williams. "Sit down," he ordered.

Detective Williams started to say something in protest but Hoffman cut him off. "Just keep your mouth shut and hope I don't decide to kill you too."

Detective Williams sat back down. He was an obedient detective.

"Hey Reid and Blackwell, how's life?" Hoffman asked with a sarcastic laugh.

"It's been better," Blackwell said.

McVede stepped across the room and butt stroked Blackwell across the face with the shotgun. Blood splattered on the chair and carpet. The blood and punch on the carpet would not make Wang happy. Surprisingly it didn't knock Blackwell out but I know it crushed his right cheekbone. "You'd better kill me," he snarled, holding his face while blood ran between his fingers. Blackwell should have been a professional wrestler and not taken up a life of crime.

McVede started to hit him again. "Not now," Hoffman ordered. "We might need him."

McVede looked at him like he wanted to say, "Oh pretty please," but didn't and stepped back to where he'd been.

"Roosevelt, one last time, where's my money?" Hoffman demanded pointing his pistol at me.

"I take it you don't plan on giving me my 20 percent," I replied.

Hoffman looked at me like whoever thought a gangster would

stick with an agreement deserved to be ripped off. "If I tell you, you'll kill all of us," I said.

"You're the one who has all these people here. Without them I would have only had to kill you."

He was trying to lay a guilt trip on me but with the integrity of the people involved, it didn't work. Although I do know that in the game of life I have about burnt up all my options. The grim reaper was at my door telling me, "Boy you are screwed," and all I could answer back was, "Grim reaper, you are right."

"I tell you what, since I'm going to die why don't you let me tell everybody what I think went on and how I know where the money is? I'd like to know if I'm right. Give a condemned man his last wish. You have to have a little decency in your larceny-filled heart," I told Hoffman, ready to fall to my knees and beg if I had to.

"Decency went out my door the day I was born," Hoffman said.

The begging idea flew out the window.

"Let him tell us," Awalt said. "I'd like to hear what the famous private detective has to say."

"Me too," McVede said.

"Me too," Reid said.

"Kill him," Blackwell said.

"Kill him," Barbara said. I didn't think she would forgive me for knocking her out the second time.

"Let me kill him," Detective Williams said.

Linda and Kevin didn't say anything, which in most situations in life is a good thing to do and shows an active mind with more than normal intelligence.

I saw Hoffman's finger start to tighten on the trigger. I tried to remember the last time I'd been to confession. The room was so quiet I could hear everybody breathing. I looked into Hoffman's eyes - they are colder than dry ice. His finger twitched, stopped, then slowly Hoffman lowered the pistol and smiled. "Ok, smart guy, fill me in. I'd like to know myself."

"Lucky, lucky, lucky," my Guardian Angel said but he did not seem overly happy that I was still alive.

Sighing in relief I gathered my thoughts, the grim reaper

frowned. I wondered if there is a way I can talk for twenty-two years. I would much rather die at 84 than 62. "Get on with it, Roosevelt," Hoffman ordered.

Twenty-two years was definitely a pipe dream.

"This case has been really complicated," I began. "Trying to figure out who killed Gloria, who was trying to kill me, and where the stolen money is, has all been a jumbled mess."

"Don't be so verbose," Hoffman said, "just get with it."

Who is he to think I'm verbose? But, I answered my own question - he is the man with the gun. "I think the easiest way to explain everything is to start with who was trying to kill me," I said.

"Oh boy, this is better than Mystery Theater," Reid said acting like a little boy at show and tell.

"Roosevelt does not tell good stories," my Guardian Angel said. "You will be disappointed."

"The first time I was attacked was at Linda's apartment. Two men, one with a knife and the other with a ball bat attacked me in the parking lot. At this time I was only looking for Gloria's killer. A few days later, when leaving the golf course, I was shot at by two men driving a four door black Mercedes. By now I knew about the bank robbery but not the fact the money was missing - according to police reports the only thing they knew for sure was certain people had not been paid."

"I wonder who those poor fools are," Reid butted in.

I wanted to tell him he was rude but figured it was too late in his life to teach him any manners and went on.

"I was also followed by a Chevy Nova but I didn't give them a chance to kill me. Then somebody tried to shoot me through my door. The next time somebody tried to kill me was in Barbara's driveway. The last attempt at my life happened the other night when a man tried to choke me to death. Once again I was leaving Linda's."

"Boy, this is really exciting," Reid said. "I've always wondered how a private detective figures things out."

"Would you shut up," Awalt told Reid.

I gave Reid a dirty look. "Too many interruptions and I'll lose my train of thought," I scowled at him.

"Get on with it," Hoffman ordered. He was losing his patience.

"I had to figure out who or what was the common denominator in all my attacks," I continued. "Somebody had to know where I was to be able to attack me. The first time I was attacked, only Linda knew where I would be, so if it wasn't a random attack, it had to be Linda who set it up and therefore she was a prime suspect in Gloria's murder. Easy enough?" I asked Hoffman.

He nodded his head.

"When I was shot at by the men in the black Mercedes nobody knew I was at the golf course except I saw Linda talking on a pay phone. This doubled my suspicion about her."

Linda frowned.

"When I was followed by the two men in the Chevy Nova they must not have wanted to kill me or they would have shot me when I ran at them. But who knew I had gone to see Detective Richards because I had been followed from police headquarters. Only Detective Richards knew and his secretary."

I smiled at Barbara. She didn't smile back - the thrill is gone.

"When I was ambushed at Barbara's, only Barbara and Detective Williams knew where I was. When somebody tried to shoot me through the door it could have been anybody. All somebody has to do is look and see if my car is here or the lights are on. When I was almost choked to death at Linda's is a different story."

"Roosevelt, you got a mess," Blackwell said, then he said to McVede, "and don't you tell me to shut up you low life."

"Who's calling who a low life?" McVede snapped.

"Shut up," Hoffman ordered.

"I had a mess, but I knew there was a connecting thread, and I found it."

"You are a good detective," Reid stated in awe.

"You have these idiots buffaloed," my Guardian Angel told me.

"Now I want anybody to correct me if I'm wrong, ok?" I said.

Everybody nodded their heads. It's nice to have a captive audience, especially when one is the captive. "Linda hired the two guys to attack me at her apartment. They weren't supposed to kill me but to hurt me enough to scare me off. Linda didn't know at the time that I don't scare easily, although now I'm scared." I added the 'now I'm scared' bit to play up to Hoffman's ego.

"Isn't that right Linda?" I asked.

She nodded her head tentatively. "Speak up I can't hear you," I said.

"Yes it is," she spat.

"You took my money," Hoffman accused Linda.

Linda didn't even flinch. "No she didn't," I told him. "Stay calm, I promise you you'll get your money."

Hoffman gave me a confused look and Linda looked bewildered.

"It was you two," I looked at Awalt and McVede, "who shot at me at the golf course. Linda called Detective Williams telling him I was at the course and he got in touch with you guys."

"No need to deny it," Awalt said.

"I know Kevin followed me in the Nova, but I have no idea who was with him."

"How do you know that?" Kevin said, trying to sound defensive.

"You were stupid enough to leave the car at your house," I told him, adding. "Who was the other guy with you?"

Kevin looked stupid to go along with being stupid. "You're right," he conceded, glancing at Linda, "but I only wanted to know what you were up to. The other guy with me was just a friend."

"How did you know where I would be so you could follow me?" I asked.

"It was purely an accident. I was going to a golf repair shop to pick up some clubs and saw your car at police headquarters."

"I'll be," I said.

"Remember, I told you to go to Kevin's house," my Guardian Angel said.

Hoffman started to say something to Kevin but I cut in. "He doesn't have your money," I told him.

"One of these thieves has my money?" he snapped.

There should be a word for the situation when a thief robs a bank, decides he won't pay the thieves who helped him be a thief and then thieves rob the original thief - but, alas, there isn't. But, if there was, it could be, 'thuved'. The original thief could go around telling all his low class buddies he'd been thuved.

"I know it was you, Detective Williams, who tried to shoot me through my door," I said.

Williams started to protest. "Don't even try," I told him. "I bet if we roll up your pant leg you have a partially healed bullet wound. Right after the police left you came by the apartment. I noticed you were limping and that your pants didn't match your jacket. When I swabbed up some of the blood on the porch I could tell it frightened you. You knew it was your blood. You had tried to shoot me, got shot, left and quickly bandaged your wound and then came back thinking it was the best thing to do to keep any suspicion off of you. I bet you went to Mexico to get your leg worked on so no gunshot report would be filed with the police."

"I wish I had killed you," he growled.

"Crooked cops make me sick," my Guardian Angel said.

"There were only two people who knew I was going to Barbara's the evening I killed those two men, Barbara and Detective Williams. There is no doubt Williams contacted them and told them where I would be. The night the two men tried to shoot me at Barbara's house I ran into you, Williams, at Heartbreakers. When I left, you sent Barbara out after me, telling her to tell me her car was in the shop and she needed a ride home. But, when Barbara found out I was going to Babe's, she tried to stop me, you had told her to stop me from going to any other topless bars. I had told you my plan on how to find Reid and Blackwell and you had a meeting with them later on."

"I didn't know anything at first," Barbara said. "I was only doing him a favor,"

"I know. The first time I went to see Detective Richards after I had punched you, you ignored me. But when I went to see him again you were all lovey dovey and I figured Detective Williams had approached you and offered you a lot of money if you would help him. With your help he could keep track of me easier."

"He told me if I didn't help him he would hurt me, I swear," Barbara said trying to look innocent.

"Shut up," Detective Williams ordered.

He did more than threaten to hurt you Barbara," I told her. "You wouldn't have pulled a gun one me tonight if he didn't offer you a sizable chunk of money and maybe, just maybe, you thought you could get your hands on all the money."

Barbara would have liked another chance to whip me with her ridding crop.

"Back to you Williams. While I was at Babe's, Reid and Blackwell came in and when you arrived, you tried not to show how surprised you were to see Barbara and me. When you left Babe's you called the two men I had had the run in with at Linda's and gave them Barbara's address. You had gone to see them in the hospital after they had tried to hurt me the first time at Linda's and you told them if they helped you, you would pay them and wouldn't arrest them, even though there were no charges."

You're a real smart guy," Detective Williams said.

"And it was also Williams who almost choked me to death the other night."

"You're the luckiest guy I've ever met in my life," Williams declared disgustedly. "But how do you know?"

"When you tried to choke me to death, Barbara had told you I had asked her for your address and you figured I would snoop around your house, which I did, and you followed me to Linda's."

"You are lucky," Reid said.

"It was also you Williams who broke into my house and left me the bad poetry. You were looking for the blood sample I kept. And the reason you knew I wasn't home was because Barbara had told you she and I were going out. At one time I thought Kevin might have broken in. I found a fingernail and the only person in the group who bites their nails is Kevin but his are so chewed down he couldn't bite off a complete nail. So I figure you bit off a nail without thinking about it."

Williams didn't say anything. "It was you wasn't it?" I asked.

"It wasn't your mother," Williams replied begrudgingly.

"I know you didn't leave me a warning note at the golf course."

"I don't even play the stupid game," he said.

"It was also you Williams that contacted Hoffman who sent his goons to shoot me at the golf course."

"Don't call me a goon," Awalt said. I'd hurt his poor little feelings.

McVede didn't say anything. He knew his status in life and

accepted it - one has to be what he's got to be.

"So, I knew Linda had tried to scare me. Awalt and McVede had tried to kill me. Williams had contacted the two men to kill me. I wanted to know why was Detective Williams trying to kill me? Why would a cop want to kill me? I did a little checking around and adding two and two and making five I had a suspicion. He was in communication with Linda, and also you," I told Hoffman.

Linda said nothing but looked at Williams like he is lower than toe jam.

"You're full of as much stuffing as a Christmas goose," Williams said.

"Au contraire," I said. "Let me explain."

"Kill him, Hoffman," Detective Williams almost pleaded, "can't you see he's telling you a bunch of lies."

"No, I think it's interesting," Hoffman said, giving Williams a deadly look.

"I went to Detective Richards and asked how long Williams had been on the force. He told me Williams had been hired out of L.A. and used to work robbery. Which I found interesting since the bank jobs had been pulled in L.A.. Then I saw Reid and Blackwell and Williams at Babe's. I followed Reid and Blackwell back to their apartment and we became partners in crime. The first night I met Reid and Blackwell they made one slip up. I was about to go home and they didn't ask me where I lived so I knew they knew where I lived. They wouldn't trust me to come and go as I liked, especially after we had made a deal and I knew everything about them."

"I told you he was good," Reid said to Blackwell.

"But why would they know where I lived and how? Their second mistake was telling me they knew where you lived Hoffman, both here in Phoenix and in Florida. I asked them how they knew and they said they had connections? There was only one connection. And it was you, Williams.

Reid and Blackwell shook their heads and looked at Williams. Awalt, McVede, and Hoffman looked at Williams and shook their heads. "You can never trust a cop," McVede said.

"He approached me too," Linda said, deciding it was time to

fess up. "The day after Gloria's body was found. He told me you were a suspect in the murder and he wanted me to tell him everything you asked me and to contact him as soon as possible every time you showed up at the golf course or at my house. I called him the day you got shot at."

I gave Linda a wry smile.

Williams wanted to write me a hate letter sealed in a letter bomb. "Where's my money Williams?" Hoffman demanded pointing the 22 at Williams.

"I don't have your money. If I did I'd be in Brazil you idiot," Williams declared.

I'll say one thing for him, he is no sissy boy.

"Does he have it or not, Roosevelt?" Hoffman asked, still pointing the pistol at Williams.

"No," I said.

"Roosevelt, you should have been a writer, you tell a real good story," McVede said.

"So now I knew who had been trying to kill me. I knew about Reid and Blackwell, but I didn't know much about you and your guys Hoffman, and I still had no idea who would have killed Gloria. What I had to do was get in touch with you, Hoffman, which I did."

"Good thing you aren't a fed," Hoffman said.

"I've been told that by other crooks," I replied proudly.

"When I was only looking for Gloria's killer I'd called you on all your phones and left an impolite message, something to the extent of I was going to be your worst nightmare. I didn't know what good it would do, but frustration leads to stupid moves."

"How did you get my phone numbers?" Hoffman asked.

"When I broke into Gloria's apartment."

"You know, Roosevelt," Hoffman conceded. "If I didn't have to kill you, I think I'd like you."

I didn't want to make him angry, but some people I don't want for friends.

"After talking to Reid and Blackwell I called you and set up a meet. I purposefully didn't tell you who I was on the phone but I did tell you I would help you get your money - at the time I didn't know you didn't have the money, I was merely playing a hunch.

But the minute you walked in I knew you didn't have the money. If you would have, you would never have showed up. It was no surprise you knew who I was and knew where I lived. You and I made a deal and you agreed to give me 20 percent of the money if I recovered it."

Hoffman smiled.

"Since I know Detective Richards is as honest as the pope, I knew the only way you could know my name and where I lived was Detective Williams had to tell you. I for sure knew it wasn't Reid and Blackwell, they had just shot you guys, so Williams was working with you also."

"I tell you Roosevelt," Hoffman said. "I am really impressed."

"I didn't know your brain worked this well," my Guardian Angel said, also impressed.

The bad thing about impressing people is the fact it really doesn't mean a thing, especially when Hoffman plans on killing me.

"The next thing I did, Hoffman, was break into your house."

"You darted me," McVede gasped and started toward me with no intention of giving me a hug.

Awalt also started toward me.

"Hold it, hold it," Hoffman ordered. "Not yet. We still don't know where the money is."

"The night I broke into your fort, and by the way, nice doggies you have, Barbara drove the get away car, or van, I should say. I knew, because of Barbara, Williams knew I was going to break in, but he didn't warn you so I knew Williams wanted the money all for himself. He was using everybody."

Detective Williams didn't even try and protest.

"So what did you find out by breaking into my garage?" Hoffman asked.

"You played golf, even though you told me you didn't, and I knew that all three cars that had come up in the case belong to you."

"I don't understand?" Hoffman said.

"I told you it was complicated. But before I go on how about a glass of punch, my throat is getting dry."

Hoffman gave me a disgusted look. "Ah come on boss," Awalt

pleaded. "I'd like some punch too."

"Me too," Reid said, "but don't forget the umbrella."

"Me too," Blackwell mumbled. His jaw was getting stiff.

"Why not," Barbara said. "I'm thirsty."

"Go get the punch bowl and glasses and put them on the coffee table," Hoffman ordered me, "and don't forget the umbrellas."

At least I know people liked my punch and Hoffman wasn't as much of a party pooper as he let on to be.

"I wish I could have a drink with an umbrella in it," my Guardian Angel pouted.

"Every job has its pitfalls," I told him.

CHAPTER TWENTY-TWO
THE JOKES ON YOU

Everybody decided to drink a glass of punch, which finished off my first batch, and I made another one. I guess since most of us figured we were going to get killed we might as well get killed in a festive mood, and the killers figured they might as well be festive when they killed us. Even Hoffman drank a glass. "These umbrellas are cute," he commented.

"They stink," Detective Williams said.

There's always a spoilsport in the crowd.

Hoffman finished his punch. "Ok, Roosevelt, what's the big deal that I have golf clubs and three cars in my garage?"

"You have to remember that the only reason I got involved in this mess was to find out who killed Gloria. Linda told me a man had come to the golf course one day, whose description matches yours, and that Gloria had been afraid of him and that he and two other men picked Gloria up after work driving a black B.M.W. with Florida plates. After that Gloria wasn't seen again until she was found dead. She also told me Linda's boyfriend, who she had never met, drove a silver Jaguar with Arizona plates. After being shot at by people in a black Mercedes I wanted to find the cars as a possible lead to the killer. That's why I broke into your garage."

"I can understand that," Hoffman said. "And seeing the three cars you knew I was the boyfriend, the ex-husband, and the mystery man."

"That's smart thinking," Reid commented

I continued. "During my conversations with Linda she told me

Gloria hated golf. But during the brief time Gloria and I had talked in the swimming pool she had told me she was going to play golf with her boyfriend the next day."

"I don't know how you could talk to her in a pool," Awalt cut in. "She wore bathing suits that were little more than two band-aids and a string."

"I have a mind like a steel trap," I told him.

"You lie like an imitation Persian rug," my Guardian Angel said. "You have a mind like a bowl of Jell-O that won't set up."

"I also saw two sets of golf clubs in your garage, men's and women's, unless some man you know has a powder blue bag with matching head covers. But I remember you telling me you didn't play golf," I told Hoffman.

"Gloria and I used to play," Hoffman conceded, "The day she was found dead we were going to play. I thought it might help her mentally. But where is all this leading?" Hoffman asked.

"When I made up my mind to find Gloria's killer, the first thing I did was break into her apartment. I stole her phone book. There were only a few numbers in the book, yours, Linda's, Tony's Pizza, and the golf course. It wasn't until the next day Detective Richards told me about you and I thought it strange that if Gloria was so afraid of you, according to Linda, why would she have your phone numbers, and why would she be living in an apartment under her real name? During my search of her apartment I also found a man's silk sock under the sofa, which had to belong to you, you're the only guy I've seen in Phoenix who wears silk shirts. There was also a pillow and blanket on the sofa and a spill spot on the floor that smelled like whiskey, but there was no whiskey in the apartment. Why would you sleep on the sofa?"

"Gloria was going through one of her deep depressions. When she had her attacks I couldn't get close to her. I slept on the sofa just to be near in case she tried something rash," Hoffman said.

"I discovered there were no purses in the apartment and no jewelry boxes. A lady with no jewelry box or no purse is almost impossible. I found a length of rope in Gloria's dresser that matched the rope that was found around her neck, and which I found out later she had bought herself. To tell you the truth, at this time I didn't know squat, I was as confused as a drunken rat in a

Skinner box."

"You don't sound confused to me," McVede said.

"Don't puff up his ego," my Guardian Angel said.

"Linda told me she had been approached by two men, supposedly detectives, who wanted to know where I lived. I knew she was lying to me, detectives would know where I lived, and people trying to kill me wouldn't have to ask where I lived - they would just follow me, plus they wouldn't want to talk to somebody who might possibly I.D. them. I knew, then, that most of what Linda was telling me was lies. This was further substantiated when I saw Kevin kissing her one evening on her porch after she had told me she hated him, but, even then I didn't think she killed Gloria.

"You dog," Linda said.

"I also didn't think you would kill your ex-wife," I told Hoffman, "and this was before I knew you had only gotten a divorce to put her name on certain assets."

"I didn't kill her," Hoffman said.

"I know you didn't," I told him. "A few days later I wanted to go through Gloria's apartment again. Wang, the apartment manager, agreed to let me in. All the wall sockets had been removed from the apartment and the carpet ripped up, making me think whoever had broken in had been looking for a key, or a map. Wang told me two men had been interested in renting the apartment the day before, but had not come back. It took me a while to figure out Detective Williams had broken into the apartment and the two men were not connected at all."

"You're full of peanuts, Roosevelt," Williams accused.

"I am not full of peanuts but I know you broke into the apartment. You were the only one who would have had to break in. Hoffman and his men wouldn't have to break in and Reid and Blackwell didn't know Gloria was dead until I told them."

Detective Williams didn't say anything.

"But I never thought you killed Gloria, Williams. You were only after the money. The only reason you wanted to kill me was I could mess it all up for you and you knew if you did kill me nobody would think about you being the guilty party."

"I didn't kill Gloria," he said.

"I just said that," I replied.

"Who did kill Gloria?" Awalt asked.

"I told you it was complicated," I said, glancing at Hoffman.

"Complicated but a good story," Reid said.

I don't think his mother told him stories when he was a kid.

"I now figured Williams didn't kill Gloria, Barbara was only a stupid flunky, Linda didn't kill Gloria, Kevin, her sidekick, didn't, Hoffman didn't kill Gloria. After I talked to Reid and Blackwell I knew they didn't kill Gloria. When I told them Gloria had been killed they were shocked, which didn't mean anything at first, crooks are good at looking innocent. But, when I told them Springer had been found dead in a dumpster with his throat cut, they said it had to be some punks because a good gangster would dispose of the body where nobody would find it. I'm sure if they had killed Gloria to get at you Hoffman there would be no body. I was in a quandary, if nobody involved had killed Gloria, who did? There was no getting around the fact Gloria had been found dead with a rope around her neck."

"Where's the money? You're getting way off track," Hoffman said.

"I'm getting there, hold your horses?"

"There are no horses in the apartment," my Guardian Angel said.

"I now had to reevaluate everything. I knew the money was gone. I figured nobody I knew had killed Gloria. So I decided to focus all my attention on finding the money and maybe I would discover who had killed Gloria instead of trying to find out who killed Gloria and then discovering the money,"

"That makes sense," Barbara said. Of course her head is twisted on differently than most peoples.

"I knew you men had robbed enough banks to make two million. I knew Gloria had driven the get away car."

"How do you know that?" Hoffman asked.

"Reid and Blackwell told me."

Hoffman gave them a look that would turn milk into cottage cheese.

"I knew you had all agreed to put the money in a coke deal and then split it and that Tony's Pizza is a front for a Colombian Gang to clean money. I knew Springer had been killed and I knew

that your plan, Hoffman, was to never pay Reid or Blackwell. Therefore, I figured you had killed Springer."

"He was a snitch," Awalt said. "I cut his snitching throat."

"Detective Williams told you he was a snitch," I said to Hoffman. "He was working robbery at the time in L.A.. The cops knew you had done the jobs but they couldn't prove it. To help keep them off Williams' offered his services for a piece of the take. When you told him you were going to invest the money in cocaine he decided to let his money ride. Of course, at the time, he figured everything was on the up and up between all of you."

"It's a good thing you have to die," Hoffman said.

Reid and Blackwell looked shocked.

I bet you wished you'd stayed a good cop," I said to Detective Williams.

Williams gave me a dirty look that didn't have much impact.

"Then I asked myself. Self, why would Gloria have her own apartment if she and Hoffman were still together? Why would Hoffman stay there at times? And then one evening it all came to me. Hoffman, you never intended to pay anybody, you and Gloria were going to keep all the money."

"What are you talking about?" Hoffman bellowed and was about to shoot me with the silencer equipped 22, but before he could pull the trigger Awalt slammed the barrel of the M-16 down on Hoffman's wrist, knocking the pistol to the floor. Hoffman winced and held his wrist. He started to say something but Awalt stuck the barrel of the M-16 in his chest. "Keep talking," Awalt ordered me, not exactly a happy Howdy Dowdy.

"You and Gloria hid the money but somebody else had to know where the money was in case something happened to you. Your plan was to tell Awalt and McVede you invested the money with the Colombians but the deal got busted, after a few months you and Gloria would slip away. With two million you would be set for life. There was only one flaw in your plan. Gloria had a relapse into her depression, got paranoid, and did something with the money before you were able to tell everybody about the fake drug bust"

"What did he tell you happened to the money?" I asked McVede.

"He said somebody killed Gloria and stole the money, but we'd get it back and then we would still do the drug deal."

"Even if you got the money back he was going to steal all of it," I said.

"He's telling the truth, isn't he?" Awalt asked Hoffman calmly. "I thought it was strange when Gloria moved out of the house."

"You know me better than that. You know I wouldn't cheat you guys," Hoffman pleaded. "Roosevelt is making everything up. It's all lies."

"He talked you guys into cheating us out of Blackwell's and my share," Reid said.

"I think Roosevelt's lying," McVede said.

Awalt smiled grimly and picked up the silencer equipped 22.

Hoffman looked over at me with nothing but hate in his eyes. I was the last thing he saw. Awalt shot him in the temple. Hoffman crashed to the floor and was dead before he knew he'd been shot - a small pool of blood formed around his head. Linda screamed. Barbara started to cry. Blackwell jumped out of the chair to leap at Awalt but he was too slow. Awalt shot him right smack dab between the eyes. For a second, Blackwell gazed at me in utter astonishment and then thudded to the floor. Kevin was frozen to the sofa in fear. Reid, calm and cool gangster, didn't look affected at all. Awalt looked at Detective Williams. "I never did like you," he said. "From the time you came to us in California. We're crooks, but there's something about a dirty cop that's lower than any of us."

He raised the pistol. There was nothing I could do - McVede had the shotgun on me. Just as Awalt was about to pull the trigger Detective Richards stepped out of the closet and I noticed he was wearing gloves. "Awalt," he ordered.

Awalt turned and Richards shot him twice with a silencer-equipped pistol that was larger than a 22. Awalt jerked around like he was a puppet on a string before he hit the floor. This time Barbara screamed and Linda cried. McVede turned, utterly surprised, but before he could fire the shotgun, Richards shot him twice in the chest. He slammed back against the wall and slid down the wall, leaving a large streak of blood as he did.

"You waited long enough to make your entrance but I must say your timing is impeccable," I said to Detective Richards.

Richards ignored my remark and walked by me quickly. Detective Williams, seeing Detective Richards, smiled and started to get up but before Williams could get to his feet, Richards shot him in the heart. Williams clutched his heart, looking in utter astonishment at the blood running between his fingers, looked at Richards as if asking why, and then pitched over onto his face.

Something was terribly wrong. I started to rush at Detective Richards but he pointed his pistol at me. "Don't try Roosevelt. Not even you are that lucky."

Lucky had no sooner come out of his mouth when he turned slightly and shot Reid in the forehead. Reid's head slammed back, he twitched a few times, and died, his eyes starring blankly at the ceiling. Barbara and Linda started sobbing. "I didn't do anything," Kevin begged. "I worked for Linda. I don't know what was going on. I was only getting paid."

Richards didn't seem to like excuses. He shot Kevin in the neck. Blood splattered all over Linda and Barbara. Kevin started to stand, making sickening gurgling sounds. Richards shot him in the head. Kevin crashed to the floor.

"I should have known you were involved," I told Detective Richards. "When you gave me the two shell casings to the bullets I fired at Linda's I knew something was strange. You knew in time I would find out where the money was."

"The jokes on you, Roosevelt," Detective Richards said.

I was not laughing.

There were four people left alive in the room - a crying Barbara, a sobbing Linda, myself, and Detective Richards. I had no doubt that soon there would only be one person left alive in the room and since Richards was the only one with a gun it wasn't going to be Linda, Barbara or me. The grim reaper had hit the jackpot

"You thought you were being really cagey when you told me your plan," Detective Richards said, with a sick trace of mirth in his voice. "But I have to admit, it was a good plan. Invite everybody over, with me hiding in the closet with a tape recorder to record everyone's conversation, and when everybody had talked enough to prove their guilt, I would jump out playing the unwelcome guest and arrest them. Ta da, case solved."

"You sneaky thing you," my Guardian Angel said. "You didn't even tell the only person in your life you can trust."

"Sorry," I said to him.

"That's why you didn't lock the door when you went for a walk around the apartments," my Guardian Angel said. "Richards came in the apartment and hid in the closet. Roosevelt, you're the fox that out foxed himself. But it was a good idea to go down on. I'll give you an A for originality and planning but an F for accomplishment. It's been nice being your guardian angel. I can say it's never been dull and I'll have a lot of stories to tell to my buddies while I'm waiting to get reassigned to some sexy young thing. If it's any consolation, you have about a 90% chance of making it to heaven."

I felt like a chimp at the bottom of the pecking order, so far down I am not even allowed to watch the alpha male eat.

Detective Richards aimed the pistol at the center of my chest. "Where is the money?" he asked me in a cool and controlled voice.

After killing four people there really was no need to shout. The point had been made quite clearly that he is a serious guy.

I looked at Barbara, she was still crying. I looked at Linda, she was still crying. There was no need to look at Hoffman, Awalt, McVede, Reid, Blackwell, or Kevin, they wished they could cry. "I bet you didn't record anything," I said to Detective Richards.

"Tell me where the money is?" he ordered.

I looked at Barbara and Linda again. Their crying was about to get on my nerves. They aren't people who perform well under pressure. "Kill me," I told Richards.

At least I will go down with dignity, which doesn't mean squat after you are dead, but sounds good.

Richards laughed. "I like you Roosevelt you've got your own weird class."

He then shot me in the left upper leg. I went down like a ten pin knocked over by a 16 pound bowling ball.

"I can't help you," my Guardian Angel said sadly and turned his back not to watch.

Richards grabbed me by my collar, yanked my head back and stuck the pistol in my face before I could say, "Lord, my leg hurts."

"Tell me," he demanded through clenched teeth. "I'll put holes in you for hours. You'll want to die before I kill you. Now tell me."

I thought of two friends of mine who were prisoners of war in Vietnam. One is home. Only God knows where the other one is. The one who is home never talks about his four year experience, but I know he didn't talk while he was being held by the North Vietnamese, and if he did, he lied. "Your mother wears combat boots," I told Richards between gritting teeth.

He hit me across the face with the pistol. Putting a large gash on my forehead and stunning me. He hit me again and again. I felt the impact of the pistol. I felt blood running down my face. "Tell me, tell me," I heard him holler, but it didn't matter.

Far off I heard a lady screaming. "Tell him, tell him."

I was about to black out when I heard a loud noise like wood splintering. "F.B.I., put your hands up," echoed through my ringing ears like a man hollering at me from across a large lake. Then there were two loud bangs, a thud, and a sound like a fish flopping around on the bottom of a boat. Then it was black, a peaceful black, no thoughts, no dreams, no memories, no wants, nothing but a deep, dark, silent black.

I did not hear my Guardian Angel say, "Well I'll be. I would never have guessed."

Coming to, I was sitting on the floor propped up against the wall. A paramedic had cut off my pant leg and had bandaged my leg. Another paramedic was cleaning my face. Linda and Barbara were sitting on the edge of the sofa with handcuffs on. Barbara probably likes the handcuffs. Half a dozen men, dressed in black fatigues and wearing flack jackets with F.B.I. stenciled on the front and back were standing around the room. A man knelt down in front of me and smiled. He also had on black fatigues and a flack jacket with F.B.I. stenciled on it. "I'm sorry," I said. "The carpets will have to be replaced. The furniture is ruined. The party wasn't supposed to turn out so rough."

"That's Ok. The government will pay for it," Wang said.

CHAPTER TWENTY-THREE
WHAT A BUMMER ENDING

The next time I came to I was naked, a nurse was scrubbing my leg, and a doctor had just given me a local. “The bullet didn't hit anything major," the doctor said.

I wonder why flesh isn't considered major?

When he was finished with my leg, he put a few stitches in my face, decided I didn't have to stay in the hospital and had a nurse get me a set of crutches while I got dressed. He walked beside me as I crutched to the waiting room.

Wang had changed out of his attack clothes and was reading a book. The first thing I asked him was, "How's Richards?"

"Dead," Wang replied simply.

"Good," I said. "How about Linda and Barbara?"

"We have them locked up. They won't get a bond hearing until late tomorrow afternoon."

Wang drove me to a Holiday Inn. "On us," he said as we went to a room. It was a nice room with a wet bar and a picture window with a view of the city.

"All your things have been moved here, including your two stun guns and pistol," Wang informed me.

"How about Matilda?"

"Who?"

"My car."

"We couldn't find the keys to that thing you call a car, so we had it impounded, but give them to me and I'll have it brought

over."

I don't think Matilda would like somebody else driving her but some concessions have to be made in life. I always keep my car keys in my pocket, then I don't I forget where I put them. "I had no idea about you Wang," I confessed as I handed Wang Matilda's keys.

Wang smiled, which in Chinese is a full belly laugh. "I will come over in the morning and talk to you. You rest."

Wang opened the door. "Thanks for saving my life," I said.

"I go out of my way to save old hippies. The world needs a few things to laugh at," he replied before leaving.

Hobbling over to the bar as fast as my crutches would carry me I made a gin and tonic. Four drinks later I fell asleep deeper than an old farm dog on the first warm day of spring after a seven month winter.

I woke up in the morning feeling like what an old farm dog does in the middle of the yard after eating a bowl of leftover spaghetti that was covered with imitation meat flavoring and minuscule amounts of mushroom stems. And, to top it off, my leg was throbbing in time with my head.

I crutched to the bathroom and looked at my face. Richards had done a good job of turning my face into what a punching bag would consider ugly.

"I bet you were wondering what to tell God so he would assign you to some over sexed young thing," I told my Guardian Angel.

"When I told you, you had about a 90% chance of making it to heaven I was lying," my Guardian Angel said.

"I knew you were. But thanks for trying to make me feel better."

"It's my job," he said.

I cleaned up and ordered from room service - orange juice, coffee, wheat toast, and steak and eggs - the steak medium rare. Since the government was footing the bill I felt no guilt about spending too much.

The eggs were cold and rubbery, the toast dry, the orange juice watery, the coffee weak, and the steak over cooked but since it was free, it was delicious. I was drinking my second cup of coffee when the phone rang. "The miracle hot line," I answered.

"You ever think about being a comedian?" Wang asked.

"People don't shoot you or beat you up if you're a comic," I said.

"Do you feel well enough to talk?"

"I don't think I can do a good two step but I can talk all you want."

"I'll be over in about 30 minutes and also bring your car."

"Matilda to you mister," I said.

Thirty minutes to the second there was a knock on the door. I crutched over and opened it. Wang and the maintenance man from the apartment walked in with broad smiles on their faces. They were as happy as I.R.S. agents that were going to take my Bob Dylan record collection and couldn't be bribed to let me keep Highway 61 Revisited.

I shut the door. "Since the government is paying for this I want a suite on the top floor and a limo service until my leg heals enough I can get into my Volkswagen," I told Wang.

Wang didn't laugh. His dry, undertone, Chinese humor, wasn't even undertone. Wang called room service and ordered another pot of coffee. I was thankful he didn't order green tea. We sat at the dining room table waiting for the coffee. Wang introduced me to F.B.I. Agent Silversmith. "You do a good job of putting on doors and painting," I told him. "Did you learn that in the academy?"

He chuckled and took a small tape recorder out of his pocket and placed it on the table.

"You should have been an F.B.I. agent," Wang told me.

"He would have to finish college," my Guardian Angel said.

"I saw you on TV," Silversmith said. "That was really some job you did in Florida. I was impressed. I even saw the reruns."

"If you're watching reruns, you're watching entirely too much TV," my Guardian Angel said.

A lady from India, complete with a red dot on her forehead, delivered the coffee. I have always wondered about the red dot. Supposedly the red dot signifies mankind's third eye or our mind's eye, but, if you put a red dot on your forehead won't you cover up your third eye or mind's eye and not be able to see out of it?

Wang poured three cups of coffee. "To the F.B.I.," I toasted. We each took a sip.

"Let's get down to business," Wang said.

Silversmith turned on the tape recorder.

"Where is the money and who killed Gloria?" Wang asked.

"You mean you don't know?" I asked, bewildered.

"Would I ask you if I did?" Wang said.

"Where is the money and who did kill Gloria?" my Guardian Angel asked.

"Before I tell you where the money is and about Gloria I want to know how you guys were in position to save me last night?"

Wang looked at Silversmith. "Go ahead and tell him," Silversmith said.

"I was assigned to investigate the bank robberies in California," Wang began. "I organized a special task force that neither reported to other federal agents in California or the state police, although I had access to all their files. Through our investigation using phone taps, bugs in houses and informants, we discovered everything, even the fact Gloria drove the get away cars. We could have arrested everybody and filed a conspiracy charge but we couldn't find out where the money was hidden. We found out Hoffman was planning on rolling the money over on a big coke deal through Colombians that own the Tony's Pizza chain. We decided to wait and see if we could bring down the Colombians, get the money, get the dope and get Hoffman and his crew all at the same time."

"That would have been a feather in your bonnet," I said.

"He's not an Indian," my Guardian Angel said.

Wang gave me a dirty look before continuing. "While we were waiting for something to happen Springer was picked up by the local cops in L.A. and we recorded a conversation between Detective Williams and Hoffman. Williams wanted a hundred thousand for his information, which Hoffman agreed to. Williams told Hoffman Springer was trying to set them up. Hoffman told Williams about the planned dope deal and if he wanted to let his money ride and keep funneling him information he would get close to a half a million. Williams agreed. When Springer was found dead, we knew Hoffman was responsible but we couldn't prove it. When everybody moved to Phoenix we moved our operation."

"You picked the wrong apartment to move into," my Guardian

Angel said. "It's strange how life is all a matter of distance."

"I learned that in Vietnam," I told him.

"Too bad Richards didn't have a tape recorder in the closet like he was supposed to," I said.

Wang smiled. When a Chinese man smiles I know something is up. "Your apartment and phone are bugged Roosevelt. Last night we even had a van in the parking lot and recorded everything as it unfolded. We know everything, so there is no need to enumerate what went on last night," Wang hesitated for a moment then added, "You do talk to yourself a lot. You should maybe go see a doctor."

I couldn't tell him I talked to my Guardian Angel. He would believe me as much as a jury truly believed O.J. Simpson was innocent - welcome to the American legal system.

"Did you bug Linda's apartment and phone also?" I asked.

Wang nodded his head.

"How about Barbara's?"

Wang nodded his head.

"How about Detective Richards?"

"We didn't know a thing about him until last night. He was the only one in the group who never made a mistake."

"How about Detective Williams?"

"We couldn't bug his office phone. We couldn't take a chance somebody would tell him. But we did bug his home phone," he said.

"Reid and Blackwell didn't have a phone?"

"We bugged their apartment," Wang said.

"Kevin?"

Wang nodded his head.

"Hoffman's?"

Wang nodded his head.

"And Gloria's?"

Wang nodded his head.

For the first time in several weeks I was speechless, but it was a good thing I didn't have any more people to ask Wang if he had bugged their phones and homes - he'd get a kink in his neck from nodding.

"But even though we had bugs planted in all the homes we didn't have the manpower to record everyplace around the clock,"

Silversmith said. "We had to play hunches, and our hunches were hit and miss, so we missed a lot of important information. And we didn't bug Linda's, Barbara's, or Kevin's until you showed up."

"Everything was going along smoothly until Gloria was killed," Wang said. "But then there was you, good old Roosevelt, famous private detective, without an active license I should add, who happened to hit a golf ball crooked. I decided to let you go your merry way and see if you would find out who killed Gloria and maybe stumble onto the money."

"Anything that Roosevelt does is by luck," my Guardian Angel told Wang.

Thank God Wang couldn't hear him, it would tarnish my famous for fifteen minutes and two reruns image.

"The way it looks, Richards got involved with Williams soon after Williams got the job in Phoenix, but we'll never really know," Wang said.

"I wonder why good cops go bad?" I asked. "Richards was a family man."

"Do I look like Confucius?" Wang asked.

"No, but if you gained about twenty pounds and put on a white suit you could pass for Charlie Chan," I said.

Silversmith laughed. Wang didn't.

"You knew Williams broke into Gloria's apartment," I said.

"Not until he confessed to you last night. We thought it might have been you. After Gloria was killed, we took the bugs out of her apartment."

"You told me two men had looked at the apartment. It was two agents taking the bugs out."

"I had to tell you something, for all I knew you had been watching her apartment," Wang said.

"Concerning last night, and why we were there, we recorded you telling Reid and Blackwell to come to your apartment.. After you left they argued over who was going to kill you after they found out where the money was. Although I should tell you they both liked you," Silversmith said.

"Sounds like most of the friends you make," my Guardian Angel said.

"And we heard Hoffman, at his home, telling Awalt and

McVede they were going to your apartment and when they found out where the money was, he wanted you killed. With all the crooks going to your apartment to see who was going to kill you we decided it was a good time to pick them all up. The plan was to let Hoffman and his crew and Reid and Blackwell come over, listen until we had all the information we needed and bust in, but we saw Detective Richards go into your apartment shortly after you left which threw me for a loop. Then you came back and everybody and their aunt showed up. With you talking and everyone confessing, we kept on recording. The rest is history."

"You guys waited long enough," I said. "I could have been killed."

"Confucius say round eye who invite five known criminals to house to drink silly drinks with umbrellas in them wants to die," Wang grinned.

"That's funny," my Guardian Angel said, laughing so hard he had to hold his belly.

"You must have good karma," Silversmith said.

"Karma, smarma," my Guardian Angel said. "In the old days Roosevelt thought karma was something you rolled up and smoked."

"Now tell me who killed Gloria and where the money is?" Wang said.

I scratched my head. I rubbed my chin. I looked up at the ceiling. I scratched my neck.

"Don't even think about keeping the money yourself," Wang warned.

I looked at him like there is no way a measly two million bucks could tempt me. I don't want to be set forever. Where is the challenge in life? I don't need a house on the beach. I love poverty and wondering most of the time where my next meal is coming from. I'm an old hippie, non-materialistic, but, wait a second, I could always under dress, fain poverty, give to the poor, drink good beer, buy a bus and become a Dead Head even if Garcia has levitated to Mars.

"Keep the money," my Guardian Angel said. "I would like driving around the country in a bus, anything would beat Matilda."

"Don't slam my car or I'll take up hitchhiking," I said.

"Roosevelt, out with it," Wang ordered.

"It's really quite obvious and has been obvious from the beginning," I conceded. "Linda has it."

"Last night you told Hoffman she didn't have it," Wang said.

"I lied. If I had told him it would have ruined my party too early. The original plan was for Richards to record everything that was going on. I had to talk as long as possible and hope people would confess."

"It worked," Silversmith said.

I hobbled over and went through my stuff and dug out my clues, photographs and love notes. I handed Wang the copy I had made of the receipt I'd found behind Linda's poster. "I imagine you'll find the money at this bank in a safety deposit box. The original receipt is behind a poster at Linda's."

"That's a stupid place to put the money," Wang said. "She should have buried it."

"Linda isn't a criminal, she fell into all this mess and got sucked in by the power of money," I said.

"Would you care to explain?" Wang said.

"Gloria and Linda worked at the Tatum Ranch Golf Course as refreshment cart drivers. Linda told me they went out one night drinking and talked about life. You know how things get after a few beers? Plus, Gloria wasn't mentally well, she was a manic-depressive and taking both Elavile and Imipramine to try and control it. I figure Gloria was having a paranoid attack, and needing a friend, she told Linda about the money. Linda agreed to hide the money. Then Gloria turns up dead and Linda has all the money and Hoffman does not know where it is. Two million is a nice present."

"Oh boy," Silversmith commented.

"She and Kevin were friends, probably more, and she told him about the money. When she found out I was a private detective, she was worried I might find out about the money since I decided to look for Gloria's killer. The worst thing about having money is you worry about it all the time. Kevin knew two street punks and hired them to scare me away. But, where Linda really made a mistake was when I found a note addressed to me in a mesquite tree close to where I had found Gloria on the golf course - it was too obvious. She was the only person who could have left the note. She also drove a new car. A Mazda that is far too expensive for a person working on a golf course. I found out she paid cash for the car. From then on I knew she had the money. All I had to find out was where it was, which I did by breaking into her house and finding the receipt. I'll say one thing for Linda, she kept her cool, even last night she never admitted she had the money. She was going to hold out as long as she could."

"I'll be struck dumb," my Guardian Angel said.

"If you are struck dumb it will make you smarter than you are now," I told him.

"If Linda would have held out much longer she would have died rich," Silversmith said.

Wang made a phone call and gave the information about the receipt to somebody. "We'll know if the money is there within thirty minutes," he told me after he hung up.

"You can get a search warrant that quick?" I asked.

"Quicker than a defense attorney can say illegal search and seizure," Silversmith said.

"It seems strange to me that nobody figured out Linda had the money, presuming you're right," Wang said.

"Linda was smart, she kept her mouth shut. Williams and Richards thought the attack on me in her parking lot was two punks trying to rob me. When Williams approached them they obviously didn't tell Williams Kevin had hired them or they might have suspected Linda - plus, Gloria had only been dead one day and Hoffman didn't know the money was gone. And when Williams approached Linda telling her to inform him every time I talked to her she remained cool. There was no way Williams or Hoffman could know that Gloria had ever gone out with Linda."

"Smart lady," Silversmith commented.

"Not smart enough," I said.

"Now, who killed Gloria?" Wang asked.

I hesitated for a few moments. Looked at Silversmith and then back at Wang. "You did," I said gravely.

Silversmith's mouth dropped open.

"Cut the garbage, Roosevelt," Wang replied not even smiling at my funny.

"All right, let's see if I can make this clear."

"You can do it Roosevelt, I know you can," My Guardian Angel said.

"When I first met Gloria in the swimming pool and after she found out I was a private detective, I could sense she wanted to tell me something, something she was afraid over. The next day when I found her dead on the golf course there were several things strange about the body. Besides being naked, she was on her back, her eyes were closed, and her hands were resting on her stomach. They had to be placed that way. Whoever had put her there did it with care. The rope around her neck was a slipknot and the end of the rope had been cut with a knife. There were no footprints anywhere - the ground looked like it had been swept clean by a dust storm. There were also large black ants on her face and not far from the body, close to the cart path, were six small holes in the ground. None of it made any sense to me. The autopsy found no signs of violence, no flesh under her fingernails, but she was full of Elavil and Imipramine. I found out she had been married to Cecil Hoffman, who was from a wealthy family, but during their marriage he had spent all of her money, which also didn't make any sense. Also, if he was so wealthy from family money, why was she working at a golf course driving a refreshment cart? There was only one answer. Hoffman had spent all the money his family had given him along with Gloria's. I bet if you check everything around Hoffman, it all belongs to his family. I know the house here in Phoenix belongs to his mother and I bet he is getting a small monthly check from her. Hoffman was smart enough he knew he couldn't bring out any of the stolen money for a long time or for sure he would get busted. He went to the Colombians who own Tony's Pizza and set up a deal and as part of the arrangement they would pay him a salary through their store here in Phoenix to help cover his bills. I saw him at Tony's Pizza one night picking up the night deposit. He wouldn't pick up the deposit if he wasn't getting paid. The drug deal would accomplish two things: It would increase the money and it would also get the stolen money out of the country. Gloria took a job at the golf course, which made her at least a hundred a day. Everything was going along fine. Hoffman, Gloria, Awalt and McVede were living in the house in

Paradise Valley, biding their time waiting for the Colombians to get the coke deal ready. But Gloria started to unravel. Reid and Blackwell told me she was always going off the deep end. Gloria rented an apartment not far from the house. At this time, I think Hoffman and she weren't getting along and she was truly afraid he would hurt her, whether it was in her mind or fact, it doesn't matter. Hoffman would come and see her but she wouldn't let him sleep with her, remember his pillow and blanket were on the sofa. By now, things had started to get tense. The coke deal was stringing out. They couldn't touch the money and Reid and Blackwell were taking pot shots at Hoffman. Plus, Gloria was having attacks of depression. Hoffman and Gloria both knew where the money was. Hoffman had to trust somebody in case something happened to him. I don't think it's strange that Awalt and McVede didn't - most crooks who aren't bosses don't know where the money is kept, and don't care as long as they get paid. But, in Gloria's growing depression she told Linda about the money and also gave Linda her expensive jewelry either as a gift or to keep for her."

"How do you know Gloria gave Linda her expensive jewelry?" Wang asked.

"When I searched Gloria's apartment I didn't find a purse or a jewelry box, which I thought was strange. Linda has two jewelry boxes at her apartment - each on top of a different dresser. One has costume jewelry in it. The other has six sets of diamond earrings for pierced ears, a ladies Rolex watch, and other expensive trinkets. Linda's ears aren't pierced. Gloria's were - three holes on each side. If Linda had stolen the jewelry, she would have hidden it, especially when Gloria was, what everybody presumed, murdered."

"How about the purse?" Wang asked.

"I have no idea," I replied.

"Go on," Silversmith told me obviously not caring about any purse.

"Gloria got the money from wherever it had been and gave it to Linda to hide. Then abbra kadabra, Gloria is dead. Hoffman goes to get the money and it's gone and all hell breaks loose. I don't think he ever planned on ripping off Awalt and McVede, even crooks need friends, especially when other people want to kill them,"

"You didn't say that last night," Silversmith said.

"I lied. Things were getting out of hand. I had to make up something so I said Hoffman planned on keeping all the money."

"It worked," Silversmith said. "A bullet to the head work."

"But you still haven't told us who killed Gloria." Wang said.

"Yes, who?" Silversmith asked.

"Who?" my Guardian Angel asked.

I shook my head in disbelief. Send some people to the grocery store and all they bring back is a paper sack. "She committed suicide. There is no murder."

"I'll be a damned round eye," Wang exclaimed.

"Amazing," Silversmith exclaimed.

"What a bummer ending," My Guardian Angel exclaimed.

"How did she get to the rough on the first hole if she committed suicide?" Wang asked. There is always a doubting Thomas in the crowd.

"When I broke into Gloria's apartment, I found in the bottom drawer of her dresser rope that matched the rope around her neck, and later I found out she had purchased the rope. When I went back with you, Wang, to the apartment, and you were playing a good role of an apartment manager, I saw two hooks in the ceiling of the closet designed to hold a bicycle. Here is what happened. Gloria was telling me the truth when she told me her boyfriend and she were going to go play golf in the morning. She told me boyfriend because she didn't want to say ex-husband. She hadn't been to work for three days so I know she was beginning to feel heavily depressed. She was also nervous. Hoffman was telling the truth when he said he was going to take her golfing the next morning but he came over in the evening and went to bed on the sofa - I found his sock and saw the blanket and pillow and found a spot where he had spilled a bottle of whiskey. Early in the morning, I'd say around 2:00, I found her around 8:30 and she was stiff, she got up from bed, having lain on top of the covers, took her clothes off, ate all the pills she had left, made a slip knot in the rope, got the chair from her bedroom, attached the rope to a hook in the closet, and when the pills started to come on she hung herself. There was no pain. Hoffman, asleep and having drunk a lot of whiskey, heard nothing. I imagine he woke up early, had to go to the bathroom and he found her. What with the bank robbery he couldn't take a chance and call the police. He cut Gloria down using a dull kitchen knife, which he put back and put the rope in the bottom drawer of the dresser. He put the chair back in the bedroom, placing her blouse on the back and hung up the other clothes she had been wearing. He was so freaked out he dressed quickly, not putting on one sock and spilled his whiskey. He drove to Williams' house. Williams always drove his unmarked squad car when he wasn't on duty and they could move the body without any fear of getting stopped. Barbara told me he always used the company car while we were sitting in the parking lot to Babe's."

"Besides wanting to use his squad car how do you know Williams was involved?" Wang asked.

"When I found Gloria she had large black ants on her face, wood ants they're called. Big black ants don't live in the desert. They need trees and water. The only place I've seen black ants in Phoenix is on two willow trees at Williams' house. They fell on either him or Hoffman as they got into the car. Hoffman didn't want to just dump the body, he really did love her. They decided they would take her to the golf course, which is logical, since she worked there. When she was found no one would suspect Hoffman. They wiped down anything in the apartment they might have touched making sure there were no fingerprints of either one of them. Richards told me later he had found Gloria's and my fingerprints in the apartment. They put her in the unmarked patrol car, drove to the golf course, carried her to the rough, Hoffman and Williams laid her out, shut her eyes, and placed her hands on her stomach. Sometime during all this, black ants fell off Williams or Hoffman onto Gloria. They then broke into the maintenance shed, I bet there is a set of bolt cutters in Williams's trunk and Hoffman knew where the equipment was because Gloria had told him everything about the course. They took a gas powered leaf blower and blew away their footprints from around Gloria, put the leaf blower back in the shed and took off.

"Wouldn't the noise alert people in the area?" Wang asked.

"It had to be getting close to dawn by then and people would be used to noise around the course."

"Wouldn't you think they would be afraid about getting caught?" Silversmith asked.

"It probably seemed a lot safer than dumping her in the desert. And, if somebody did come up, Williams could say he was a cop who had found the body."

"What a deal," Silversmith said.

"Roosevelt, I think you're right," my Guardian Angel said in astonishment.

"How about the holes you said you found in the rough the day you found Gloria. What caused them?" Wang asked.

"They were made by an old man who uses a cane. He walks the course every day for exercise."

The phone rang and I answered it. "Pete's Towing."

"What?" somebody said.

"Bob Roosevelt."

"Is Agent Wang there wise guy?"

"It's your mother," I told Wang as I handed him the phone. "And she doesn't have a sense of humor."

Wang didn't talk but listened, said goodbye, and hung up. "All two million dollars was in the safety deposit box," he said.

"How can that be? Linda paid cash for a new car," I asked, slightly confused.

"Don't ask me. I'm not a private detective. I'm only an F.B.I. agent."

I sensed an undercurrent of hostility but could understand where he was coming from. It's tough being the bad guy all the time.

Silversmith turned off the tape recorder. "You know your story about Gloria sounds good but we will never really know," he said almost sadly.

"I bet the D.A. swallows it and closes the case," I said.

"It makes a good ending for a gangster's wife," Wang said.

Both he and Wang stood. "You can stay here for another day and then you're on your own," Wang told me. "But you should contact the federal prosecutor and see if they will need you."

"You guys should go to my old apartment. Hidden in the doorknob to my bedroom is a plastic baggie with a cotton swab in it. The blood on the swab should match Williams' blood. I took it off of my front porch."

"It doesn't really matter," Wang said.

"I also have the piece of fingernail I found on my floor."

"Keep it for a souvenir," Silversmith said. "This has been the perfect case. If all the bad guys always killed each other we wouldn't need jails."

"What are you going to charge Barbara and Linda with?" I asked.

"That's not up to me. My job is to arrest people," Wang said as he and Silversmith headed for the door.

I crutched along behind them. Wang opened the door and held out his hand. We shook hands. I shook hands with Silversmith. "I guess I should tell you now. The banks have a $25,000 reward for whoever recovered the money," Wang informed me. "It's yours."

As I shut the door, I should have been elated, but I wasn't. There is a lot of blood on the $25,000.

"Don't worry Roosevelt," my Guardian Angel said. "It'll wash off."

My Guardian Angel has a true understanding of money. And I don't know any old hippie alive today who would turn the money down - blood or not. Time is a sad teacher.

CHAPTER TWENTY-FOUR
LOST IN THE SIXTIES

I spent the rest of the day and the next morning in the room. When I checked out I could walk without using my crutches, although it wasn't comfortable. The bellman, with all of my worldly possessions on his cart, seeing Matilda, looked bummed out. I guess he figured not many Volkswagen bug owners tip. After he loaded the car I gave him a ten just to mess with his mind - once you think you have it all figured out life gives you something to think about.

Matilda was happy to see me and started right up - it's nice to have a good reliable female friend.

I didn't want to go to my apartment, even though the rent was paid, so I rented a room at a Motel Six. I unloaded all of my things except my golf clubs and golf shoes and drove to the Federal Building. I cleared the Federal Prosecutor's secretary, who acted like she had eaten cactus for lunch spiced with alum, and was escorted into the Federal Prosecutor's office, which was large and filled with expensive office furniture - another case of government over spending.

Mr. Randolph Glory, the Federal Prosecutor, was all business. "I have contacted the banks in California and your reward money will be here in a few days," Mr. Glory said in a dull monotone, which matched his dull gray suit, his dull brown shoes, and his dull solid tie. "Linda Adams has told us everything and everything you figured out is true. Since she had nothing to do with the actual robbery, we are only going to charge her with obstructing justice, which she has agreed to plea, and she will get a few years probation. I suppose we could charge her for several other crimes, but we see no need."

"Me neither. She isn't a bad person. I don't know many people that wouldn't try to keep their hands on two million bucks if it fell in their lap like it did hers," I said.

"Barbara told us everything she knew, which really isn't much," Mr. Glory said. "Barbara is also pleading guilty to obstructing justice and in turn we will drop all other charges. It really is amazing how right you were about everything. The state is going along with you that Gloria did commit suicide. You did a good job, Mr. Roosevelt."

"Mr. Roosevelt, can you imagine," my Guardian Angel said.

Standing, Mr. Glory held out his hand to shake, letting me know it is time for me to go. He probably has a meeting with some white-collar types who want to know how to commit bank fraud without getting caught.

"Since there will be no trials I won't have to stay in touch once I get my check," I said.

Mr. Glory nodded his head.

On the way back to the motel I stopped at Joe's Easy Money Pawn Shop and pawned my golf clubs and golf shoes. It had been fun thinking I could become a normal human being, but I'd only been kidding myself. I felt lower than a pelican's belly driving back to the motel. I bought a coke from a machine at the end of the hall and sat in my room looking at a print of two deer standing in a meadow. "This whole idea to take up golf and come to Phoenix for the winter was nothing but a double bogey," I told my Guardian Angel.

"I have to agree," he replied. "A double bogey murder."

"I have to get out of here."

"Where to this time oh one who is lost in the 60's and can't seem to find his way back?"

"I don't have the faintest idea," I replied. "Where can I go where there is no hate, no crime, no fear, no prejudice, no news, no taxes, cheap beer, and hopefully find love?"

I felt like the last unclaimed item at a lost and found.

"I know where you can go," my Guardian Angel said.

"I'm all ears one who has to stay with me till death do us part."

"You can go where frogs don't croak in the winter."

I chuckled.

Two days later I got my check for $25,000. Matilda putted down the interstate. "You know, you really did a good job deciphering all the clues in this case," my Guardian Angel said.

"I might be getting better. I was more organized."

"No, just another case of luck."

"Maybe at the next stop I won't fall into a crime and need clues."

"Sorry to say, I doubt it," my Guardian Angel said.

"Someday I will find the love of my life."

"It is a good dream, you can't stop dreaming."

I started to sing, my Guardian Angel joined in - "He's a real nowhere man, living in a nowhere land......"

The wind blew through my hair. I am not happy or sad, but I am ok. Love, love, where art thou?

THE END

OTHER BOB ROOSEVELT MYSTERIES

DOULBE BOGEY MURDER – BOOK ONE
TROUT FISHING FOR BODIES – BOOK TWO
DOUBLE BOGEY MURDER – BOOK THREE
FROGS DON'T CROAK IN THE WINTER – BOOK FOUR

COMING SOON
BEACH BUM TANGO

For more of Robert K. Swisher Jr's many novels visit
http://www.swisherbooks.com/

www.ingramcontent.com/pod-product-compliance
Lightning Source LLC
Chambersburg PA
CBHW051919110726
47902CB00002B/336